EMPLOYEE'S BOOK
PROGRAM

Christ's Santa

Volume 1

©
COPYRIGHT 2002

First Edition

By: Glenn R. Elion

ISBN # 0-9747815-0-9

Published By:
Life's Journey of Hope Publications
P.O. Box 1277
Groton, MA 01450

Email: sales@lifesjourneyofhope.com
Phone: (978) 448-1252

Scripture taken from the HOLY BIBLE, NEW INTERNATIONAL VERSION ®. Copyright © 1973, 1978, 1984 by International Bible Society. Used by permission of Zondervan. All rights reserved.

Christ's Santa

By : Glenn R. Elion

About The Author

Glenn received degrees in Religion and Chemical Engineering from Tufts University in 1970. He then earned a PhD in Chemical Engineering at Princeton University in 1973. In 1987 he also received an OPM Certificate at Harvard Business School. His issued patents cover a number of different science fields. He has previously authored technical books sold worldwide.

The author's aunt, Dr. Gertrude B. Elion, won the Nobel Prize for Medicine along with many other awards. The work that she first became known for internationally was in developing what was then the first drugs to treat childhood leukemia, a once incurable disease. She also discovered the drugs to permit organ transplants without rejection. For this effort she received numerous letters from all over the world thanking her for the gift of life. Her work has provided an opportunity for renewed health, and her drive to get more people of all ages willing to give the gift of life is the inspiration for Christ's Santa. How wonderful it would be to get everyone signed up to donate their organs to others to relieve the international crisis that now exists from a shortage of eligible donors, and how sweet a tribute that would be for a woman who dedicated her life to helping others.

The author has cooked and served meals at homeless shelters in Massachusetts and New Jersey. Each time he went, the one phrase most prominent in his mind was "There but by the grace of God go I." Seeing children dying in hospital beds in desperate need of organs, wouldn't all of us say the same?

The author has organized blood drives on Cape Cod in Massachusetts. In 1995 he created what was known as the "Blood Drive Of The Century" to get as many of the town's people and the school children involved as possible in donating blood for those in need. He has also cooked breakfast for blood drives and Boy Scout fundraising events.

Glenn has remained dedicated to helping others by sharing his spirituality and working to get people registered for organ donation as well as giving blood through the Red Cross.

The author has donated his time to helping children at the Shriner's Burn Center in Boston Massachusetts and has been profoundly moved at the medical miracles that happen when the efforts of many become focused on helping children from all over the world. Seeing the look of hope in the eyes of such children has been a major inspiration in writing Christ's Santa.

The author has two sons who always enjoyed Christmas and their joy at the holidays has also been inspirational not only in the writing of this book but in getting school children throughout the country excited about taking the lead in organ donation.

Glenn is also the author of De-Evolution, a science fiction, spiritual adventure that presents a new Christian perspective on the subject of evolution.

About The Cover

The cover art was created by artist and illustrator John Mantha. He has worked for book publishers, magazines, corporations and television. John's art has been seen throughout North America. He lives in Toronto, Ontario. You can contact John through his agent carollee@cableone.net and to see some additional artwork created by him you can visit www.pennystermergroup.com and click John Mantha.

Christ's Santa

Chapter		Page
1	The Early Life Of Nicholas	1
2	Nicholas As A Young Man	5
3	Nicholas Chosen	12
4	Jesus And The Cross	19
5	The First Christmas Gifts	27
6	The First Easter	34
7	Santa Travels North	40
8	The First Christmas Tree	46
9	The Gifts Of The Cross	55
10	The Stories Of Santa's Gifts	63
11	Santa's Sleigh	67
12	Shriner's Burn Center	76
13	Always Represent God	100
14	The Olympic Vision	129
15	The Last Journey	158
	Epilogue – The Gift Of Life	175
	Organ Donor Cards	179
	Order Form	183

Christ's Santa

Preface

The greatest story ever told was about the birth, life, death and resurrection of Jesus Christ. No other historical event has so touched and shaped this world and the next. From the dawn of Christmas, many stories, songs and legends have emerged over the years. The most widespread throughout the world is the story of Santa Claus or St. Nicholas, a man, a spirit, a Saint of many names. Children of all ages love Santa Claus. By any name, the story and his deeds have grown since Santa delivered his first Christmas gifts two thousand years ago.

There are so many questions about Santa Claus. Who is he? Where did he come from? Where does he live? Is he real or just a legend? Is he a spirit, a man, a Saint or an angel? Why do the stories about him still fascinate people of all ages around the world? What were his origins and how did all the wonderful stories about him originate in so many countries?

This book provides insights into the nature of the man and the spirit of giving that has captivated the world on a magnitude difficult to comprehend. At Christmas time all around the world, there is no one who creates more excitement in the eyes of children of all ages than the anticipation of Santa Claus. Somehow, over the years, who he is and why he is here amongst us has almost been forgotten. Christ's Santa helps us to remember.

The story of Christ's Santa is not just a Christmas-time tale. Rather, it is meant for year-round, to encourage us all to follow his lead. From those rich in material wealth to those filled with spiritual gifts, there is an overwhelming sense of joy in getting to know St. Nicholas. As we get to know him, we learn much more about ourselves and each other and what we were intended to be in this world and in heaven.

Christ's Santa is a new way to explore parts of the past and the bible that encourage us to put into practice the art of giving and the joy it brings to our hearts. We all need to become an integral part of the

Christmas spirit. This story also lets us know of the importance of sincere spirit-filled prayer, not just for ourselves but also for the spiritual welfare of people everywhere. We all have an obligation to help those in need. It is now time to act.

Children of all faiths should discover from Christ's Santa that there is a lot more to the twinkle in Santa's eye than the joy of giving. At the end of this book, each of you will be asked a simple question. Do you want to be like Santa and would you like to help him? For you see, this is much more than just a book. It is a doorway into a new life, one in which you can directly help others. Maybe they are your next-door neighbors. Maybe they are in your town. Maybe they are in a country far away. Wherever there is a need for a child to find food, clothing, shelter or find loving parents or friends, wherever there are people of any age needing organs to live renewed, healthy lives, this book will offer a way for you to become one of Santa's helpers.

This book is about the Santa Claus that came to the world at the time of Jesus Christ two thousand years ago. It is from this origin that all other stories have been developed over the years. His life, his story, is unique. There is enormous depth to his spirit. It begins at the Cross and continues for all eternity.

Call him by any good name and he will be with you because St. Nicholas is about understanding the giving of love to others, in your family and in the much larger family of God.

There is a God in heaven.

St. Nicholas is here with us on earth today.

Santa, Christ's Santa, is here to stay.

Chapter 1

<u>The Early Life Of Nicholas</u>

St. Nicholas stepped out of his workshop to look up into the heavens. The angels who were helping him put together his Christmas list had whispered that the northern lights could be seen dancing above the snow-covered pines. As he turned his eyes towards the heavens, the cold night air filled his lungs. His rosy cheeks turned bright red in the winter wind. He felt so excited that another Christmas eve had come and that after hundreds of years he was still on earth. The northern lights glowed like curtains of green and blue, shimmering in the night. His reindeer pawed the ground anxious to begin their journey.

Santa kneeled to pray as he wondered about the future of Christmas and the miracles that had brought him to this very moment in time. How it is that he still remained on earth as a simple Godly man who knew one thing better than all others, how to give and how to love giving. As his eyes looked down he saw a beautiful reflection of the northern lights coming from his old buttons. He touched them tenderly with his white-gloved hands and remembered the day he cast them. He had taken the nails of the cross and re-formed some of them into the buttons he would use for centuries to hold his coat together for warmth on his journey through the snowy skies.

As he became quiet, he could hear his leather boots creak a bit from their age. The black leather was becoming worn but still in good shape considering its age. His scarlet coat was a bit frayed but kept in good repair for Christmas Eve. His wife Anna had done a wonderful job in making his clothes years ago. Around the pants there was some black dust from a chimney or two but the color showed clearly even in the night sky beneath the moon, the stars and the heavens. His breath formed little clouds of white mist just like the deer as they snorted and raised their heads getting ready for the annual journey. He thought about all the events in his life that led to this moment in time.

Nicholas was born in Antioch. Look at a map of the Ancient world. If the island of Kittim, now called Cyprus, was a hand with the eastern tip a finger, that finger would be pointing to exactly where Nicholas was born. Antioch was 300 miles north of Jerusalem. In the ancient world, it was a wonderful blend of cultures and a crossroads of people traveling by land and sea, trading goods made all along the Mediterranean Sea and even from Africa.

In the times when Nicholas first lived, men were called by their first name and the town or place where they were born. Thus, our beloved Nicholas would simply be known as Nicholas of Antioch.

Nicholas was the first-born son of eight children born to parents Claudius and Meredith. As a baby, Nicholas found it difficult to pronounce his father's name and learned to call him Claus. His father often called his mother Mere for short, or sometimes Meri, which in modern times became known as Merry, for she was always uplifting to her husband and children. Meredith truly was a wonderful asset to her family and was superb at many crafts. Over the years she taught Nicholas things a boy would not normally know. He learned how to spin wool and to create clothing from leather.

Nicholas became a good baker and could prepare meals for many people through his work at the temples in his area. Nicholas learned how to forge metals from his father and became an excellent finish carpenter. He did delicate crafting for the temples and families in his town and the surrounding areas.

His other brothers soon became good farmers and shared in the labors for their family. Nicholas spent his time with most of the artistic crafts and over time his reputation for quality work spread throughout the countryside. He was a hard worker who could work from sunrise to sunset and he was a wonderful son to his parents who loved him dearly.

For some of the people who spoke Hebrew, he crafted small spinning tops called dradles and hand painted the symbols onto the wood. He also made ornate wooden boxes and sometimes crafted metal hinges for the priests to use for the Ark that held the Torah or for doors to the inner sanctums of the temples. He learned to carve delicate scenes and patterns, often working late into the night.

By the time he was two years old, Nicholas had developed a contagious laugh. It was a delightful belly laugh that made all the adults laugh with him. He soon became loved by everyone he knew, not only for his laugh, or his tireless work to help his family, but for many other things. Nicholas had an almost angelic way of settling disputes and arguments, not only with his brothers and sisters but even with total strangers. At dinner time, Nicholas was the one to divide up the food for the family making portions that were fair, based on everyone's size and needs, not equal in size, but proportional. Often, to settle an argument, Nicholas would give up his share of food, or payment, to give to another, so that everyone would leave satisfied and never part in anger. Nicholas was a joy to Claus and Meri who came to rely on his honesty, hard work and his unique ability to keep the peace in their household.

Nicholas was not able to go to school. There were few in his day who could attend. However, the priests and rabbis in the temples taught him how to read and write at an early age. With his artistic hands he was soon able to work part time as a scribe. Sometimes he would prepare long detailed lists of things that were needed to build the temples. Nicholas became very good at remembering long complicated lists of things for the church. He could memorize a hundred things and later in the evening write them all down for delivery to other cities and the surrounding countryside.

Nicholas loved birthdays and holidays. As part of his enjoyment, he learned new skills to bring others joy. In his day, all paper was made to be an off-white color or light yellow, depending upon how it was made. To everyone's delight, Nicholas discovered how to make many pretty colored papers to wrap around gifts to make them more appealing, especially for young children. He gathered flowers that were violet, orange or red and mashed them in stone bowls until they yielded their bright colors in warm water. He then took rough woven cloth and poured the mash through it, and then squeezed it to get as much of the color as possible into a water bath that he then used to tint the paper. He also dyed strings for colorful wrappings. Since there was no sticky tape, everything was wrapped using twine or colored strings. To add to the pretty papers, Nicholas would carve shapes of angels or animals and use the flower dyes to color the carved wood he used as stamps. In this simple way, he was able to make beautiful colored paper with pretty patterns. The end result was that every gift looked unique and special.

3

Even as a young boy, Nicholas invented many things. For the shepherds in his town, he created a new type of miniature bell that made a quiet sound that would not wake up neighbors, yet would allow them to keep track of their flocks at night. These tiny bells were put onto leather or twine and placed around the neck or legs of the sheep. As they grew older and bigger the twine could be loosened to expand. Each time they took a step it would make a sound, not like a clanging bell, but more like a jingle.

At the time the star of Bethlehem hovered over the manger where Jesus was born, Nicholas was also born far away in Antioch. Nicholas would not understand his unique link to Jesus until many years later at the time of the crucifixion. Nicholas was not born in a manger, nor was his a virgin birth. He came from a family that loved church and was close to God through prayer. At an early age, Nicholas had developed a very powerful voice in his prayer life and often the adults called upon him to begin a meal or celebration with a wonderful prayer. His solemn and sweet voice in prayer seemed in stark contrast to the playful and laughing Nicholas most of them heard in public. At times in prayer he would have tears in his eyes. He always felt close to God and lived his life as if God was walking by his side not just watching from afar.

As a young boy, Nicholas heard stories about a Messiah and how three wise kings visited a manger in Bethlehem and that he had the same birthday as this chosen one. Nicholas could not imagine that he would be chosen by Christ to serve the special purpose of spreading joy and the true spirit of giving. At the same time, he was chosen to perform one of the most horrific tasks that could possibly be imagined.

Matthew 2:9-11

After they had heard the king, they went on their way, and the star they had seen in the east went ahead of them until it stopped over the place where the child was. When they saw the star they were overjoyed. On coming to the house, they saw the child with his mother Mary, and they bowed down and worshipped him. Then they opened their treasures and presented him with gifts of gold and of incense and of myrrh. (NIV)

4

Chapter 2

Nicholas As A Young Man

When Nicholas was young, a boy made the transition to becoming a man usually between the ages of 12 to 14. It depended in part on the religious faith and local practices of the town. For the Jewish boys, this transition often happened at the age of 13 when they read the Torah in front of the other men gathered at the Temple. In Antioch, the transition for Nicholas came when his father told him that he would be responsible for preparing the meal for the harvest festival that included making a sacrifice for God and then saying the prayer before the meal. It was an exciting time in any boy's life. At the evening meal in front of gathered friends and family Nicholas would become a man by tradition. It was also a time for young women to look over the new crop of young men to see if any were to their liking to consider as a future husband.

At the age of 14 Nicholas prepared the harvest meal for a gathering of over one hundred men, women and children. Nicholas made the event quite unusual. Instead of the people in town giving him small gifts to celebrate him becoming a man, he decided to make them something special. During the summer he cast candles into which he added the fragrances of flowers and perfumes he had made by hand. He made many fanciful colored papers and dyed twines with bright autumn colors of red, oranges and yellows. For his young brothers and sisters he carved wooden toys and figures. For his parents he cast a small metal box in the shape of a heart and placed a small colored scroll of some of their favorite verses written by King Solomon and David inside of it. For the ink he used violet colors squeezed from flowers he found in the mountains where the sheep roamed to feed at night.

On the night of the great festival, Nicholas and his whole family gathered together. During that summer, Nicholas had met a new girl who had moved to Antioch from Jerusalem with her parents and sisters and brothers. Her name was Anna Marie. The very first time they saw each other, they couldn't help but stare. They were drawn to each other as if by some unknown power that they did not understand. Sometimes they had the chance to talk with one another. Nicholas wanted to know everything about her as well as her hometown in Jerusalem. He was surprised to find out that they had something very special in common. Anna Marie was also born on December 25th. She was born in her parent's house in the city. From Jerusalem that night, her parents could see the star that was shining brightly over the sky in Bethlehem and took it as a sign of good fortune for Anna Marie and her future.

For the night of the great festival, Nicholas made a special present for Anna Marie. He cast small figurines in thin metal and attached them to a short thin chain to become a bracelet. The figures included doves, angels, cherubs and stars. He polished each of the pieces so it would catch the light of the sun during the day, or at night the light of the candles or the fire to make it sparkle.

As was the custom in those days, marriages were arranged between parents and relatives. Knowing this year he would become a man, Nicholas had gone to his parents and asked them their opinion on whether he was ready to be married and to tell them he really liked Anna Marie. He asked them if they thought it would be good for the family if he were to marry her. Claus and Meri considered this in their own quiet way.

At the right time Claus and Meri met with Anna Marie's parents. After getting to know them for a while, they brought up the subject of Anna Marie and whether she had eyes for anyone in the town in terms of marriage. Both parents were surprised and pleased to find out both Nicholas and Anna Marie had secretly expressed a desire to be married to each other. It seemed this was a marriage not really arranged by parents but by a higher power.

As a young child Anna Marie had a rare infection that made her sick for several weeks with a high fever. She had no way of knowing it, but that infection had rendered her unable to bear any children. Both she and Nicholas would grow up loving their younger siblings and other children in the town and would thus eventually want to have children of their own. At first it would seem a cruel fate to prevent them from having their own children, but God works in mysterious ways. Ultimately, they would have more children than any one else in the history of mankind.

On the night of the great festival, as the sun was setting in the western sky, Nicholas stood up before friends and family with his father and mother by his side. The smell of roasted lamb and fresh baked breads filled the air with delicious scents that made everyone both hungry and excited.

Claus spoke first to the gathered crowd.

"Dear friends and family, we are gathered here tonight to celebrate the bounties of the earth God has provided for us. This night is a special one for our family, for our son Nicholas shall become a man this evening. The meal he has prepared and the sacrifices he has made show us he is ready to enter into a new period of his life, one that eventually will lead him to leave this place, our house, our home, and go out into the world to have his own family. After Nicholas gives the prayer to bless our food, Meri and I have a little announcement to make to everyone. This is going to be a night we shall all remember for many years to come."

Claus stepped back and turned his loving eyes to Nicholas. As Nicholas stepped forward he removed his apron to say the prayer that would begin the evenings festivities. His chest swelled with pride.

"Heavenly Father, God of Abraham and Isaac, Lord of Moses and giver of the ten commandments, creator of all things that live and grow, we come before you tonight to give thanks for the great bounties of the harvest for this year. You have given us ample rain and sunshine and nourished the ground. The wheat this year has been plentiful and our flocks have multiplied. Truly we are blessed as your people. We shall follow your commandments. We shall worship no other. We shall remain your people and praise and thank you always for all your treasures here on earth. We ask that you bless our food and our people that we may continue to honor, serve and worship you for all the years to come. Amen."

In unison, everyone from the youngest child to the oldest man, said "Amen!" As soon as Nicholas had finished his prayer the crowd was anxious to begin the meal, but Claus quickly stepped forward once again and raised his hands asking for silence.

"Dear friends, as is our custom, by preparing the harvest meal, making the sacrifices to God and leading us in prayer, Nicholas has become a man this evening. And all good men should work hard and prosper in our community as we serve God and learn to follow all His ways and commands. To go forth into the world as a man, it is fitting that he should one day marry and join us in making our community grow and prosper. This evening we take great pride in announcing that after asking the parents of Anna Marie if Nicholas may one day marry her, and after giving the marriage dowry, we are pleased to tell you that Nicholas and Anna Marie are now officially engaged."

Everyone stood up and cheered and clapped. Nicholas turned beet red and didn't know what to say or do. Anna Marie quickly emerged from the crowd with her parents, who placed her hand into the hand of Nicholas and raised their arms up high for all to see. Nicholas looked carefully at Anna Marie. He was very happy to see that she was smiling and clearly welcomed the wonderful announcement. They sat next to each other all evening and tried to talk over the loud noises of the celebrations, music and dances.

During the next year, Nicholas and Anna Marie got to see each other very often. They became great friends and shared all their hopes and dreams. When Nicholas went to other towns to work on special projects for the priests and work at the Temples, he would always write to Anna Marie. He would entrust his letters to merchants as they passed through to give the letters to those going to Antioch. After months of learning about each other, Nicholas and Anna Marie fell in love. It was a special love. They had grown to greatly respect each other and took great joy in spending time together. They both loved young children and would often meet when they were caring for their younger siblings. They made up many new games to play and where ever they went, the household would fill with laughter. Their engagement was a blessing to the entire community. Everyone in the town seemed to almost adopt the young couple as their own, because both individually and as a couple, Nicholas and Anna Marie brought out the best in everyone.

After being engaged for almost a year, both parents set the date for them to be married. They decided that given the unusual fact that they shared the same birthday, the marriage should also occur on December 25th. That way, no one would ever forget about birthdays or anniversary dates.

Back in those days, calendar years were known in different ways. Different countries counted the years in different ways. Even to this day in some Asian countries they use two ways of counting and marking years. By today's calendar, in the year 15 AD, Nicholas of Antioch and Anna Marie of Jerusalem were married in the Temple.

As part of the wedding celebration, Nicholas made many small gifts and wrapped them in colored papers and dyed strings and twines. Each guest at the wedding was presented with something Nicholas or Anna Marie had made by hand. The wedding was a happy time. They sang many songs using harps, cymbals and bells. The hills echoed with the sounds of laughter and singing late into the night.

After the wedding they lived together in a small house Nicholas had built himself. The house was built on a piece of land given to Nicholas by friends of his father. They thought the young couple should have a place of their own to begin a new life together. Traditionally, they would have started by living in the house of one of the parents. So in this way, they were more fortunate than most young couples of that era.

Nicholas was a very good husband for Anna Marie. He was always faithful and worked hard to provide for her needs. As time went on, his reputation as a fair and Godly man, as well as a good husband spread throughout the land. He loved the harvest festival celebrations but most of all he thought that December was the best time to rejoice. As time passed, he turned December 25th into not only a date to celebrate his birthday, Anna Marie's birthday and their wedding anniversary, but also a joyous time for children throughout the town, and eventually the world. Since he and Anna Marie did not yet have children of their own, he spent all year round making toys for children and stored them in a shed behind his house. The shed grew over time into a workshop to carve, paint, assemble and decorate the numerous gifts made from wood and cloth. As word spread of his giving nature, many people started to drop off gifts to be distributed to local children. Sometimes they were new, sometimes used, so Nicholas, Anna Marie, and their helpers would repair them and fix them up to look like new.

Claus took great pride in seeing his son turn so much energy and time into helping other children each December. As he grew older, he spent more time helping Nicholas. Some nights they would work late into the evening singing, laughing and making toys. As a gesture of respect, Nicholas carved a little sign for his father and put it on the shed. It was a simple plaque he painted long ago in red on white - CLAUS WORKSHOP.

As the years went by Nicholas became a true artisan sought after by many men within Antioch and as far away as Jerusalem. The children in Antioch followed him almost like a piper with a magical flute. They would sing and dance and play. Sometimes they would gather on holidays at the house of Nicholas, and Anna Marie would spread a table with flour and dough made from wheat, rye and other grains, and together they would make cookies. Nicholas crafted dough cutters in the shapes of stars, angels, lambs and donkeys. The children would then coat them with honey or sugar or colorful spices like ginger dipped in flower juice extracts of marigolds, to make bright yellows, oranges and reds. Though they had no children of their own, they soon acted as the parents of hundreds of children who were homeless, lost or forgotten.

On the Eve of December 25th, the night before his 29th birthday, Nicholas loaded up a caravan of donkeys with huge sacks of gifts for children. He and his father spent the night going to all the houses with young children. Sometimes he didn't have enough paper to wrap the gifts and some toys were odd shapes and difficult to cover, so he often just placed them on the mantle of the fireplace to be sure they were safe from the sparks of the logs heating the house. Every now and then, he would find the children's clothes on the floor and wrap the gifts inside the clothes, even inside of their socks, though few had socks in those days, since most wore sandals of leather.

They would come home exhausted from the wonderful journey of giving, knowing in the morning that many children would find a surprise which would make them smile.

Claus was particularly proud to bring Nicholas news on his birthday. The priests and governor in Jerusalem had sent word they wanted Nicholas to come live in Jerusalem to work in the temples as a Master Craftsman. So, after years of living in Antioch, Nicholas moved to Jerusalem just as Jesus was becoming known throughout the land. At 29, Nicholas settled into Jerusalem in a nice house with enormous workshops next door. In this way he could work on projects with wood and metal on a grand scale. On his land there was a stream that flowed with clear water. Nicholas also built a barn that became an animal shelter. He learned through years of experience how to help heal animals with broken legs or wings. Over time, even wild animals sensed that they had nothing to fear from Nicholas.

Nicholas developed his new talent with animals of all kinds. Many people in town noticed his rare ability. Occasionally wild animals would come right up to him in the forests and fields, much to the amazement of friends and family alike. He also had a special way with horses. If a horse was too wild and too dangerous to ride, they would leave the horse with Nicholas. With great kindness and patience, he was able to tame any horse. He ended up with a reputation of having the largest and fastest horses in all the land. If a donkey was too stubborn, it would end up with Nicholas as well. Nicholas found that these once wild animals had a special connection with the orphaned children and often protected them from strangers. Somehow their wild or stubborn nature yielded to the sadness, loneliness, or need for love so visible in these children. Perhaps in the world today, the only animal that loves unconditionally is a dog. Back in the times of Nicholas, and even for St. Nicholas today, there remained that unique ability to have all kinds of animals love and respect not only him but also the children he cared for with such love and tenderness.

1 Timothy 6:17-19
Command those who are rich in this present world not to be arrogant nor to put their hope in wealth, which is so uncertain, but to put their hope in God, who richly provides us with everything for our enjoyment. Command them to do good, to be rich in good deeds, and to be generous and willing to share. In this way they will lay up treasure for themselves as a firm foundation for the coming age, so that they may take hold of the life that is truly life. (NIV)

Chapter 3

Nicholas Chosen

By the time Nicholas reached Jerusalem, the entire city was full of rumors, stories and activities all related to Jesus Christ and his disciples. The number of disciples was growing daily and many left their houses and earthly goods to spread the good word. As the number of people seeking Jesus grew to thousands, the distribution of food became a problem. Men, who were once fishermen and farmers, left their boats and their fields to become fishers of men.

It was in these exciting times of the gospel that Nicholas became known to the twelve disciples as word had spread of his good deeds and superb craftsmanship as well as being known by all as eminently fair. So Nicholas became chosen along with Stephen, Philip, Timon and others to help distribute the food fairly among the disciples, widows and children of all faiths. The apostles of Jesus laid their hands upon Nicholas to pray for him to give him wisdom and to seek to be Godly in all his actions with other men on earth.

Thus, Nicholas of Antioch became known for all time as a man chosen, selected by the Apostles, a man to be honored for his wisdom and fairness, a man known for his generosity and giving spirit, a man who uniquely shared the same birthday with Jesus, who had also chosen Nicholas.

The Apostles did not know about Nicholas when they chose him. Well before being chosen, Nicholas was known as a man of God. He spent time each day in prayer. He spent time each week seeking out children who were in need of food or clothes or simply to be uplifted. His workshops became the depositories of a never-ending supply of vast amounts of clothing, food, and children's gifts. Even merchants from far away, hearing of Nicholas and his deeds would seek him out. Sometimes, if they arrived in Jerusalem late at night, they would simply leave sacks of food and clothes on his doorstep to be delivered to those in need.

By the age of 32 and having been married for many years,

Nicholas and Anna Marie resigned their fate to never having children of their own. But more than any man of his time, children sought him as a friend, not because he gave them gifts, but because they could see in him a man who loved children and who was always a child on the inside. You could always see his eyes sparkle in the presence of children and many would run to him to give him a hug or a kiss on the cheek.

One day, as the disciples met with Jesus in a field near Jerusalem, Nicholas happened to pass by. Behind him was a trail of children, some healthy, some crippled, some lost or unwanted by the outside world but all singing and playing and laughing. As they passed by the field where the disciples and Jesus were talking, the Apostles all stopped and watched as Nicholas passed by with his caravan. At the back of the line was a little girl in simple clothes, with bright red cheeks leading a donkey laden with goods. She was holding a long rope to guide him along. The little girl's name was Rosie. The donkey's name was Old Faithful. As Nicholas went by, Rosie stopped and stared at the men underneath the tree. She had often seen Nicholas take food from the sacks and give some to the poor and needy. All Rosie could see through her eyes, as she stared at the men under the tree, were men in need. In her eyes they had no place to sleep or food to eat and in one sense were worse off than she was because she had a home with Nicholas and Anna Marie. So in her innocence she went off the road, leading Old Faithful to the disciples. They were stunned when Rosie interrupted Jesus while he was speaking. She smiled and looked into the eyes of Jesus. Slowly she walked up to him and handed him the end of the rope, thus offering Christ all she had in the world. She did not know who He was, only that it looked like He needed help. The disciples immediately stood up, being protective of Jesus. There was a prolonged silence. Tears came to the eyes of Jesus. Rosie went to him and hugged his knees since she was so short then. Then Rosie ran back to the road to find her place once again at the end of the caravan.

It was at that very moment in time that Nicholas was chosen for the most amazing task in history. It was one that was so perfect for him, and for all of us. It was in this gesture of kindness and giving from a little girl, a child who had learned the true spirit of giving from Nicholas, a man who had no children of his own, that would lead Nicholas to ultimately become a Saint, unique among all others. He would become an immortal Saint who would roam the earth among men, long after the time Jesus ascended into heaven after rising from His tomb.

On the way back to town along this ancient path, Nicholas and his little caravan would discover Old Faithful tied to the same tree, waiting. Rosie gleefully ran to him, so happy to see her friend again. She gave him long green grass she found in the field. She never quite understood how the sacks now on the donkey became so heavily laden with food and clothes. She just untied the rope and led Old Faithful back to the workshop at the Nicholas' house. It would help feed the many children who stayed with them, never formally adopted, but always loved and cared for with a tenderness usually only given to a son or daughter.

Many other married couples in that era were also not able to have their own natural children. There did not seem to be any particular reason for this and although a random occurrence, it led many couples to be sad or to think they were being punished. For those who had to do the daily tasks of work on farms or in the city, having children to help with these chores was an important part of family life and sometimes even a necessity. At that time, there was no such thing as an orphanage run by the state or government. If children were separated from their parents or their parents had died, they were taken by the rich to be slaves, unless relatives could raise them. To Nicholas, this was a tragedy and an unbearable heartache. So in his own way, he set about to change the system to one based on kindness and freedom, not on greed and slavery. It would take many centuries to complete that task.

Over time, the property where the house and workshop stood became an unusual gathering place for infertile couples who wanted children of their own. At the Saturday noon meal they often gathered in large numbers to partake of the food and merriment but more importantly it provided an opportunity for people to meet and to get to know the children under the care of Nicholas and Anna Marie. It was the first true orphanage based on love that offered hope to both the children and the couples who sought to adopt them. Nicholas never accepted a fee for these children. Rather the parents would promise to return them each year to prove the child was safe, happy and well cared for. At that time, many brought gifts of food and clothing for the other children waiting to find a couple with whom to go home. Each time people offered gold or silver, Nicholas would put his hands on his belly and laugh as his way of saying that payment has already been received in ways money cannot buy. Sometimes he would suggest the money could be used to buy the children clothes, seeds for the next harvest, or for a fund to help build a temple or church for worship.

To keep track of so many children, Nicholas would make long lists with their names, where they went and what they needed. Each year he would update their sizes. When he couldn't see them, he would receive word by letter on how they were doing. Most of the original letters to Nicholas were not asking for anything. Rather, the first letters to Santa were letting him know of their families or to let him know about other children in desperate need of food, clothing, shelter or medical care. Nicholas learned how to make long narrow papers for these lists. They could be rolled up like scrolls and were records of service for thousands of men, women and children not only in Jerusalem but also far north of Antioch and eventually in all directions of the known world.

Despite his responsibilities at churches and temples, and the growing obligations of the orphanage and the bulging workshops, Nicholas always found time to play. When he decided to be really silly and playful, the screams of joy and howls of laughter from the many children could be heard from miles away.

One of the difficult on-going tasks at the orphanage was doing laundry. They were fortunate to have a fast flowing stream of clean water that passed near the house and workshops. Sometimes in the summer Nicholas made up games to clean the clothes. He crafted a large mound of dirt with a wooden ladder leading to the peak that the children would climb up to with joy. He diverted some water with a wheel and buckets to splash on top of the mound creating a long slippery fast chute of water and mud. Each time the children washed five pieces of clothing they got to climb the ladder and take a wild slippery ride down the chute. As they hit the bottom of the chute they were going very fast and would create a giant splash at the bottom. At the end of the day, all of the clothes were washed and the children were exhausted from having so much fun. He made everyone take a bath on those nights, so in the evening the air was filled with the fragrance of soaps and oils and everyone just glowed with joy. On these nights Nicholas would sometimes sit in a rocking chair he had made, on his front porch and tell stories to the children for hours. With a young child on his lap, rocking back and forth, he soaked in the sounds of children laughing, giggling, sleeping, eating, reading and playing until sleep overcame them all, all except Nicholas.

Some nights he could not sleep. He felt a change was coming over the land. He knew something enormous was about to happen. Perhaps it had to do with the man who shared his birthday, the man everyone now spoke of as the Messiah, King of the Jews, the Son of God.

As merchants and travelers passed through the city they would bring news of Jesus. They would tell stories about where He was and what He said and of the many miracles He performed. Nicholas loved the stories of how Jesus fed so many from so little, a task that was always on his mind in terms of feeding the children who stayed with him. Nicholas, being an excellent scribe, wrote down each of the stories he heard about Jesus and His disciples. Over time it became stacks of papers and scrolls filled with parables, the Sermon on the Mount, and of the many teachings of Jesus to those people He encountered over the years. Nicholas would spend time during each meal with the children to talk about what he had heard. It wasn't just relating the stories that Nicholas heard about Jesus. It was that Nicholas made an effort to ask each of the children to think about how such wonderful ideas affected their daily lives. He realized the children loved learning more and hearing more about Jesus. It made them happier and they realized that although they were poor by human standards, they had great wealth in the spiritual realm. Making the transition from material wealth to being joyous in the spirit is hard for us all, but Nicholas had a rare gift of encouraging children and adults to achieve that goal in life, as the most important thing they could ever do.

After hearing the stories about John the Baptist and that Jesus himself was baptized, Nicholas decided that the children should be baptized. Nicholas could not find one of the disciples that day so he learned what to ask of each of the children and how to baptize them. On a warm summer's day, they all worked together to place rocks across the stream to make a pool of water deep enough to baptize them by total immersion in water. One by one, Nicholas baptized everyone including Anna Marie. When he had finished with the last one, all the children stood by the stream quietly looking at Nicholas. He had grown a long black beard and had long silky black hair that glistened in the summer sun, wet from the waters of baptism. Rosie, always being one to speak her mind openly, asked Nicholas first.

"Poppa Nicholas, who is going to baptize you?"

Nicholas looked a bit surprised and scratched his head.

"Well you know, I hadn't really thought about that. I was so concerned about baptizing each of you, I forgot all about myself."

Anna Marie called to all the children.

"Come now. Everyone make a circle around Poppa Nicholas. We're all going to baptize him together."

Quietly, all of the children circled Nicholas in rings of bright shining faces. They did not splash or play in the water. They knew it was a solemn and serious occasion. They held hands and bowed their heads as the oldest boys stood behind Nicholas to symbolically lower and raise him into the baptism pool. In unison the children repeated the same questions that Nicholas had asked them.

"Do you believe Jesus is the Messiah sent by God and that Jesus is the Son of God?"

Nicholas: "I do."

"Do you believe in the Virgin birth?"

Nicholas: "Yes."

"Do you repent all of your sins and accept God as your Savior?"

Nicholas: "Yes, I do."

And with that Nicholas was immersed in the baptism pool. When he arose his body and clothes were dripping wet. He had a giant smile on his face. It felt wonderful. It was as if a weight had been lifted from his heart.

After Jesus died on the cross, baptism was changed to be more centered on salvation than repentance, but whether they were baptized before or after the crucifixion, all the children of Nicholas felt a closeness to God. One of their many blessings of the house of Nicholas and Anna Marie was that it was always a house centered on God, and therefore a house filled with love and joy.

Nicholas performed thousands of baptisms over the coming centuries. As the years passed, some of the questions or words changed. In some countries the ritual was different as well as the language. The objective was common in any language, in any country at any time -- to give your heart and soul to the Lord, to follow His ways, to seek light and truth, to accept Jesus as your Lord and Savior and to believe in Him and to have faith. Faith is to accept things which cannot be been, but which have an enormous impact on your life. Nicholas was strong in God as a man, as a husband and as the temporary father to thousands who lived under his roof in the centuries that would pass. He had no idea how God had chosen him for the most special task ever to befall human hands. Nicholas had no idea of how soon his life, his legend, his immortality would influence millions of people and how he would become an integral part of the holiday that would eventually be called Christmas.

Acts 6:1-7

In those days when the number of disciples was increasing, the Grecian Jews among them complained against the Hebraic Jews because their widows were being overlooked in the daily distribution of food. So the Twelve gathered all the disciples together and said, "It would not be right for us to neglect the ministry of the word of God in order to wait on tables. Brothers, choose seven men from among you who are known to be full of the spirit and wisdom. We will turn this responsibility over to them and will give our attention to prayer and the ministry of the word." This proposal pleased the whole group. They chose Stephen, a man full of faith and of the Holy Spirit, also Philip, Procorus, Nicanor, Timon, Parmenas, and Nicholas from Antioch, a convert to Judaism. They presented these men to the apostles who prayed and laid hands on them. So the word of God spread. The number of disciples in Jerusalem increased rapidly, and a large number of priests became obedient to the faith. (NIV)

18

Chapter 4

Jesus And The Cross

By the time Nicholas celebrated his 33rd birthday, the entire area in which he lived was flooded with the excitement generated by Jesus of Nazareth. Every merchant who passed through the house and workshops where Nicholas worked, spoke to him about the Messiah, the miracles, and the physical healing that had been done. Nicholas was excited like everyone else about the man with whom he shared a common birthday, but at the same time he had an overwhelming sense of concern for his safety and the future of his church and the local government. Underneath the surface of excitement Nicholas could see the underpinnings of jealousy and even anger that such a wise and humble man like Jesus might usurp the power and authority of the Rabbis and the Roman governors in his area.

He could feel the increasing level of unrest everywhere he went. Known as a man who prayed, known as a man who was generous and loving to children, in the eyes of the local government and churches, Nicholas became a disciple of Christ and a suspect in a possible uprising against the established religious and government authorities. As a result, the number of requests for his services as a finish carpenter slowly diminished to the point that Nicholas struggled to maintain the orphanage and workshops. Yet despite his problems, he was always amazed to find that people quietly and silently left donations at his house to continue supporting his good works.

To try to subvert his will to the local government, the heads of state in Jerusalem gave Nicholas some work for their needs. To his dismay, it was tasks such as forging metal doors and bars for prisons, which housed political and religious men as well as thieves. They also gave him menial jobs, such as making wooden crosses for crucifixions of prisoners.

To Nicholas and his family, Jesus offered the hope of salvation for all mankind. More importantly, his efforts at the orphanage taught men and women to be kind and generous and to love their neighbors. It was such good and honest teachings that gave them all hope that the world in which they lived would improve and offer his many children a chance to find good homes with loving and caring parents. At the same time, Nicholas realized that the more he gave to others, the more he received, not only in physical secret donations from strangers, but in ways that could not be measured on any earthly scale. He felt a deep sense of love and his heart was overfilled with joy. It was perhaps Nicholas more than any other man on earth who sensed the coming and the first presence of the Holy Spirit sent by Jesus at the time of his death and resurrection.

On a cold and windy day in late March, right at the time of the evening meal, there was a loud knock on Nicholas' door. He had just finished his prayers over the evening meal. The children stopped eating and stared at the door as Nicholas opened it cautiously. It was a group of Roman Guards who shouted their demands at Nicholas, who spoke not a word.

"You must make three wooden crosses immediately. Two are to be of the usual size and one of them is to be taller and heavier than any others you have made before. And we need some nails. This time longer spikes to make it easier to pull them out when we are through. Speak to no one about this."

As the one mean guard shouted at Nicholas, two of the others who escorted him kept looking at Rosie and Peter, two of the children in the kitchen. In return they stared back. Both of them seemed curious because there was a striking resemblance between the two guards and the two children. Nicholas never looked up into their faces but looked sadly at the floor, nodding his head that he would comply with their request. He was crushed and saddened at this request, although he had no idea for whom these crosses were meant, nor of the immense impact of the upcoming world event centered around the man for whom the large cross would be used. He only knew that he must obey or else the local governor would remove him for disobedience and leave all the children without food and shelter. The Roman guards disappeared into the night and slowly Nicholas closed the door. He was not hungry any more. He sat in silence during dinner, which instead of the usual noisy excitement was respectfully quiet. Somehow the children understood that it was a sad, solemn evening.

The next day, Nicholas went out and took Old Faithful to haul back the lumber for the crosses. He took Rosie, who had once given that very donkey to Jesus when it was laden with food, with him. They walked and talked and sang until by coincidence they came upon the very tree under which Jesus and his disciples had rested when they encountered him some months before. They decided that this tree would be good wood for the crosses and for future gifts that Nicholas could craft by carving. It was a tall oak tree with many straight branches. Nicholas had often spoken to the children about being an oak of righteousness when they grew up.

Nicholas spent the morning cutting down the tree and then cutting it into pieces to be bundled and dragged back. The burden was too much for Old Faithful so Nicholas went back with a load and then returned later in the day with more donkeys to haul the rest back to the workshops. The wood was dense and heavy, and the journey back to the workshops was over a bumpy road. By the evening he had brought all the wood from the tree back to the lumber shed and was working on making the crosses. There was a sadness that seemed to fall over the house, as Nicholas was unusually quiet.

After the evening meal, Nicholas went to the woodshed and worked well into the night to finish the six pieces of lumber needed for the crosses. Then he forged the nails to be used to attach the pairs of pieces together and the longer spikes. As he forged the last of the nails and poured the molten metal, some of it formed drops that bounced up out of the mold. Nicholas was burned with small circles on the tops of both his hands and feet. He quickly placed them in buckets of water to soothe the pain. The burns were not deep but they would leave permanent scars. In the coming winters he would often wear gloves that covered these scars not only because his hands were cold, but more so out of the shame he felt for forging the nails and making the cross upon which God's only son was crucified.

The Roman guards came at dawn and collected the lumber for the crosses with a wagon drawn by large white horses. They threw down into the dust a small bag of coins to pay Nicholas for the lumber and nails. He used the money to buy wheat to feed his many children. He cleaned up the pouch of leather that held the coins and decorated it with pretty patterns. He then filled it with colorful glass balls which would one day be known to young children as marbles, and placed it in the stack of gifts being saved up for the coming December.

Nicholas and his many children did not work that day. For this was no ordinary day but the day all on earth shall remember forever. At noon on this day, they saw the sun go dark in the sky. At three o'clock that afternoon the earth shook and the tremors were felt for hundreds of miles. On this day, Jesus, the Son of God, born to the Virgin Mary, was crucified along with two others on a hill at Calvary. Nicholas felt a darkness fall over the earth. He felt sad for a reason he would soon be made to understand. The wounds on his hands and feet hurt and for the first time started to bleed. He washed them and tenderly Anna Marie bandaged them. Both of them were silent and simply could not speak. They knew the darkness and earthquakes could only be a sign of something tragic happening in their land.

At nightfall, the sound of the Roman guard was once again heard at his front door. They were returning the lumber used for the crosses. Once again they were shouting and once again Nicholas could not lift his head to look into their eyes.

"Now the blood of Jesus in on your hands. Some king! He could not even save himself on the cross. You can have your wood back and your nails too. The iron pierced his body like butter. So much for the King of the Jews."

It was at this moment that Nicholas and all the children realized what had happened. Nicholas was stunned and could barely move. Rosie and Peter stared at the two Roman guards who looked so much like them and wondered what kind of men could do such a thing to a man of God, a man who loved children and healed the sick.

Is there anyone on earth who could bear the pain of knowing he had made the nails and the cross used to crucify the Son of God? Nicholas would not hear for several days that Christ would rise on Sunday morning and would once again walk amongst men. As far as Nicholas knew at that moment he would be forever known as the man who helped to crucify Jesus. That pain, that sorrow, that knowledge was more than he could bear.

For miles around the house of Nicholas, people could hear the sound of wailing. The cry was almost not human in sound. For his whole life, Nicholas was known for his belly laugh and his singing. No one had ever heard him cry let alone wail and with such volume and intensity that it scared the children who hid inside the house and cried, huddled on the floor. All during the night, Nicholas cried and tore at his clothes, begging God's forgiveness.

At dawn he dragged the lumber stained with blood into the wood shed. He closed the door and locked it from the inside so no one could enter. At sunrise, the light of the sun struck Nicholas on the face as he remained on his knees in prayer, begging the Lord to strike him down for what he had done because he could not bear the pain any longer.

Our God is a merciful God. Our God is a wise and kind God. He knew of the tree before the disciples had gathered under its branches for shelter. He knew that Nicholas would forge the nails and cut the tree before the earth was formed. And He knew now, seeing Nicholas so repentant and full of sorrow, what He must do to fulfill the destiny of the man who would hereafter be known not as the man who built the cross, but as the saint we all came to know and love as Christ's Santa.

As Nicholas knelt upon the ground, the sun from a new dawn streaked through his workshop window. The dust floating in the air formed bright white spots in the midst of the streaming light. Rarely in our lives can we hear the voice of God speaking to us, but for Nicholas this would be one of those special moments.

"Nicholas my child, weep no longer, for I know of your sorrow and pain. The destiny of my son has been fulfilled and for your part in the salvation of all mankind, it is not your fate to suffer for forging the nails and crafting the cross. No Nicholas, stop your weeping for your work has yet to begin. Arise now and work until your bones can no longer move. Work as I command of you and all that has happened shall become for the good."

Nicholas could not lift up his eyes for fear of the Lord and out of deepest respect and an overwhelming sense of remorse and humbleness. He spoke as he had never done before.

"But Father, I have made the cross and forged the nails upon which your son has died. How can I live with this sin? It is more than I can bear, rather strike me down as I kneel before you that this pain may be taken from my heart."

As Nicholas spoke he could feel the workshop get warmer and although all windows and doors were shut, he could hear a wind blowing inside. Soon that wind wrapped him in sound, force and light. His body felt re-energized and warm, and his belly felt nourished as if he had just partaken in the harvest festival meal. He opened his eyes for a moment to see his whole body enveloped in dancing sparkling light which made pins of light all over his skin and clothes and which seemed to jump into his body, penetrating every pore. His eyes filled with tears and he could no longer look upon the dancing lights of so many colors streaming and streaking throughout the workshop and his body.

Finally the wind subsided and Nicholas could hear the voice of God once again.

"Nicholas, I have this day taken from the tree of life and given unto you what few other have known on earth. You have become a true Saint, immortal, living upon the earth amongst other men. Your destiny shall be to show all people the true meaning of giving. You will know what to do, which is to continue along the path upon which you have already embarked. Remain that oak of righteousness and surely goodness, joy and laughter will follow you for many centuries into the future until my son comes once again. Though the blood of my son is upon the cross you fashioned by your own hands, you must now take it upon yourself to turn all of that into gifts, the greatest gifts you can bestow upon those believers who are worthy."

With that, the workshop suddenly became still and silent. Anna Marie was very worried about her husband, and went out to the workshop and knocked on the door. She was surprised it was locked. He had never done that before. Nicholas got up off his knees and opened the door. As he swung the door open and as his wife saw his face, she started to scream and quickly put both hands over her mouth to dampen the noise. The night before, Nicholas had long black hair and a long curly beard. Now, standing before her was a man who had a long white beard and curly white hair with a touch of silver. His violet eyes sparkled and she knew it was Nicholas and knew in her heart something very wondrous had just happened. Nicholas held out his arms and smiled and Anna Marie hugged him tight and cried. Nicholas rocked her gently back and forth and slowly in whispers told her what had happened.

"Anna, something wonderful has just happened. I am not sure how to explain it or why it has happened to me. I am responsible for making the cross upon which Jesus was killed. I am the man who forged the nails that corrupted his flesh and held him to that cross. Surely, in all the history of mankind there can be no more horrible a crime that a man could commit against his God, than to be the one who helped crucify His only son. Yet...yet our God is so amazing. I cannot help but weep for joy. He has forgiven me for what I have done. How is that possible? How could anyone on earth forgive me for such a crime? I cannot forgive myself. How could God, how could Jesus then forgive my sins? I understand now this cross, this sacrifice. His sacrifice was not just for us, but for all of mankind and all of time. I know now it was the greatest event in all of human history."

Nicholas paused for a moment then stepped back and put his hands on Anna Marie's shoulders. Her bright red hair had a glow to it even in the dimly lit workshop lighting. He was always a man of truth but hesitated over the words God had spoken to him that fateful morning.

"Anna, there is something else. God spoke to me just now. He told me I am forgiven. He did something to my body and heart inside and out. He said I am now immortal and shall know what to do. I have an immediate task that is to transform the cross from a symbol of death and sin, into one of joy and love and the spirit of giving. I must not let anyone in this principality know we have this cross, nor its meaning, nor what we shall do to transform it for all time. People will see that I am changed. We cannot stay here forever because everyone will see that I remain while others pass on. That is part of the reason why He has made me appear so old now. It will take years for you to catch up in aging my sweet wife. Please don't worry about this."

Anna Marie gently touched his face with her fingertips.

"Nicholas, I do not understand. What is it God wants you to do? And if you are now immortal, what shall become of us? I will grow old and die but you shall live on. How can that be good?"

Nicholas gently kissed her cheeks and held her shoulders.

"All I know is that God has given us a great task to do. This task, this work will bring us joys even greater than we have ever known before. We shall have many children with us and our blessings shall be greater in number than you can count. Just believe in your heart that God works out everything for the good. Now, I have a great deal of work to do. Please watch after the children today. Let me know if you hear of any news from the city. I will remain in here today. Do not let anyone in or know I am here. Tell the children not to fear my new looks, rather to rejoice in a new and marvelous task that God has sent me to do for them, all of them, all of the children on God's earth."

1 Peter 4:8-11

Above all, love each other deeply, because love covers over a multitude of sins. Offer hospitality to one another without grumbling. Each one should use whatever gift he has received to serve others, faithfully administering God's grace in its various forms. If anyone speaks, he should do it as one speaking the very words of God. If anyone serves, he should do it with the strength God provides so that in all things God may be praised through Jesus Christ. To him shall be the glory and the power forever and ever Amen. (NIV)

Chapter 5

The First Christmas Gifts

Nicholas spent the entire day with the cross. He had trouble touching it at first and still had trouble accepting his responsibility in the death of Jesus on the cross that he had fashioned of wood and nails. He began his task by slowly pulling out all of the nails from the large cross. When he gathered them all together he could still see bright red blood on the cold iron. He slowly and respectfully collected them altogether and then re-forged them. He had to devise a way for them to no longer be recognized as the nails used to hold Christ by his hands and feet to the wood. He decided it was best to recast them as buttons. That way they could be seen clearly yet no one would ever know from whence they came. Later on, Nicholas would use those buttons for his red coat that has now become a symbol of his traditional clothing. Few understand the significance of the large buttons used to keep his coat snug and warm on his body while traveling to deliver gifts of kindness and love. He would never touch the buttons again by hand, only with his tools or with gloves on to show the greatest respect for their holy origins.

Next Nicholas worked on the two large pieces of the cross of Christ. He cut them into small blocks that he could later use to carve bowls, cups, toys, spinning tops, animals and other gifts for children to be given on December 25th as a remembrance of the birth of Jesus, not his death. That day in December would later be known as Christmas.

At dusk, Rosie came to the door and brought Nicholas some food. She knocked softly and called him by name and finally he answered. He hid behind the door, afraid to show his face to Rosie, concerned that she might be frightened. Finally, he slowly peered from around the door and saw Rosie standing there waiting for him to show his face. Rosie beamed and held up a bowl covered with a kitchen cloth.

"Look Poppa Nicholas! I made it myself. It's bread and butter with some cooked vegetable stew. I put everything I could find in the kitchen into it."

She smiled waiting for him to take it. He slowly leaned forward looking carefully at her eyes. There was no fear. She would not run away. He wondered why.

"Rosie, doesn't my new appearance frighten you?"

Rosie just kept on smiling and pointed to his face.

"Oh no Poppa Nicholas. Now we're the same. Look! You have big rosy cheeks just like mine."

Nicholas went to look into the mirror in his workshop. He hadn't noticed. He touched his cheeks with his hands. He could see the reflections of his circular scars on the topside of his hands. He started to cry.

"Don't cry. Please Poppa Nicholas. Everything is going to be all right. You'll see. Trust me. I'll take care of you."

Nicholas stopped crying and lifted his head.

"You'll take care of me?"

Rosie nodded her innocent head. Her curly hair bounced as she nodded up and down. Finally she ran and hugged Nicholas. He picked her up and kissed both her cheeks. Then he started to laugh.

"Oh, I see. So you're going to take care of me are you? Then who is going to take care of you?"

As he spoke to Rosie he touched his finger to the tip of her nose and smiled in a kind gesture, almost teasing her. Rosie shrugged her shoulders. Quietly but with authority she spoke to Nicholas.

"Jesus. He told me to tell you not to worry. I'm going to stay with you until I get married. Then I'm going to have lots of children too. And when I die, Jesus will send me back to help you. So you see, there's nothing to worry about!"

Nicholas nodded his head in part agreeing with her yet wondering where in the world she came up with that.

"What do you mean Jesus told you Rosie? Jesus died on the cross, the cross I made. Don't you think he would be very mad at me for doing that?"

Rosie shook her head no as her curls bounced side to side.

"Oh no. Jesus died but He's going to come back just like He said. By Sunday morning he won't be in the tomb any more. And he told me He loves you Poppa Nicholas. Everybody does. And now we can call you Santa because you're a Saint. Is that all right with you? I like that. It sounds a lot better than just Poppa Nicholas. But Santa, when I come back to help you, can I just work in the kitchen and take care of the animals? I really don't know how to make toys."

Rosie sometimes could go on and on holding up both ends of a conversation at the same time. Nicholas loved her for her enthusiasm but most of all, for her faith.

"You can do whatever you like Rosie. We both work for the Boss from now on. What do you think?"

Rosie looked a little puzzled by this.

"Who is the Boss now Santa? You mean Momma Marie?"

Nicholas laughed at her wonderful view of their family.

"No sweetheart. I mean Jesus. From now on we are all going to work for Him. It will be like before, only different. Now we know that we are saved. If He can forgive me, then He can forgive anyone."

Anna Marie suddenly walked into the workshop looking worried.

"Nicholas, I have just heard from our neighbors. The Roman guards are going to return for the crosses. They want to burn them to destroy any evidence that Christ ever lived. They want to destroy anything that He touched so that He will soon be forgotten. What should we do?"

Nicholas stared out the window and then looked at the blocks of wood scattered on the floor and tables that came from the cross. Then he smiled and turned to Rosie.

"I need your help Rosie. I am going to send you on a secret mission. I want you to go to our neighbors and ask for the blood of a lamb. Someone has surely killed a lamb for the Sunday meal. Bring the blood back to me in a wineskin, so that no one may suspect what it contains. Can you do that for me?"

Rosie stood at attention, so happy to go on a secret mission.

"Yes boss. Oh, I'm sorry. I mean yes Santa."

She looked up at Anna Marie and then dashed out the door to complete her task. By then it was dark but she knew her way by heart. Anna Marie looked at Nicholas and folded her arms across her chest.

"Nicholas, what does she means by calling you Santa and who is the Boss?"

Nicholas was too distracted with the tasks now confronting him.

"I'll explain later my dear wife. But right now I must hurry to prepare another cross."

Nicholas started to prepare some more lumber in the workshop but Anna Marie was getting concerned about all this.

"Nicholas, you are not going to pull this off like a magician. The Roman guards can be very dangerous if they realize you have fooled them."

Nicholas nodded in agreement.

"Yes, you are right. But do not worry. I will use the blood of the lamb and pour it onto the timbers so that no one shall ever suspect the cross of Jesus is actually here in pieces, waiting to be made into very special gifts. These gifts shall always give. No gifts will ever be made after this that shall be more powerful and more spiritual than these. They shall remain in loving hands and passed on for generations until He comes again. Ah, I realize now how perfect all of this is and shall be. I can see now it was planned so long ago. We are just willing players in the greatest story ever told, ever known. It is so wonderful. Now I see. We are so blessed."

That night Nicholas made a duplicate of the original tall cross from the same oak tree lumber. He used the lamb's blood to stain the surface of the wood where he had made nail holes to duplicate those where Christ's hands and feet were nailed to the cross. Then he placed the pieces stained with blood, next to the fire used to cast the molten metals so that they dried quickly.

In the morning the Roman guards came banging on his door. Nicholas was completely prepared. They would never suspect him of the switch he had made. Anna Marie opened the door. Quickly the guards started shouting,

"What have you done with the timbers from the crosses we brought back to you the other day? You are to return them at once. Those are our orders."

Anna Marie, looking afraid of the soldiers, just pointed to six pieces of wood in the front of the workshop. The guards dashed over to examine them, then satisfied they were the right ones, signaled to the wagon to come over to pick them up.

"Take all of this lumber and burn it, burn it all, and then scatter the ashes over the ground so that no one can ever recover it. Go as fast as you can and report back to me when you are finished."

In a few moments they scurried away and once again there was silence in the house and courtyard. Nicholas opened his workshop door and Anna Marie just nodded to him. In their haste to recover the cross, they never suspected that Nicholas had preserved the original cross in pieces, which would be given out over the centuries.

Rosie came to the door and smiled at Anna Marie. She looked very proud.

"Mission accomplished! But what are people going to say when they see Santa? Everyone will see it is no longer just Nicholas. Maybe they will be afraid of him when they see what God has done. What are you going to tell the other children and our neighbors and all those who come seeking him? So many come here bringing children or wanting to find children of their own to adopt. Will they still come?"

Anna Marie wiped her hands on her apron and looked lovingly at Rosie.

"I don't know, Rosie. Those are good questions. When Nicholas comes back into the house we can ask him about that. Right now though, I think he needs to catch up on his sleep after staying up too many nights working in the workshop. For now, we will just tell the other children Nicholas is sleeping and everyone must be quiet."

Later that day, miles away, the Roman guards burned everything they could find that Jesus had touched, including the new cross. They never found out about the switch Nicholas had made. They thought by turning all that Jesus had touched to ashes they could somehow erase His memory from the men and women who had witnessed the miracles and the crucifixion.

It would take years for people to better understand what really happened that day. They had no idea the magnitude of the events that were taking place. In fact, Jesus was with his disciples again for a short while before He finally ascended into heaven. As He promised, He sent the Holy Spirit to earth so that we could feel His presence in us at all times. More than other men, more than other Saints, the soul, the spirit of Nicholas became overflowing with a double dose of the Spirit. Though he was immortal amongst other men on earth, truly there was never a more kind and giving soul. All who crossed his path from then on knew they were in the presence of a great and gentle soul, a quiet giant and servant to all mankind.

That night Anna Marie gathered all the children and explained simply that God had turned Nicholas's hair white and not to be afraid of his new appearance. She also explained about Jesus and the blood of

Christ and how He died on the cross for our sins. They all decided as a group to show their love for God for sending His only son. They decided to wear clothes of scarlet representing the warmth of God for church services. Every December 25th for his birthday, they would return from wherever they had traveled and would celebrate with Nicholas and Anna Marie. The gathering place would thereafter be known as Santa's Workshop. It may be in a different place every year but they would find it or be guided there by praying and asking God to show them the way.

Many years from then, Nicholas would often think about those events and about how wonderful his dear wife Anna Marie was during their time together. Centuries after the bible was written, during the times Nicholas thought about these things, he would sit and read from Proverbs 31. In his own mind, the woman of noble character referred to in this part of the bible was none other than his Anna Marie. He would love her always. He would never marry again. They were soul mates for eternity.

To this very day, every Christmas Eve, the angels of those special children still gather with Saint Nicholas at Santa's Workshop, wherever that may be. Some people have seen the gathering of the angels and over the years have reported seeing strange glowing lights on December 24th, sometimes in the desert, sometimes in the mountains, sometimes on the plains and even in the northern places covered with snow. Today, Santa still roams all over the earth.

In the coming months after the events of the cross, everyone got used to seeing Nicholas with white hair. Some thought it was from the stress of being so poor and working so hard. Thus, the donations to the orphanage came in faster than ever before. Many of the children found homes with good families. Nicholas always made sure his children were loved and cared for. In one sense, he never had any biological children of his own. Yet he would have more children than any man could ever imagine or even count in a single lifetime.

He slowly crafted the blocks from the cross into gift boxes, toys, tops, animals and figurines of Joseph, Mary and Jesus. He kept them in a special bag that Anna Marie sewed from scarlet cloth. Even after several years not all of the blocks had been carved into gifts. Nicholas had a hard time with the pieces that had blood upon them. On those blocks the blood of Christ had seeped into the pores and cracks of the oak. Those Nicholas left as natural in color and for all time, the blood remained red and never darkened. All those who touched those special gifts would have their lives changed forever. For these were the first true gifts of Christmas. They were not fancy electronic toys nor expensive things purchased from a store. No. They were from the cross and the blood of Christ. It is from this cross and his blood that all true gifts to mankind have their origins. Traditions from different countries have confused these origins. The spirit of giving takes many forms. But the first true Christmas gifts came from Christ. It could be no other way.

Proverbs 31:10-21

Epilogue: A Wife Of Noble Character

A wife of noble character who can find? She is worth far more than rubies. Her husband has full confidence in her and lacks nothing of value. She brings him good, not harm, all the days of her life. She selects wool and flax and works with eager hands. She is like the merchant ships, bringing her food from afar. She gets up while it is still dark; she provides food for her family and portions for her servant girls. She considers a field and buys it; out of her earnings she plants a vineyard. She sets about her work vigorously; her arms are strong for her tasks. She sees that her trading is profitable, and her lamp does not go out at night. In her hands she holds the distaff and grasps the spindle with her fingers. She opens her arms to the poor and extends her hands to the needy. When it snows, she has no fear for her household, for all of them are clothed in scarlet. (NIV)

Chapter 6

The First Easter

After word spread that Christ had risen and was indeed the Messiah as foretold in the scriptures, the number of disciples increased at a rapid rate. Men, women and children all over the known world started a movement that has persisted to this day. They asked Jesus to take control of their lives and lead them. They accepted Him as their Lord and Savior and they became baptized. Many learned the words of Jesus that he had spoken to the multitudes gathered during His last years of His earthly form. Even today people are learning the importance of loving thy neighbor, His greatest commandment. Others are taking up the challenge of the Great Commission, which is to go out and disciple to all nations and baptize the people of this good earth to be true children of God.

Nicholas had now become a Saint and personified the love Jesus had preached to all his followers. Saint Nicholas loved to make others happy, not just with physical gifts but also with spiritual gifts which had a much greater eternal value. Nicholas became the symbol of giving and loving thy neighbor. In his early days as a Saint, his work was never more needed. As governments tried to suppress the movement that swept the known world like a wild fire on a dry summer's day, it left in its wake more homeless children and orphans than ever before.

To address the huge number of children who had lost their parents by crucifixion or murder by the state, St. Nicholas realized he needed to mobilize the forces of goodness in people throughout the world. He had to show them how to join together to form a support network for all of these children who needed help. More than just food or clothing or shelter, they needed love and attention and role models to teach them to lead a righteous life. It did not matter to St. Nicholas what religious faith people were, for he knew in his heart, all paths lead to God. Some organized religions over the years ended up calling themselves Catholics, Protestants, Christians, Baptists, Methodists,

Quakers and thousands of other names. To St. Nicholas, our beloved Santa Claus, all those names didn't matter. The only important thing to him was -- did a child of God need help and how could he get that job done. There were too many children then and especially now who need help. So Santa learned to help grown-ups take on many of the needed tasks. This included building homes for needy children and teaching them about taking a part of their earned wealth and sharing it with others. Most importantly, Santa symbolized the most wonderful fact that Jesus had taught us all, that the more you give, the more you receive. This concept seems odd to speak of, and difficult to understand. Yet everyone who has offered a drink of water to a thirsty stranger, shared food with a child or a family in need, offered shelter to a weary traveler, or given money, time, or labor to their church, already knows the sheer joy and the tremendous blessing such acts bring to your spirit. The more you give, the more you grow until it eventually spills out over your soul and spirit to the point others, even total strangers, can see it and sense it.

Santa realized now, as an immortal, that he was given a worldly task. He could not stay in Jerusalem forever. He was needed everywhere to help show the way. Christ had chosen well, when He picked Nicholas to become one of His special Saints. Santa would become an international icon, a symbol of love and giving.

In the year following the crucifixion and the resurrection of Jesus Christ, St. Nicholas gathered his family of children and spoke to them about their choices. He waited until after the evening meal, at the time he would normally read stories or play with the children. Anna Marie looked worried about what he was going to say. They had talked about it for months but they both knew now was the time. Nicholas gathered all the children in a small circle around him as he sat in his rocking chair with Rosie secure in his lap, half asleep.

"Well, dear children, what a wonderful evening. That was such a wonderful meal. Maybe I'm eating too much lately because my belly seems to be growing."

Rosie patted his big belly and all the children quietly giggled.

"Alright, alright. So I need to eat a little less. But when you cook with Momma Marie it just tastes too good."

Slowly his smiling eyes turned to a more serious gaze. All the children were quiet waiting for his words.

"During the past year since Jesus died and rose again before going to heaven, it has been both a wondrous time and a difficult time. Many children in lands near and far away are suffering from the loss of their parents. We need to do something. We need to show other people how to love one another, how to give, and how to share in a way in which everyone benefits. Our place here is unique and very successful. Anna Marie and I are just so happy, so blessed to have you all as our children. At the same time we wish for all of you to find good homes with parents and families who will love you and care for you, and in return you will show them the wonderful blessings they shall receive by showing what it means to truly love your neighbor."

The children sat quietly and gazed at Santa's white beard, rosy cheeks and listened to his soft and kind voice. Whenever he spoke they always knew it would be kind and truthful. They knew in their hearts he loved them all.

"It is time for Anna Marie and I to move on to other lands. For some of you we need to find homes now with good people who love God and who will love you and care for you. We all know each of you eventually will grow up and seek your own future. It is hard for parents to see their children leave the nest but we accept in our hearts that it is inevitable for each of you to one day seek your own destiny."

The children all turned to each other in quick and quiet whispers. Santa knew what was on their minds. He smiled and for the first time began to laugh with a "Ho, ho, ho." He remembered how Jesus had said in what is now the book of Zechariah 2:6, "Ho, ho, come forth and flee from the land of the north, for I have spread you abroad as the four winds of heaven." Indeed, he was about to begin his own journey of going forth to many lands, all over the world. From this same passage in the bible, Santa would later remember when he commanded his deer and spoke "Up, up and away" because in some versions of the bible when Jesus speaks He is interpreted as saying "Up, up" and at others "Ho, ho". In both cases he is trying to get our attention, and Santa has a wonderful way of doing this with hands on hips, and a smile on his face.

"Ho, ho, ho. There is no urgency in this. We just need to make this our long-term plan together to achieve what must be done. Everyone will be fine. Please do not worry. Some of you will find families here in Jerusalem and nearby towns. Others will come with us on our journey and over time you will find homes in other cities or countries. But, trust me, we will all be serving God in our own way and each of you has His love, His protection and mine. So there will be no frowns nor worries, only excitement about all the wonderful things that will come to pass."

Anna Marie looked at Nicholas and smiled to assure everyone things would be fine. Then she remembered their private discussion about Easter and excitedly reminded him.

"Tell them, Nicholas. Tell them about Easter."

Nicholas nodded and smiled to Anna Marie, thankful for her reminder.

"Oh yes. I almost forgot. As you remember in a few weeks it will be the anniversary of when Jesus died, was resurrected and then went to heaven. This will be remembered as the greatest event in history, greater than the day He was born in December. The disciples of Jesus have spoken to me about what to do to celebrate this event. Everyone who does something special on the Sunday anniversary of when He arose from the tomb will be taking a chance. Those who want to stop the spread of the word will be watching for people who gather in His name or who make themselves known in public such as on the eve of His birth in December. They will be watching out for those who have declared themselves to be Christians. Because I love you and must protect you, we are going to stay here and have our own celebration before we move on."

Rosie got all excited about moving and then hearing about a new celebration, a new holiday for all people of the new faith.

"Poppa Nicholas, what are we going to do to celebrate? We don't have enough gifts yet in the workshops and we are running low on food to eat. What can we do when we have so little?"

Santa laughed, one of his jolly belly laughs.

"Well, we are going to have so much fun I just don't know where to begin. First of all on Friday we shall have a special day of prayer in remembrance of the crucifixion and death of Jesus. I will expect all of you to put on special clothes for that day. There will be no work in the workshops or fields that day."

Rosie could not contain her excitement and interrupted.

"But Poppa Nicholas what games are we going to play? What are we going to do for Saturday and Sunday? When are we moving?"

Nicholas smiled and patted her head with all those big curls.

"Well, you know all those pretty colors we make each year to color the wrapping paper and twines? We are going to use them to make colored eggs. Everyone will collect eggs this week and on Friday we will boil them. Then on Saturday we're going to color the eggs and decorate them. On Saturday night, while you're sleeping, the eggs are all going to disappear."

The children looked confused. Peter spoke up first.

"What do you mean, disappear? You mean they're going away? Why are we going to color them if they're going to disappear?"

Santa leaned back and laughed once again.

"Trust me, it will be fun. On Sunday morning we will all gather here and then everyone will go on an egg hunt. We can use the baskets we have to gather vegetables in the field so everyone gets a chance to bring some back here. Then we'll have a big Easter feast."

Peter looked happy about this but still seemed puzzled.

"If this is the first Easter, does this mean we're going to have the first Easter Egg Hunt?"

Santa wiggled his eyebrows and chuckled quietly. He looked all around the room at the excited eyes of his children and lowered his voice.

"Sometimes it is easy to put names and labels on things we do that are symbolic, things that represent greater events in our lives than we can ever imagine. Children, we are going on the first Easter day egg hunt, but let us never forget what we are doing. We are seeking a new life in Jesus, symbolized by the egg. We are not hunting for objects but seeking the good in other people, represented by eggs of every color. Easter is the day to celebrate our love of God, to worship Him and remind ourselves He is the greatest good, He is the greatest love of our lives."

Rosie who always spoke from her heart or her stomach, that too often lately was almost empty, couldn't help but ask one more question.

"Poppa Nicholas, when we come back with the eggs, can we eat some? I think I'm going to be very hungry."

Anna Marie laughed and covered her mouth so as not to laugh too loudly in front of the other children. Then Santa spoke kindly to her.

"Yes sweetheart. You can eat some. But we have to share to make sure everyone gets some. Maybe you can help me make some rye bread to make sandwiches, so if it's nice weather, we can all go for a walk into the countryside and have a picnic. That way we can play in the field before it gets too late in the day. Maybe we could pick some flowers to decorate the house. That is a nice way to show new life, just like the eggs."

All the children nodded their approval. So the first Easter came to pass in the house of St. Nicholas. There was prayer, thanksgiving for all of God's gifts including the greatest gift, salvation. There were colored eggs, bright fragrant flowers, Easter baskets and the sounds of laughter throughout the countryside, wherever Santa and his children traveled.

Matthew 18:1-4
At that time the disciples came to Jesus and asked, "Who is greatest in the kingdom of heaven?" He called a little child and had him stand among them. And He said; "I tell you the truth, unless you change and become like little children, you will never enter the kingdom of heaven. Therefore, whoever humbles himself like this child is the greatest in the kingdom of heaven. (NIV)

Chapter 7

Santa Travels North

After the first Easter there was another wave of religious persecutions against the followers of Christ. Santa knew it was no longer safe for his wife or children to remain in Jerusalem as such visible symbols of living a life as Christ intended for us all.

Nicholas worked tirelessly to place as many children as possible with good families. At the same time, he packed up his workshops to prepare to migrate to other places that were safe from the dangers of the Roman guard and men who plotted against each other for believing in Jesus as their Lord and savior.

Without notice to his neighbors, so as not to alert the local authorities, he prepared everyone to travel north. Anna Marie made clothes to keep them all warm, as they would travel into countries that were much cooler than Jerusalem. Together they created a caravan of donkeys and wagons laden with food, clothes, Santa's workshop tools and everything from the house. He took with him sixteen children who still had not found good homes.

At dawn they ate their last meal in the house they knew as home. Santa removed the sign on the workshop he had made years ago - CLAUS WORKSHOP - and packed it into one of the wagons. When everyone was ready, he went into the workshop with Anna Marie. Carefully, Santa lifted up a few of the floorboards in the workshop and removed a few special red sacks that glowed in the early morning light. Inside were the toys and gifts Nicholas had made from the cross. There were still some blocks that had not been carved. They were the ones with the blood and holes from the nails. It would take Nicholas some time before he could carve them or attempt to alter their surface. There is power in the blood of Jesus, power far beyond what we can understand as mortal men, power difficult to comprehend even for a Saint like Nicholas.

He replaced the floorboards and held Anna Marie's hands and prayed to Jesus.

"Heavenly Father, I am your humble servant. I come before your throne of grace this day to thank you for our many blessings. I thank you for choosing me to do your will on earth. May I be worthy of your trust in me. Thank you for the gifts of the cross, the salvation of all mankind for all time. I am taking Anna and the children to places north of here and away from danger. Father, I pray for a safe journey wherever it may lead us. Please watch over us, protect us and show us the way. Show us how to better bring others unto you Lord, that we may be true disciples of the word."

Anxious to get going on a new adventure and worried that Nicholas and Anna Marie were taking too long, Rosie and Peter got off their wagon and came inside the workshop. They could see Nicholas and Anna Marie holding hands and they could hear him praying and saw the red sacks glowing with a strange light. Rosie had listened to them talk late at night. She knew much more than the other children. Sometimes children pretend they don't know things to make their parents feel more at ease. Children know their parents are trying to protect them, but most children know far more than their parents believe they do.

Rosie pointed above Santa's head to his halo and then to the sacks on the workshop floor.

"Look Santa. Your head is glowing and so is the sack. Is it because you touched the cross of Jesus? I told you Jesus was not going to be mad at you for making the cross. Why would he make you a Saint and cause you to glow unless he loved you?"

Nicholas was surprised at what he heard. He stared at the sacks containing the gifts carved from the cross. Rosie was right. They were glowing and so was he. Then Peter pointed to Santa's hands.

"Look Poppa Nicholas! Those funny dots on the tops again, just like at your birthday. Maybe when you touch the cross you become like Jesus. Is that a good thing Santa?"

Nicholas reached out his arms to Rosie and Peter who ran and jumped up into his gentle bear hug. He had tears in his eyes.

"We can never be like Jesus, Rosie and Peter. We can only try. Even if He gives me many lifetimes on earth, I will still be trying. It is one of those goals you always strive for but never achieve. That you must always remember. But what you have seen now, you must keep a secret from everyone. No one must know we have the cross of Jesus.

They think it was burned and the ashes scattered to the winds. In the years to come I will pass on these gifts to special people who need the power in them more than others. Can you help me keep that secret?"

Rosie and Peter smiled and nodded yes. Rosie smiled and spoke in a whisper.

"You know I have a secret too?"

Santa opened his eyes wide and raised his eyebrows.

"Really? Can you tell me? I know how to keep secrets too."

Rosie looked over at Anna Marie and Peter.

"Do you promise too?"

Anna Marie thought for a moment. Then she raised her right hand and touched it to her heart first, then her forehead, then her belly, then her right chest and finally her left chest, making a sign of the cross. Rosie, Peter and Santa looked at Anna Marie for a moment a bit puzzled and then understood. From that moment on, making the sign of the cross became a solemn moment and a commitment to being in the spirit of Jesus. It did not mean death or the cross itself, but the remembrance of leading a life as shown to us by God's only son.

Rosie finally spoke very quietly, looking down at the sacks on the floor.

"After I grow up and have my own children, and when I finally go to Jesus in heaven, I'm going to ask Him for something special."

Santa touched her curly locks of hairs and kissed her forehead.

"And what would you ask of your Lord and Savior then that He could not give you now sweet Rosie?"

Rosie hugged Santa tightly, and then spoke with a stronger voice.

"When I go to heaven, I'm going to ask Jesus to send me back so I can always be with you. Being with you always makes me so happy."

Anna Marie had tears in hers eyes and took both hands and placed them on Rosie's face. Anna Marie spoke with the same determination in her voice.

"Me too Rosie. When I go to heaven I'm going to ask God if He will send me back to Santa. After all, how is he going to get along without us?"

And with that they all laughed and hugged. Time to go. Time to begin a new journey. They carried the sacks to the wagons and carefully hid them under clothes so no one would suspect what they really contained. On that day, they began a long journey north. In four weeks they reached Antioch where Nicholas was born. There they found homes for some of the children and many friends from the past.

Seeing the need was great, they also gathered the people of faith in the city and helped them to establish a new orphanage. It took a lot of hard work to get started. But the reputation of Nicholas had spread throughout many lands and when people recognized his name and felt his goodness, they worked together to create wonderful things. Soon in every big city that they traveled through, they were able to organize shelters and homes. More than that, they showed people how to give and by so doing received so much in return. People everywhere have goodness in their hearts. If you show them the way, a way that is full of love and kindness, they will follow.

In the centuries to come, the people of many countries learned to create safe homes for children and the practice of adoption by love, rather than selling children into slavery, changing forever the practice of the old ways. Nicholas stayed in Antioch until the following Easter and then once again packed a caravan to go farther north. This time they knew wherever they went, people would be blessed by what they had to share with them.

At the same time, each December 25th became a special day of giving gifts made by hand, giving food to the needy or providing clothes to those who were cold and hungry. The tradition of Christmas was here to stay. Over the years it would grow into a worldwide phenomena. It started with Nicholas. It became eternal through Jesus and the cross, and the spirit of Christmas remains alive today, in part because Nicholas became a Saint whose spirit lives on forever, and in part because it allows each of us a time each year to express what is deep within our hearts and souls.

Each year Santa and his changing group of children and Anna Marie would pack up and travel to other cities. During those early years, while Rosie and Peter were still children, they mostly traveled north. Later as the centuries passed, Santa would travel throughout the world, to every land and every country.

By the time Rosie was old enough to marry, Santa had reached a place further north than the country now called Norway. It was here that the legend of Santa's Workshop in the North Pole first began. Over time, Santa helped create workshops all over the world. Most of them are not marked with signs. Rather, they are marked by people's hearts and actions. They are found by those who give and choose to love and honor God and Jesus. The language and the religion does not matter. What matters is whether the spirit of loving thy neighbor is in your heart and whether you act upon that spirit, sharing it with others.

In the year 62 AD, Jesus called Anna Marie home to heaven. Nicholas cried because he missed her so much, yet rejoiced knowing she was with Jesus in heaven. He waited for Anna Marie to rejoin him on earth as a living and immortal saint. But she never returned as a living being, rather God sent her back as an angel to help Santa, the answer to her prayer in Jerusalem. As an angel, Anna Marie traveled the earth finding children of all ages who might need the special gifts that Santa or his helpers could offer. Sometimes, she would appear to Santa in his dreams and speak to him about those in need. Other times she would pick up a special pen Santa left by his bedside and she would write down the names, locations and special needs of those children. Santa always knew she had visited because no one else would use the special pen with scarlet ink. The pen was actually made from the feather of a dove that nested near their first home in Antioch.

Although today most people use computers and electronic networks to transmit such messages, Santa, even to this day, relies on his special angels and helpers to deliver messages. For you see, many of those children in need do not have houses or computers, but they do have hope, they do have faith, and sometimes it takes a special effort to let Santa know who really needs help.

Over the past two thousand years, many people who have prayed around Christmas time have reported seeing visions of a woman dressed in royal robes and garments. Most of the time they are probably seeing Mary, mother of Jesus. But every now and then when a child has a special need, and when they say a special prayer, a few may see Anna Marie, wife of St. Nicholas, an angel, a messenger. For more than any woman who ever lived, she was the mother to thousands of children, none of whom came from her womb, but all were deeply loved and cherished and close to her heart.

You may never see an angel your whole life, though they are all around us. Perhaps one day or one night, you may see a glimpse of an angel with red hair and scarlet and purple robes. Then you will know that you have seen the blessed wife of Santa Claus, Anna Marie, who some in the northern countries today still call Mother Christmas.

44

Matthew 6:8-13

Do not be like them, for your Father knows what you need before you ask him. This, then, is how you should pray: Our Father in heaven, hallowed be your name, your kingdom come, your will be done on earth as it is in heaven. Give us today our daily bread. Forgive us our debts, as we also have forgiven our debtors. And lead us not into temptation, but deliver us from the evil one. (NIV)

Chapter 8

The First Christmas Tree

After Nicholas had left Jerusalem and traveled north, far beyond Antioch, he arrived into lands where evergreen trees grew in abundance. He loved to see the beautiful greens and blues of these trees in the winter, especially when wet snow clung to the needles and branches. During the winter he sometimes gathered the branches and hung them in the kitchen and around the house and workshops to fill the air with the scent of pines. During the late fall after the first hard frosts had flattened some of the annual growth on the forest floor, Nicholas would gather the children for a pinecone hunt. It was something like the Easter egg hunt except to make it fun he would create special rewards for finding the biggest or the silliest shape. The children would scurry about the forest but always close enough for Nicholas to call them to return to him. A few times they found cones that were almost a foot long and very thin. Other cones were short and stubby, but with beautiful spiral shapes. A few were twisted and looked very odd.

After the pinecone collection, they would go home for hot drinks usually made with hot water and mulling spices that Santa gathered from the merchants who traveled to the east. While they drank in the warmth of Santa's workshop the children would take the pinecones and roll them in colored paints so just the ends of each part of the cone would have a different color. Then they put them on strings and hung them from the rafters to let them dry. They used the colored cones to help decorate the gifts.

Rosie stared at the many strings of painted pinecones hanging from the ceiling. Suddenly she had a wonderful idea. She went running over to Santa and tugged on his coat to get his attention as he sat at his bench carving toys from wood. She could barely catch her breath, she was so excited!

"Santa, Santa! Can we go get a tree and put it in the house and decorate it with the pretty painted cones? It would make the house smell like Christmas and we could paint our own special pinecones just for the tree. We don't have to put them all on the presents, just let some of them hang from the branches. It will be just like being in the forest, except the tree will be very happy!"

Santa thought for a moment and then began to laugh and talk at the same time.

"Well I don't know why I never thought about that. That's just about the best idea I've ever heard. It's perfect!"

Rosie began to giggle and tease Santa a little bit.

"And you know, in case any of us get presents, we could put them under the tree, so we will know where to look in the morning. Otherwise, they might get lost!"

Santa laughed so hard he had to hold his belly as he tried to speak.

"Oh I see! Just by some amazing coincidence you think about a pretty tree and suddenly it becomes the best place in the house to put gifts. Isn't that amazing?"

Rosie felt embarrassed, turned red and looked down at the floor. She spoke in a quiet voice.

"I'm sorry Santa. I didn't mean it that way at all."

Santa smiled. Rosie had always been a special child. How he wished she had been born to Anna Marie yet he was so proud that Rosie had become such a joy to everyone who knew her. Santa walked over to her and raised her head up and gave her a hug, placing her head on his shoulder as he knelt down beside her. His voice was deep and soothing.

"Rosie, you are such a blessing to me. I am so fortunate to have found you. How marvelous it is that you have always been the best friend a man could hope to have in his children. I learn from you every day. And I'll tell you a secret. Sometimes at night when I pray, I ask Jesus to make me more like you. Because I know you, above all others, show us what it means to be in the spirit of giving and how to act like a true child of God."

Placing his arm around Rosie's shoulder, Santa called the other children.

"Alright, everyone gather round. I have something exciting to tell you."

All the children formed a tight circle around Santa and Rosie stood by his side. Nicholas spoke with pride about Rosie's new idea.

"Today, Rosie has invented something that I know is going to become a tradition in the years to come. Instead of hanging all the colored pinecones from the ceiling rafters, Rosie has a great idea. We are going to bring back to the house an evergreen tree from the forest. I think we'll call it a Christmas tree, which we can decorate each year to celebrate the birth of Jesus. How does that sound to you?"

Everyone nodded their heads in approval and started to whisper to each other. Quickly Peter spoke up with some ideas of his own.

"Santa, can we decorate the tree with other things too?"

Santa nodded yes as he was getting more interested in the whole idea of a decorated tree for Christmas. Santa was inquisitive with Peter.

"What did you have in mind Peter?"

Peter thought long and hard and then his eyes lit up as a flood of new things came into his creative mind.

"In the forest we saw holly trees with bright red berries. We could make long strings of red berries and hang them around the tree."

That thought took Nicholas by surprise and for a moment he had a distant look on his face. Some things about his personal pains he did not share with the children. In private as part of his personal repentance, he had made a wreath out of holly leaves that had prickly points on them. To him it symbolized the crown of thorns placed on the head of Jesus by the Roman guard on the day of his crucifixion. He had thus always associated the holly with the pain Christ suffered at the hands of man. He had never thought about using the holly to make something beautiful. He realized that there is grace in many things on earth, especially those things that Jesus touched. You just have to open your eyes and your heart to see them.

Santa focused back on what Peter was saying.

"Then we could cut little star shapes from the left over wood and we could make them glitter and sparkle."

Santa was very interested in this concept and asked Peter to explain a little bit more.

"How can we make the stars glitter Peter?"

Peter smiled proudly. He couldn't wait to tell everyone, especially Rosie.

"Next to the road that leads down to the village, there are rocks that sparkle in the sunshine. We can take them and hammer them

48

gently to make dust that will glitter in the candlelight. We can use pinesap to glue it to the stars. We can even paint the stars to make different colors of the rainbow."

With this contagious excitement all the children scurried off to make many kinds of new ornaments to decorate the tree they would get from the forest. Some made angels from the feathers of birds. Others made ginger bread cookies and decorated them with colored sugars and spices. Part of the original fun of Christmas was to create beautiful things from scraps and things lying around the house. It is a far cry from pulling out a box of pre-made ornaments purchased at a store, mass produced and unoriginal.

The next morning, they went into the forest to find a tree. They took the wagon led by a giant horse they called Pegasus, since he was white and when he ran in the open fields he was so fast it was almost as if he could fly. Pegasus took them as if he already knew just the right place to go, a gentle slope with many small trees. The children ran and looked at all the trees and shouted to Santa.

"Pick this one Santa. Look, it's perfect!"

"No, take this one, it's much taller."

"Santa, over here, this one has many branches."

"Poppa Nicholas, look at this one! It is just a perfect shape."

"No Santa, look, this one has long pretty blue-green needles."

The children gathered around their favorite choices, jumping up and down trying to convince Santa to come chop down their choice as the best one. In all the excitement, no one noticed Peter and Rosie staring at a small tree at the edge of the forest. Santa, who was used to counting his children often, noticed they were missing from the main crowd. Finally he spied them far away from all the others.

While the children were jumping up and down and shouting and laughing, they soon started making snowballs and tossed them back and forth across the field, making the entire scene full of laughter and flying snow. In the excitement and noise, Santa slowly walked down the slope to where Peter and Rosie stood before a simple tree. He approached them quietly and stood a few feet behind them before he understood that they were praying. Always respectful of anyone while they were in prayer, Santa took off his cap, held it to his heart, and bowed his head.

In a few minutes, the other children saw Santa at the bottom of the snow-covered slope with his head bowed. Slowly, they stopped playing and walked down until they encircled the tree with Rosie and Peter standing in front of the tree. Most of them shook their heads and could not understand why Peter and Rosie would want this tree. It was small. It had few branches. Its shape was not perfect but an odd shape with branches that twisted and turned. The tree along the center had some small knobs protruding where branches had broken off and the bark sealed around the old wounds.

Finally Rosie and Peter, who were holding hands, lifted up their heads and opened their eyes widely and looked at everyone gathered around them. Peter usually spoke quickly in a high-pitched voice. But this time, he spoke slowly, carefully choosing his words in a calm lower pitched voice.

"Santa, I know the other trees are prettier than this one, but can we please bring this one back? Even if you pick another one for the house, can Rosie and I have this one to decorate? We could leave it outside the workshop so it won't take up any room or bother you or anyone else. Please, Santa?"

Silence came over the slope. Only the wind could be heard whispering in the pines. Santa slowly circled the tree. All the children watched his every move. It seemed like time stood still, one of those magical moments we all have every now and then. He stroked his white beard with his left hand and nodded. In a deep voice, still looking at the tree, Santa spoke.

"Tell me, my son, why this tree?"

Santa rarely called anyone son or daughter. Usually he just used their names knowing some day they would be adopted by other parents or grow up and leave to go out on their own. It made it easier for all of them to part company when their time arrived. Peter knew this time was special for all of them. He sensed for the first time in his life that he was no longer a boy but a young man. It was a new and wonderful feeling. He spoke with youthful wisdom.

"The trees are like children. Some are so pretty like Rosie, that they don't need any decorations. They stand alone. Some look perfect but none of us are perfect. We all make mistakes and inside we are all trying to be more like Jesus but none of us are as good as He is. We are just His children."

Peter stopped talking, awaiting some response. Then Rosie

spoke, very quietly, almost in a whisper, barely heard above the sound of the wind. At the top of the slope on the road, they could hear Pegasus, tapping his hooves on the frozen road and snorting as he nodded his head up and down, anxious to go back home to his stable and food. Rosie realized for herself that she was changing. She was no longer a little girl but was becoming a young woman and her voice and mannerisms were changing with each passing day.

"We are going to celebrate the birth of Jesus. He was the only perfect man ever to live. At Easter we celebrate that He rose from the tomb and we know that He now lives in heaven. So we think the tree should represent His birth, His life everlasting and His resurrection. When Jesus helps us, He can take anyone, no matter how big or small, no matter how scarred, and make them beautiful. So we can't start with something already beautiful. We need to start with a simple tree so when we decorate it, it will seem more like a real change, a little miracle, like transforming us into something new in Christ."

Everyone smiled and nodded their approval. Santa lifted his axe and stepped close to the tree and got on his knees to cut it close to the base. He looked up at Rosie and Peter. He reminded himself that wisdom can come at any age.

"You know my children, I have forgotten how old I am today. But I found out that it doesn't matter how old you are, you can always learn something new. I think we are all going to remember today with a big smile in our hearts."

On the way home, most of the children curled up in the wagon next to the first Christmas tree that bounced up and down as Pegasus trotted home. Rosie fell asleep dreaming about Christmas morning and the decorated tree. Peter sat next to Santa who was holding the reins and guiding them home.

As the snow got heavier during the winter, Santa switched to a longer sleigh instead of a wagon, to glide over the snow. When the snow got too deep for Pegasus alone to pull the sleigh, Santa would use teams of reindeer who lived on the mountain slopes during the summer. He built shelters for the animals for the harsh winters and provided them food that he stored up just for them. Santa liked to give names to all of his animals and they would always come running to him when he called.

Santa handed the reins over to Peter. Looking straight ahead, seeing things Peter could not yet see, he began to talk.

"Today, you take us home Peter. Pegasus knows the way. All you have to do is guide him and let him know you are not afraid. He has speed and power. He has enormous strength, but he still loves you. Just as I do. I'm very proud of you today."

Santa rubbed the top of Peter's head that was covered with a wool cap knitted years ago by Anna Marie. Peter was still getting accustomed to his new role in life as a young man. His voice was calm even though he was excited if not nervous holding the reins of Pegasus, a horse that stood 19 hands high.

"Santa, could we decorate the Christmas tree with colored eggs too? That way we could be reminded of the true meaning of the life of Jesus. I discovered we can remove the egg white and yolk inside of the raw eggs if I make tiny holes on each end and then blow on the egg gently. The eggshells won't be heavy on the branches and we could place a colored string through them to tie the colored eggs to the branches. Then we could mix the raw eggs with some milk and cinnamon to make a thick creamy smooth drink. Then maybe we could make toasts to each other like you and Momma Marie used to do, when you would tell each other what you liked best about each other. Do you think that would be something Jesus would like us to do?"

Santa looked far out to the horizon and into the future. He had abilities as a Saint that he rarely liked to use so he could remain more focused on the needs of the children. Santa's voice seemed to vibrate in the cold winter air.

"Peter, Jesus will love everything you do when in your heart you seek to praise Him, thank Him or glorify His name. He loves us all."

Peter was clearly thinking about new things today and Santa could tell Peter was becoming a man. In a curious tone Peter had some personal questions for Santa.

"Santa, when you got married you told me it was arranged by your parents and Anna Marie's parents. Is that right?"

Santa nodded as he stroked his beard, already knowing where the conversation was going to lead.

"Well, yes Peter. It was a custom in Antioch and the surrounding lands to arrange marriages in such a way."

Peter paused for a moment, trying to figure out the best way to ask the questions on his mind.

"Well, what happens when two people want to get married and they don't have any parents that they know about?"

Santa tried as hard as he could not to smile. He knew this was a serious moment in Peter's life. He just looked at the surrounding hills covered with snow and pine trees and raised his eyebrows and whispered. You could barely hear his voice over the sound of the jingle bells tied above the hooves of Pegasus as he trotted home, making a clip-clop sound on the frozen dirt road covered with snow.

"When you become a man, and you are ready to marry Rosie, I would be honored to arrange for your wedding in the church. I can be both of your parents that day. After all, I am a Saint, you know."

Peter sat up a little straighter in the seat of the wagon and made a clicking sound as he snapped the reins. Pegasus began a slow gallop as snow flew behind the wagon wheels.

In a later year, Peter and Rosie would have the most unusual wedding ever in the history of church marriages. It would be the only time Santa Claus gave away the bride and groom in a church wedding with a giant white horse as the featured witness. There were no elves or fairies present. But there was a host of angels rejoicing to the sound of the wedding bells as they vowed to bring up all their children as Christians to be baptized in the holy waters of the church of Christ. Pegasus stood outside the church with his head poking through an open window. He whinnied and stomped his hooves on the ground. His beautiful mane was braided and filled with flowers. Anna Marie was there too. The children could not see her but Santa did. His eyes can always see things beyond our vision. The twinkle in his eyes after all is the result of seeing both the spiritual and physical realms at the same time. Many generations after this wedding, a child was born in the lineage from Peter and Rosie. He became an officer with the Canadian Army who would one day decide Santa's fate.

As we think about the life Santa has led all of these centuries, in our hearts we too want to be like Santa. All of us have that hidden desire to be a Santa Claus in our own special way. Even you.

1 Corinthians 13:4-13

Love is patient, love is kind. It does not envy, it does not boast, it is not proud. It is not rude, it is not self-seeking, it is not easily angered, it keeps no record of wrongs. Love does not delight in evil but rejoices with the truth. It always protects, always trusts, always hopes, always perseveres. Love never fails. But where there are prophecies, they will cease; where there are tongues, they will be stilled; where there is knowledge, it will pass away. For we know in part and we prophesy in part, but when perfection comes, the imperfect disappears. When I was a child, I talked like a child, I thought like a child, I reasoned like a child. When I became a man, I put childish ways behind me. Now we see but a poor reflection as in a mirror; then we shall see face to face. Now I know in part, then I shall know fully, even as I am fully known. And now these three remain: faith, hope and love. But the greatest of these is love. (NIV)

Chapter 9

The Gifts Of The Cross

After Peter and Rosie were married, they had many children. Each December they made the trip to visit with Santa to share each other's joys. For Santa it was like having his own special grandchildren. He played with them on the floor of the house and took them on sleigh rides. Sometimes he woke them up in the middle of the night to show them a display of the northern lights that often filled the sky with fanciful curtains of colors. He sewed their names on the tops of red stockings that he filled on Christmas Eve with little gifts, being careful to give each one something special, just for them.

He taught his grandchildren the importance of sharing their bounty and their love with others. He also taught them to pray in wonderful ways. Before every meal, one of the children would take a turn to lead the prayer of thanksgiving.

As time went on, merchants from all over the globe would visit with Santa to share their knowledge of how to make new gifts for children. Two of his favorites were puzzles and candy canes. To make the puzzles he cut rectangles of thin wood and polished them with sandpaper. Then his helpers would paint scenes on the wood such as an image of a forest or a winter scene with snow. Then, when the paint dried, he cut the flat pieces into odd shapes with a thin jigsaw. The edges were sanded on each piece to be smooth and to remove any splinters. When they were done, the puzzles were pretty scenes with interlocking pieces. For young children the puzzles only had eight to sixteen pieces. For older children some of the wooden puzzles had hundreds of pieces and were perfect for rainy days when they couldn't go outside to play or when it snowed so much they couldn't go to school.

To make the candy canes, a merchant from Mongolia, a land now known as China, came to Santa's workshop to show him a new machine he had invented. He used syrups boiled from sugar beets with oil extracts from peppermints and spearmints. They mixed different vegetable dyes into the blend including beet reds, to make bright colored designs. The machines would twist and twirl the hot taffy-like strands of thick syrup. When they cooled they formed sticks with fancy spirals with two or three different flavors or colors. Santa's favorite was red and white with cinnamon. To hang them on the Christmas tree, he put a little hook or loop on one end of the sugar candy stick. These eventually became known as candy canes, but originally they were edible tree decorations.

To help children learn how to read and write, Santa made small blocks with different letters on each of the six sides of a cube. Over time, he had his helpers make the blocks using the letters from alphabets of many languages including English, Russian, Greek and Hebrew. Although he himself never had the privilege of going to school, Santa has always encouraged all of the children to learn as much as they can, for in knowledge there is wisdom and in wisdom there is love.

Over the centuries, his workshops spread throughout the world and were run by caring adults and children alike. Many of them have no sign on them so many people pass by every day and do not know they are there. Except for the flurry of activity on Christmas Eve, they are often invisible to human eyes, just lost in the hustle and bustle of activity of the cities in which they dwell.

The hardest task of Santa's early life as a Saint was to work on the special gifts made from the wood of the cross of Jesus. He often found every possible excuse to do something else. Finally, in one visit when Rosie and Peter came with their grandchildren, Rosie asked Santa how he was coming with the special sack from Jerusalem once hidden beneath the floorboards. Santa almost looked embarrassed. He spoke quietly, trying to avoid the issue.

"Oh, I'm still working on them. They're still not finished."

That night, after the children were all asleep, Peter and Rosie walked with Santa out to the workshops. The three of them sat quietly talking about the past and the future of Christmas. Finally, Peter looked at Rosie and they smiled at each other and knew it was time. Peter stood up and held out his hands for them to form a circle, and spoke with kindness but firmness.

"Santa, it is time for us to pray together. We need to thank Jesus for all of our blessings. And we need to ask Him for a very special kind of help. Shall we?"

They all stood in a circle and held hands and bowed their heads. Peter began to pray, just letting the spirit take over and lead him to speak what was in his heart.

"Heavenly Father, we thank you for bringing us all together for one more year to celebrate your birth, with your chosen messenger of love, Saint Nicholas. We know you chose him to lead the way for us all to learn how to love thy neighbor and how to give to others. He has done remarkable things all over the world. Hundreds of orphanages now thrive thanks to his work made possible by you. Hundreds of workshops now create gifts for children all over the world, spreading joy and hope even during hard times."

Peter squeezed Rosie's hand gently, signaling for her to begin to pray. Rosie had aged well. Even after having many children, she maintained her rosy cheeks and curly hair and her giant smile. She prayed with grace.

"Father, we come before your throne of grace to praise you, worship you and thank you for all of our blessings. We know Santa is having a hard time touching the sacred cross upon which you gave your life to forgive the sins of all mankind. He is really having difficulty with the task you gave him, but we are led by the Spirit to encourage him with your help to guide his hands now. It is time. It is a part of your joint heritage. Please let Santa finish the task and craft the gifts of the cross so that your special power may be passed on to others for centuries to come. We do not know their purpose or what will happen, but we do know it will be wonderful, for those selected to receive these special gifts."

Santa took in a deep breath and sighed, almost relieved as God spoke to his heart. He felt a wave of warmth flood his body.

"Yes Father, I understand. I will do as you ask. I am sorry it has been so difficult for me to do your will. It is just that I have never felt worthy enough to touch the blood-stained cross that I made which was used to take you from us. There has always been that sense of guilt and sorrow and embarrassment at what I did. Please forgive me Jesus. Please forgive me Father. I will do my best now. Guide my hands with your will, your gifts will be done."

Santa took another cleansing breath and finished his prayer.

"Thank you Father for bringing Rosie, Peter, and all of their lovely children into my life. They are a constant reminder to me of the fruit of the spirit, of love, and the fruits of giving joy. I have received so much more than I ever expected. Please help us all to continue to spread your word and most of all now Father, show me what to do with the special gifts made from your cross. I am yours. Show me and I will follow. Tell me, command me, and I shall do as you say, where ever it shall lead, to the ends of the earth and to the end of time. Amen."

They all hugged each other. The warmth of the Holy Spirit inside each of them, made their bodies tingle all over. It is comforting to know that the Holy Spirit is with us all of the time.

Rosie and Peter looked at each other. They had discussed something before they went on this journey and thought now was the time to ask. Peter sat down next to Santa, as he started to tinker with one of the new toys he had invented. There was a bit of a quiver to his voice, as if he wanted to ask something but was afraid of the answer.

"Santa, Rosie and I have always wanted to ask you something. I think you know what it is. We never asked you as children. We know you loved us and cared for us, so we never wanted to ask you while Anna Marie was alive and with us on earth. Now that all this time has passed, can you tell us?"

Santa put down his work and looked deep into the eyes of Peter and Rosie.

"I assume the questions on your minds have been, where did each of you come from and why didn't Anna and I adopt you. Is that what's on your minds this evening?"

Peter and Rosie nodded without saying a word, listening intently to every word from Santa's lips. He folded his arms over his belly and glanced one more time at their faces, making sure they were really intent on knowing the truth he had kept secret for so long.

"I was wondering if you were ever going to ask. Strange you should wait all this time, but I understand. It is natural for each of us to seek our origins. It does not change who you are inside or who you are in Christ. It may offer you comfort or sorrow, I do not know. At least it will fill in a gap and maybe it will satisfy your curiosity."

As he spoke, Santa looked out into the workshop. Peter and Rosie could not see that Anna Marie was there smiling at Nicholas. She had more messages about children who needed help but she would wait patiently until Peter and Rosie heard what they wanted to have

Santa reveal to them.

"Anna and I were not able to have our own children, at least not like other parents. Instead we ended up with thousands over time. We helped many to find parents of their own. For those sick and crippled it was difficult. For the strong and handsome it was easier. Yet it was always hard for us to see any of you go. After I was made a Saint, I believed I could no longer adopt any children. I would remain the same age and Anna would grow older. It would be confusing and difficult to adopt any child under those circumstances. Though I must confess we talked often about adopting you both. We decided not to because we both knew one day you would fall in love with each other, so you had to remain with different parents or else not be adopted at all to allow that future to unfold."

This explanation seemed to satisfy Rosie and Peter's curiosity. But Rosie needed to know the answer to one more question. She smiled at Santa and held his hands and looked at his gentle face as she asked the burning question on her mind.

"Santa, where did we come from? Who are our parents?"

Santa hesitated for a moment and drummed his fingers on the workshop table and glanced over at Anna, who nodded to him to proceed to tell them.

"Yes, I believe you are old enough now to understand. You know of the burden I carried years ago when I found out the cross and nails I made were used to crucify Jesus, our Lord and Savior. I cannot convey, I cannot ever describe how that felt. Yet I am so blessed that I was forgiven and not only forgiven but given a whole new life in Christ. It is not just that I am now immortal, but that He took away the pain and gave me a wonderful purpose in life. What more could any of us ask?"

Peter and Rosie looked anxious, suddenly wishing they had not asked him about their parents. Maybe it was something that should remain a mystery. But Santa continued.

"Do you remember all the turmoil in Jerusalem that surrounded Jesus and His disciples? They were difficult times for us all. During those times the Roman soldiers who kept order in Jerusalem were very cruel. When their wives had children, sometimes they would die in childbirth or would die a few days after their labors, for reasons I do not understand. The Roman guards would bury their wives and then give the newborn children to a relative in the city. But if they had no relatives, they would sometimes kill the infants or leave them in a field or out on the streets, abandoned. Both of you came from different families. Each of them abandoned you, leaving you in a small basket at our doorstep. You know the baskets we used to gather the Easter eggs? The ones you used were the baskets in which you were held when we found you. I have kept those baskets for you. You should have them. When the guards came to pick up and return the cross, you probably noticed two of those men looked a lot like you. I thought you knew back then that they were your fathers."

Santa walked over to one of the shelves in the workshop and pulled down two old baskets and placed them on the workshop table in front of Peter and Rosie. They were the baskets he had kept for years, waiting for this day.

Rosie spoke quietly as she touched the old baskets now sitting in front of her and Peter.

"But Santa, what were our names? Who were our parents more precisely?"

Santa looked a bit sad but knew the time had come. He tried his best to soften the blow to come. He spoke like a father to his child.

"All I know is the group of men they came from. I never knew their names, nor has it been recorded in either history or the archives for reasons you shall understand. The Roman guards who whipped Jesus, and tore off His clothes, who made the crown of thorns, who made Him carry the cross and who nailed him to that cross, those men were your fathers. Your mothers had died at childbirth. You were born six years before the event at the cross. You will never know the names of those men, only what they did. You must know in your hearts, Jesus loves you so much. He would not want to see you suffer from this knowledge. It is why you have always been so special to Him and to me. It is why you knew about the first Christmas tree before all the others, and why you have returned to me each year. It is why you and you alone know that the cross was not burned but has been transformed into marvelous gifts that shall transcend the centuries. Forgive me if this news upsets you. You have asked and I have spoken the truth."

Peter and Rosie just smiled and held hands. Peter spoke in a low but strangely calm voice.

"Thank you Santa. It is what we expected. But we know Jesus

60

forgave our sins at the cross. We are not ashamed of who our parents may have been and what they did. All that matters is that we have chosen to walk on a narrow path that leads from a narrow gate. We have been so blessed to be children of God and to live through these miraculous times and to survive them with you. We have now helped start many orphanages ourselves and each year we help give so many gifts because of you. The greatest gift has been sharing the love and knowledge of Jesus Christ with our children. They shall grow up loving Him and loving you. Few children have been touched by a Saint and seen the angels of heaven. Thank you Santa."

After this, Santa worked many nights after the Christmas season to finally finish all the blocks of the cross into wondrous gifts for children of all ages. He kept them stored in the red sack under the floorboards, out of sight from all who entered his workshop.

Over the coming centuries, he slowly began to give them to people with a special need. It was not necessary for them to believe in Santa since many still think he's just a fairy tale or a myth. It was not necessary for them to be rich or poor or of any particular religious faith. All those who ultimately received these gifts did have something in common though. They all were people who prayed to Jesus, true, deep, spirit-filled prayer. And it is the most important thing to understand from this entire book, that they all were people who were not asking for something for themselves but to give to someone they loved.

These gifts bestowed remarkable power to those who rightly received them and who passed them on to those they loved. It is incredible, but all of the original gifts of the cross have survived to this very day. They are scattered all over the globe in different countries and hidden like treasures in secret places or left in the open for any to see and in their simple innocence remain safe. Some of you may have them or know someone who has been touched by these gifts. You will know these people as those who give lovingly of their time and resources to help children in need or to help at medical or burn centers or pediatric hospitals all over the world. These are special people whose hearts have been touched by the gift that keeps on giving, yet in return gives back to you far, far more than you ever imagined.

There are hundreds of stories of those who have encountered these gifts. A few of them can be told. Others must forever remain a secret until Jesus comes again.

Romans 12:9-13

Love must be sincere. Hate what is evil; cling to what is good. Be devoted to one another in brotherly love. Honor one another above yourselves. Never be lacking in zeal, but keep your spiritual fervor, serving the Lord. Be joyful in hope, patient in affliction, faithful in prayer. Share with God's people who are in need. Practice hospitality. (NIV)

Chapter 10

The Stories Of Santa's Gifts

As the centuries passed, different cultures changed the original traditions of Christmas. Some survive today and others have been lost in the commercialization of the celebration of the birth of Jesus.

The tradition Peter started with decorating colored eggs on the Christmas tree is still used in some countries but most places have substituted colored balls for the ornaments. The raw eggs from emptying the shell have been used to make eggnog which has become a popular drink at Christmas time, though most forget its meaning of new birth in Jesus.

The tradition of placing an evergreen in the house has been expanded greatly worldwide where now more than forty million Christmas trees are sold each year in North America and Europe. However, many people now use artificial trees and those conscious of conservation have begun to use live trees which have their roots wrapped in dirt and burlap to enable them to be planted outside after the holiday.

The tradition of ornaments made of stars and angels has been passed down over the years. Instead of hand-strung holly berries, now most people use colored lights or string popcorn and drape the strings on the branches of the tree. Many kinds of colored lights are now used throughout the world that require electricity and wire, a far cry from the stars made by Peter with wooden pieces and pine sap glue and crushed mica for glitter.

Many children still hang stockings by the fireplace or on the mantle. The tradition Santa started was to provide small thoughtful gifts hidden inside of socks that could be used to keep the feet warm during cold winter days. Some stockings do have the names of children sewn on the top just like the original Christmas stockings.

Christmas is a wonderful time of the year for most people. Some with families make an annual journey back home to visit with brothers, sisters, mothers, fathers, grandparents, aunts and uncles. The

Christmas meal is usually festive just like Thanksgiving, which was similar to the early harvest festival back in Europe. On Christmas Eve many people go to church and children often put on plays depicting the birth of Jesus.

Many wonderful Christmas songs have been written in the past few centuries. Choirs are at their best at Christmas with so many happy and joyous songs, some sung with bells, flutes, organs or tambourines, and all are uplifting.

But for those without a family, who live alone, or for whom it is too far or too expensive to travel home, Christmas can also be a lonely time. The original Christmas was not meant to shower gifts on those who already had more than they needed. Rather it was a time to share with those who could really use some help or share some joy. The original Christmas focused on homeless or orphaned or hungry children who needed food and clothes. Today, all that seems to have been lost under a veritable flurry of retail profit-oriented merchandising, and far too many people think only of themselves at Christmas. This is something Christ's Santa wants to change and it is something we can all act upon to bring a new era in Christmas celebration.

For the homeless, the orphans and the lonely, one of the toughest times is the day after Christmas and the weeks and months that follow. People who get in the Christmas spirit for just one day of the year, often go and serve food at a homeless shelter on Thanksgiving and Christmas. They feel very good about it. But what happens the day after the holiday? The same people are still in need and are now forgotten. One day of remembrance or service is not enough. It is something that each of us can help to change. It is what Santa wants for us all.

Of the special Christmas traditions, the ones that are now most rare are those involving the toys and boxes made from the cross of Jesus. These have been dispersed all over the globe. After Santa had finished his work on these wooden blocks from the cross, he decided to give one of them to a very special person once every twenty years. To us that may seem like a long time but for Santa the beauty of giving is eternal. Now in the 21st century he has already given about ninety-four of these special gifts of the cross to those he decided needed them the most. But their affect on the world has been exponential. When one person receives the gift, their lives are profoundly changed. They in

64

turn affect the lives of other people who then pass on the love and understanding Jesus wanted each of us to have for each other and for Him. Over hundreds of years, it has created a cascade or an enormous explosion of special love all over the world. Moreover, as time goes on, these special gifts have been passed on to other families to accelerate the phenomena of how the power of the blood and the cross can change a life and offer salvation.

Many stories were told about the deeds of Saint Nicholas, ranging from the time of Jesus to today. One of the most famous stories, and one repeated in many languages and cultures around the world, was about how Santa rescued children from a wicked innkeeper. A key part of this story and others is Santa's close ties to Jesus and the cross, often using the power of the cross to do miracles witnessed by others. Other stories that have been passed on through the ages are just countless examples of his love for giving to others. In one story he found a kind nobleman with three daughters who had lost everything. Due to local customs the daughters could not get married without a dowry. Santa secretly threw three bags of gold down their chimney and they landed inside their stockings that were hanging up to dry. This helped the three beautiful maidens to get married. The nobleman witnessed Santa doing this and vowed never to reveal his true identity.

For many countries, December 6th is the feast day of St. Nicholas. This is based on one of Santa's many friendships with leaders of the church. In this case, when Santa was in Turkey, he became great friends with a man also called Nicholas whose uncle was the Archbishop of Myra. The Nicholas from Turkey was born in Patera. When the Archbishop died, he left his great wealth to Nicholas of Patera, who then turned to his friend St. Nicholas for guidance. Through prayer they determined that he should give all the money to help children. Due to these good works, Nicholas of Patera eventually became a Bishop in the church, a man well revered for his kindness and generosity. In remembrance of Nicholas, people in many countries exchange gifts on December 6th as a re-enactment of the three Magi, or wise men, bringing gifts to Jesus in Bethlehem. To this day, there are churches in Rome dedicated to St. Nicholas. This is the direct result of Santa's historical link to Jesus through the cross and the many kind acts of St. Nicholas towards children all around the world.

There are thousands more stories that Santa could tell us that could fill many books, but he is a humble and quiet man. Many of these stories have a similar theme resulting from the action of giving of the gifts to a child at Christmas. There are also thousands of examples of those who have benefited from these gifts by passing them on to other families in need and to their own children. There are a few stories that can be shared that show Santa has indeed survived all of these centuries and that even in the 21st century with all of its science and technology and political problems, the spirit of St. Nicholas continues to thrive and prosper. One of these stories is called the Good Samaritan and another is called the Shriner's Burn Center. There are thousands more stories that Santa could tell us that could fill many books, but he is a humble and quiet man.

What Santa really wants is for each of you to go out and do something for a person in need. That person may be a child, a teenager, or an adult. The age does not matter. By reaching out to someone, you are in essence writing the end of this book, for it is an everlasting and ever growing story. It is not difficult to find someone who could use your help. Sometimes it takes a little imagination to figure out what to do, especially if your physical or financial resources are limited. It is not right or proper to advertise or brag to others about what you have done. When you fast, pray, or help someone in need, that is between you and God. Perhaps the person you help will never know it was you or perhaps you will see them face-to-face. In any case, you must be humble and kind. Many are proud and will refuse the help they need unless it is done with dignity, in a Godly and a spiritual manner. You know in your own heart what you have to offer is good and kind and that is all that truly matters.

Hebrews 11:1-3
Now faith is being sure of what we hope for and certain of what we do not see. This is what the ancients were commended for. By faith we understand that the universe was formed at God's command, so that what is seen was not made out of what was visible. (NIV)

Chapter 11

Santa's Sleigh

All over the world, even in the early years of Nicholas, before Christ was risen, men and women who could heal the sick were greatly treasured in their local communities. Doctors who were gifted have always been few and far between. Jesus has the power to heal not just when He walked the earth as a man, but now, through prayer and faith.

Few people know that Nicholas was an excellent craftsman who could work in stone and wood as well as clay. He also was a superb painter. As a child his father taught him how to navigate by the stars, a skill that would come in handy over the centuries when Santa drove his sleigh through the skies all over the world.

Working in stone, laying bricks, painting and crafting in stone, took its toll on his hands. When he was with his wife, Nicholas would put on soft white gloves to cover the rough skin from his long hard labors, to make his beloved feel special and to show his sensitivity to her comfort. Thus, the white gloves Santa wears that everyone recognizes as part of his outfit, are actually a remnant of his dedication to his wife and marriage. Later, after Jesus died and rose from the tomb, St. Nicholas wore white gloves to cover the scars on his hands from the molten metal used to cast the nails. These white gloves, originally worn to cover his rough hands and scars, have become a symbol of purity over the centuries and something people accept worldwide as part of Santa Claus' clothing.

St. Nicholas lived through many dark times in human history. He lived through the Crusades when thousands of men, women and children died. He was in Europe during the great plagues when almost one-third of all those in the cities died. He was in China when earthquakes killed hundreds of thousands. He was in France, Belgium and Russia during World War II and saw millions die. It was so painful for him to be there. He was not a magician or a doctor or a healer. He was just a simple man of God who brought joy and taught the gift of the spirit and of giving to those who believed in God. But Santa had something no doctors on earth had available to them. He had faith beyond our imagination and he had the gifts of the cross. Not only the gift of salvation but the power of the blood in the gifts carved from the cross upon which Jesus gave His life for all mankind. Nicholas chose well. Over the centuries he carefully selected men and women who would become doctors and researchers in medicine who would care for children everywhere on earth.

Over the years though, Santa took a very big interest in the Shriner's Burn Centers. They treat children from all over the world whether or not they have the money to travel there. At other Shriner's Centers, they also do pediatric surgery for those in need regardless of their financial abilities. Overall, the Shriner's hospitals have cared for thousands of children and families and performed surgeries and skin graftings too numerous to keep track of in an amazing environment of love and giving.

One of the greatest emotional experiences you could imagine at any age is to walk through a Shriner's Burn Center Hospital. They do give tours for those interested in their good works but few actually take advantage of this. For those who do take the time, the scenes are so incredible, so powerful, few if any could possibly leave there without being profoundly affected. The images of young children who are burned all over their bodies and then after surgeries and skin grafts go on to lead productive lives is simply amazing. Santa went on that tour once, looking for children to add to his Christmas list. He was changed profoundly. It resulted in the only time he gave out two gifts of the cross in the same place at the same time, instead of spacing them out over his usual twenty-year period.

After Nicholas took Anna Marie and his children and migrated north from Jerusalem, he did not return to Jerusalem for many centuries. Over large spans of time, he saw enormous changes in the land he once loved and called his home. The house and workshops where he lived long ago were torn down and replaced with large buildings. The farms once visible for miles all disappeared, engulfed by the expanding population from the city.

It seemed with each visit he found new conflicts in his city. The cast of characters and the ruling bodies changed, but the air of conflict remained. It shall remain so until Jesus returns for his chosen people. His workshops for that area of the world have been forced out of the city and into quiet areas where people can come and go in relative peace. In the workshops men, women, and children leave their religious and political differences at the door and come in peace to donate their time and services to help children of all races, colors and faiths. The workshops of Santa Claus are in reality like churches where people come to worship, praise and glorify God. What better way to serve than giving of one's time, energy and spirit to helping the needy? God smiles on all of Santa's works.

One day in Jerusalem, a young woman who was fooled into believing she was of greater value dead than alive, took her life along with others. God, called by any name, has no place in heaven for such people. In the process of her self-destruction, a true act of violence, a small Israeli girl was badly burned. Her name was Beth. Both of her parents died that day and she was left alone in the world. She had no relatives and no place to go.

Santa has many helpers. They are in every country from the North Pole to the South Pole. They are there to help those in need. One of Santa's helpers in a hospital outside of Jerusalem found Beth one day, as she was staring out of the window of her hospital room. Her face and body were wrapped in bandages. She could barely talk because her lips had been burned in the explosion. Surgery had removed the metal pieces from her body and stitches had sealed the skin, but she needed serious work to repair her skin, body and broken spirit.

Santa's helper in Jerusalem contacted the Shriner's Burn Center in Boston. Soon a chain of others joined in to help Beth to see what they could do. Beth had no funds, and no family. Worse, there was no one in the Israeli government willing to sign papers releasing a Jewish girl to go anywhere, not even the United States for treatment. They were worried that it would send a message of weakness to their enemies. And so, poor Beth sat day after day in excruciating pain awaiting her fate.

After the year when Anna Marie died, Santa rarely delivered Christmas presents outside of his local community on Christmas Eve. There was such a large network of workshops and Santa's helpers worldwide, that he left the delivery to millions of children to thousands of other kind and generous people. Of course he did, and still does, make the journey to hand deliver the gifts of the cross every twenty

69

years to those carefully chosen after a great deal of research and prayer.

Santa still receives messages from his workshops in cases where only a miracle could help them, because it is beyond their means to handle the situation. Beth's case was certainly one of those cases that seemed impossible and yet so sad it cried out for mercy and for action. Though most think of Santa as a jolly fat man, few understand that beneath the white gloves, behind the twinkling eyes is a great man of God. He is himself when his spirit moves him, so at one with God and the spiritual realm that he is far more powerful than you can imagine when he sees a crying injustice and a child in terrible need.

Word came to Santa of Beth's problem. The Shriner's Burn Center would accept her as a full charity case if they could get her out of the hospital in Jerusalem and into the U.S. But the Israeli government kept arguing with the U.S. Immigration Department and would not allow her release and the publicity it would bring. Too often politics takes precedence over common sense and the Greatest Commandment Jesus gave to mankind - love thy neighbor.

As Christmas Eve approached, Santa pondered what to do about this case along with thousands of others. Finally, the day before Christmas he received an emergency delivery at his secret location in northern Canada. He still received mail from all over forwarded by his vast network of workshops. The mail was always extreme cases of need that only he could possibly handle.

In the sack of mail was a simple letter written in Hebrew from Beth. It was addressed to Santa Claus. He read it twice before putting it on the table.

> "Dear Santa,
>
> My name is Beth. I am Jewish. I don't know if I am allowed to write to you. I was told there is no Santa Claus, so I guess there is no one in the world to help me but I just had to try. I have burns all over my body. People turn their heads when they see me. They don't want to let me know they can't stand looking at me. I understand. I hurt so bad every day I just want to die. So I am writing to you because there is no one else in the world to write to. You see, I

may be ugly on the outside and no one wants me, but they forgot one thing. I have a heart, a good heart. I also have other organs someone else could use, even my eyes. All I see is the pain on the faces of others as they look at me. Maybe another child could use them and see good things, happy things. That would bring me joy. So I am writing to ask something maybe only you can do. Santa, help me to die and give all my good insides to those children in need. I could save many lives and make many families happy who are waiting for help. I was told I have a rare blood type and organs like mine are very much in demand. This way I could die knowing I helped someone. After I die, I don't know if I can go to heaven. Please take this letter as my legal permission for you to do whatever you need to do to make this happen.

If you could put in a good word for me to Jesus I would really appreciate it. I don't know how to pray anymore but I know you do. Maybe some day you could teach me. Thank you very much Santa. Please make this happen soon. I can't stand the pain anymore. I am willing to give my body to those who really need it. I really need your help Santa.

Shalom and Merry Christmas,
Love Beth

After reading that, any one of us would expect Santa to just put down the letter, close his eyes and pray. Well, you're close.

Santa ran out of his workshop. The men and women of the local town who were there to help noticed how focused Nicholas seemed to be. It was a look foreign to their eyes. He had not acted like that in their presence before. Nicholas walked briskly to the barn where he provided food for local animals all year round. He went behind the shed so no one could see him and instantly dropped to his knees and bowed his head, and he prayed as never before.

"Oh Heavenly Father, creator of heaven and earth. Jesus my Lord and Savior, I come before your throne of grace seeking your love, seeking your guidance. You have given me immortality. You have given me gifts too wonderful to ponder. You have entrusted me with giving the gifts of the cross to those special people in need. But Father, I think I have been on earth too long. I no longer recognize the places where I once grew up as a child. This world has introduced technologies, weapons of mass destruction, and political strife that kills innocent children. I am truly lost in this world where I have created vast networks of workshops and orphanages, yet it never seems enough. I barely sleep. There is not much left to do. I am overwhelmed. Though I am a Saint amongst men, I have no power like yours. I am but your humble servant. Father I must ask your help now. If I am too old and just too outdated for this new earth, so far from my home, my days of old, then maybe it is time to call me home to you in heaven. I am not sure my use here is of any further value. The thousands of Santa's helpers worldwide will grow without me. I am almost finished giving the gifts of the cross, though it has taken me nearly two thousand years. I am tired Father. Who can bear to read one more letter to Santa as the one I have received today? I love you so much Father. I am yours. Command me, and I, your humble servant, shall do as you instruct me to do."

Santa could feel the Spirit inside of him linking his thoughts to God. He continued his heart-felt and spirit-filled prayer.

"I sense my time on earth is soon to be at an end anyway Lord. The sack of gifts of the cross is almost empty. I shall never give up. I shall do my best. It's just lately Lord, it seems like my best simply isn't good enough. You know my heart. You know my thoughts. I treasure you as my best friend and my Lord and Savior. Send me a sign Father. Call me home if that is your will. If I am to remain then tell me if I am still of use on this earth. Guide me. I will, until my last moment in this realm, continue to be your disciple. I have tried to make disciples in all nations. I have failed you in making disciples of all nations Lord. Forgive me, if I have fallen short of your expectations of my work. Thank you Jesus. Take me home now or give me the fire of my youth to stay and do your will, as you would have me do in your Holy name. Amen."

After his prayer, Santa stood up with his head still bowed and his red cap firmly in his humble hands. The sun was low in the northern winter sky. For a moment, the world suddenly seemed to stand still.

The sun did not move in the sky. The clouds froze in their windy paths high in the skies. The small birds of the forest stopped chirping. The waters under the frozen streams stopped their motion and silence, total silence fell over the land.

Santa lifted his eyes to witness his answer to his prayers. The sun turned blood red. The earth trembled. Santa's helpers in the workshops ran outside to see what was happening. A beam of red light shot from the sun to behind the animal shelter where Santa stood. Then bolts of lightening with wave after wave of thunder pealed in roars all around them. Everyone fell to their knees in fear of the Lord. After many bolts of lightening, the earth became still and the lightening stopped. The sun turned into an orange globe once again.

Everyone ran to see if Santa was alright. Some expected him to be gone for he had talked often lately about going home to Jesus. Instead, as they rounded the animal shelter, a most curious sight greeted them. There in the snow stood Santa, a changed Santa. He was walking around the sleigh he used each year to carry gifts to the local children. The sleigh was glowing, sparkling, just like the day Santa himself became immortal. All around the sleigh, the reindeer he fed during the winter and protected from the wolves of the forest, were gathered. The reindeer glowed and as they pawed the ground, sparks of orange and yellow light jumped up from the snow. Santa quickly was harnessing them to the sleigh, and he seemed to be moving with great determination. As the helpers approached the glowing, sparkling scene, Santa looked up to them and smiled.

"Fear not, dear friends. I myself do not understand all of this, but I know what each of us must do. Please get some blankets from the house and a bag of food and drinks to bring on my journey. There is no time to explain now. I do not know how long this power from God will last."

Santa turned to his oldest helper, a kind man named Paul, from the local town in Canada.

"Paul, old friend. Tonight is your night to be Santa to the local children. You know the town, the fields and roads. The list is on my workbench. You know where the sacks of gifts are in the workshop. Do your best and I will see you tomorrow. Go with God's speed. I am taking the deer but you can take the team of horses in the barn. They know the way. You can use the old sleigh. I fixed it up this past

73

summer in case we needed two for this year. You will need to start early. Wear my clothes from the house. You'll be fine."

The next few minutes were a flurry of activity with Santa's helpers running to the workshop, the barn, the house and the kitchen. The horses were quickly hitched to the other sleigh and Santa was packed with food, blankets and drinks for his long journey. At last Santa went into his workshop and lifted up the floorboards. The red sack containing the gifts of the cross was now very small compared to two thousand years ago. So many had been given to those in special need. The red sack still glowed in the dim light of the workshop. Before touching the sack, Santa knelt down to pray.

"Heavenly Father, my oldest friend, how great thou art. You are an awesome God. You are the sun and the stars, the creator of all that lives and breathes on earth. To you goes all the glory. Let every man, woman and child bow before you and praise your holy name. I have just a few of your gifts of the blood of the cross left to give, Father. I have chosen well with your guidance. We have done so much good together. How blessed I am to serve you. I know you want me to go on a mission tonight Lord. Jerusalem is so far away for an old Saint and a wooden sleigh. But I have faith. I have enough faith to fill my heart and touch all of those whom you send my way. I am old, Father. You keep me young, but tonight especially I must put myself completely in your hands. Lord, guide me and protect your children. If this is to be my last night on earth Lord, let me come to you victorious. Whatever the cost, I am yours. You know my thoughts. I fear not joining you in heaven. I shall be overjoyed to be in your light forever. But tonight Lord, tonight Father, I do what I must do. I do it for Anna and for Peter and Rosie and all children who have been abandoned or who are in need, in need of you. Give me strength and give me wisdom. Tonight, Jesus, I wear the helmet of salvation, the belt of truth, your breastplate of armor and the shield of faith. Time to battle for you, Lord."

With that, Santa gently lifted the sacred sack from its hiding place and briskly walked outside to the sleigh. His helpers all gathered next to the sleigh, as was their tradition, to wish Santa well on his journey. He secured everything in the sleigh and turned to all gathered. Many eyes turned to his kind face. His violet eyes were almost on fire, his cheeks bright red and his face determined, yet for the first time almost sad.

"Dear friends. I do not know what will happen tonight. I have to go on a special mission. I am uncertain if it is my destiny to return. Should I not come back, you know you must continue on your own. You all know what to do. You do not need Santa Claus any more to deliver presents. Each of you is capable of that. We have thousands of Santa's workshops. Help others each year to become greater in the spirit to keep expanding to every corner of the earth. Do not slow down. Do not stop. Always find those in need and help them, and in so doing you will be helping yourself beyond all earthly measure. One day Jesus will come again. On that day I shall see you all. Should I not return tonight, none of them will know I am gone. The spirit of giving is infinite. It is not limited to one man or even one Saint. It lives forever in each of us. Seek, and ye shall find. Knock and it shall be opened unto you. God bless you all. Since the time of the Apostles, God's first disciples, has there ever been a more glorious gathering of saints as surrounds this sleigh tonight? What a wonderful world we live in."

Tears filled everyone's eyes as Santa raised his white-gloved hands to the heavens, tilted his head back and raised his voice.

"Into thy hands I commend my spirit Lord. Guide me now. I am yours."

Silence gripped the darkening evening sky as the sun began to set. Santa jumped into his sleigh and took the reins.

Mark 10:13-16

The Little Children and Jesus

People were bringing little children to Jesus to have him touch them, but the disciples rebuked them. When Jesus saw this, he was indignant. He said to them, "Let the little children come to me, and do not hinder them, for the kingdom of God belongs to such as these. I tell you the truth, anyone who will not receive the kingdom of God like a little child will never enter it." And he took the children in his arms, put his hands on them and blessed them. (NIV)

Chapter 12

Shriner's Burn Center

In an underground facility hidden in Canada, lies one of the NORAD centers that coordinates the defenses for North America. Their job is to protect the people from attacks by missiles and enemy aircraft. As soon as Santa lifted his sleigh above the level of the surrounding mountains, the NORAD Command Center in Canada went on alert. Colonel Peterson was on duty that night. He was a descendent of Rosie and Peter. It was his turn to stay underground on Christmas Eve. He had lost his wife and son in a car accident a few years before and remained a bitter and angry man. He took out his anger on everyone who crossed his path.

The radar operator at NORAD saw a blip on the screen as soon as Santa was above the tops of the mountains that circled his workshops.

Radar Operator: "Colonel Peterson. We have an unknown bogie traveling east, southeast."

Colonel Peterson sat in his command chair sipping a blend of hot chocolate and coffee. He was a combat veteran from the Gulf War. It took a lot more than a strange green dot on a radar screen to alarm him.

Col. Peterson: "Alright. How fast is it traveling?"

There was a moment of hesitation and then a stumbling answer.

Radar Operator: "Ah... well sir. It started out at about 60 miles and hour."

Colonel Peterson cut in right away.

Col. Peterson: "Don't worry about it. Probably some local flyer going home for Christmas who forgot to register a flight plan."

Radar Operator: "Yes sir, but is going faster every second.

Colonel Peterson sat forward in his command chair, a bit more interested.

Col. Peterson: "Oh really? What's its present course and speed?"

Radar Operator: "Same vector, but its speed is now 250 miles an hour."

Col. Peterson: "Okay. Let's keep track. Lock in on it. Let's not scramble unless we have to."

Radar Operator: "Yes sir, but ..."

Col. Peterson: "But what?"

Radar Operator: "Well sir it's now at 500 miles an hour, 600...700...now going super sonic."

Colonel Peterson jumped up and stood behind the radar operator.

Col. Peterson: "This better not be some flock of geese giving a false reading or an equipment glitch, or else we're both going to look awfully stupid."

He watched the screen and confirmed the observation.

Radar Operator: "Sir, it's heading towards Boston or New York."

Col. Peterson: "I see. I see. Alright, full alert. Code Red. Scramble intercepts. Alert the American centers. Ask for a scramble out of Hanscom in Massachusetts. This thing may be too fast for us to catch here."

Colonel Peterson watched for another minute and then got worried.

Col. Peterson: "Track down all commercial flights in its path. Divert them all out of the way. Let's give this baby some serious air space."

He picked up the red phone, connected directly to the American underground secret facility. A few seconds later, a voice answered at the other end.

Col. Peterson: "Sorry to bother you tonight sir. I have a bogie coming your way. It's gone supersonic. I know you have something faster than we do. This is the time to use it, I know it's Christmas Eve Sir, but it's now at Mach 1.5 and headed your way...Yes sir. Have him encrypt his radio messages and patch it in to us here to coordinate. We've already scrambled intercepts out of Montreal and Toronto. At this speed it's all going down fast sir."

He hung up the phone. The room got quiet.

Radar Operator: "Sir. Radar now confirms multiple bogies. It's not just one missile. It's a cluster. It's the real thing."

Col. Peterson: "Okay, tell our fighters to arm. Permission to open fire long range at my command. Repeat, only at my command."

In the next few minutes many jets launched. They had no idea what they would find. All assumed it was the unthinkable -- a terrorist attack with multiple missiles. One burst and it would all be over. It could trigger a response that would be unprecedented in human history.

American Superjet: "This is Thunderbird 2 to group leader, over."

Col. Peterson: "This is Peterson. Your orders are to intercept but do not fire until I give the command, over."

American Superjet: "This is Thunderbird 2. Confirmed. Intercept, lock in and wait for your orders."

Col. Peterson: "How long to first intercept?"

American Superjet: "About two minutes."

Col. Peterson: "All right Thunderbird 2, listen up. I want you to reverse course, so they will catch up to you. I want a good long look before I order this. I don't want to shoot down a commercial airliner on Christmas Eve. Got that?"

American Superjet: "Confirmed. Doing a loop now sir."

Col. Peterson: "How long to first visual?"

American Superjet: "30 seconds before first visual contact."

Col. Peterson: "All right. Go to missile lock. Repeat, lock on targets and wait for my command."

American Superjet: "Confirmed. Roger that."

Clouds covered the area. The pilot of the Thunderbird 2 put his finger on the button to launch his air-to-air missiles. Silently he prayed it wasn't a commercial airliner, such as a hijacked jet or worse a cluster of enemy missiles.

Col. Peterson: "You should have visual contact now. Do you see anything?"

There was an eerie silence.

Col. Peterson: "Repeat. Command to Thunderbird 2. Do you have a visual on multiple bogies, over?"

Another silence. Finally, a strange message in a strained voice.

American Superjet: "Ah, command. This is Thunderbird 2. I have a visual now."

Col. Peterson. "Is bogie hostile? I repeat is bogie hostile? Over."

At 10,200 feet above the ground, the Thunderbird 2 pilot at close to full throttle, pulled next to Santa and his sleigh and reindeer. Santa turned his head, nodded and then waved. A shield of some kind surrounded the sleigh and reindeer. Inside the shield there was no wind and it was cool but not cold.

Col. Peterson: "Repeat. Is bogie hostile? Over!"

American Superjet: "Ah, well. That's a negative. Not hostile. Repeat. Not hostile."

Col. Peterson: "How many are there?"

American Superjet: "Well sir. I see eight up front and one in the sleigh."

Col. Peterson: "Repeat. Repeat message. Did you say sleigh or side?"

American Superjet: "Well sir, I think one can safely say some kind of object, but I can't really say for sure just what it is."

Colonel Peterson was starting to completely lose his temper and had trouble restraining himself.

Col. Peterson: "What do you mean? I've got half of the North American intercepts launched at this thing, I've got over 30 anti-missile batteries ready to fire at any possible target and you're telling me you don't want to say right now? Are you drunk?"

American Superjet: "No sir."

Col. Peterson: "Well as of right now you're relieved of your duties. Return to base. I've got the first Canadian squadron ahead of you and the American intercepts coming up fast now."

American Superjet: "Permission to escort Santa, sir."

Col. Peterson: "Son, your days in the Air Force are over. Return to base or I'll have you shot down too!"

Col. Peterson: "This is Colonel Peterson, NORAD Command to Canadian and American attack groups. You have permission to open fire once you have a visual. If that American idiot stays up there and gets in the way, shoot him down too."

The Canadian and American intercept flight leaders had been listening.

Canadian Leader Levi: "This is Levi, Canadian intercept leader. We are armed. We have missile lock. Visual in 60 seconds."

American Leader Samuels: "This is Samuels, American intercept leader. We have missile lock and understand your orders sir."

The Thunderbird 2 pilot had remained on his course. He had to speak.

American Superjet: "Colonel Peterson, are you a father?"

Col. Peterson: "I told you to back off or I'll shoot you down too.

Get out of there now. The fireworks are going to start any second."

American Superjet: "Sir, I repeat, are you a father?"

Col. Peterson: "None of your business. I lost my family in a car accident. What does that have to do with any of this?"

American Superjet: "Sir, I am a father. Tomorrow morning if I'm still alive, I am going home to have Christmas with my son and daughter and my wife. I sure don't want to be the one to tell them that last night their daddy shot down Santa Claus because Colonel Peterson did not believe in Santa and gave the order to fire."

Col. Peterson: "What did you say?"

Colonel Peterson covered the radio microphone with one hand and turned to his co-workers in the Command Center room.

Col. Peterson: "This guy is nuts!"

Canadian Leader Levi: "This is Canadian attack force one. We have visual"

American Leader Samuels: "This is American attack force. We have a visual too now."

Silence.

Col. Peterson: "Well? Would someone like to tell me what's going on up there?"

American Leader Samuels: "Well sir, since we're in Canadian air space, I think we should let them speak first."

Col. Peterson: "What's with all this polite stuff? Is everyone nuts up there tonight?"

Canadian Leader Levi: "This is group leader Levi. We confirm visual. There are eight bogies up front and one in the back. Permission to return to base sir."

Col. Peterson: "What do you mean return to base? The bogies are headed straight over Boston! I can't risk it. Fire! Fire now! That's a direct order, do you hear me?"

High in the sky a dozen men had to make a choice. The Canadians went first. Then everyone understood and followed suit. Every jet launched one missile high into the clouds, far from Santa and then pressed their Auto Destruct button so that the missiles blew up, harmlessly lighting up the night sky with pulses of orange.

The reindeer panicked but Santa understood and laughed out loud. All the pilots waved goodbye and headed for home.

Canadian Leader Levi: "All attack force jets have fired their missiles sir."

Col. Peterson: "We're still showing a bogie heading east! Did you all miss?"

Silence.

American Leader Samuels: "I guess there was really nothing to shoot at tonight sir. Merry Christmas."

Santa had accelerated to Mach 3. He zoomed out over the Atlantic.

Radar Operator: "Sir, we have satellite confirmation of a fast moving object over the Atlantic. It must have been a comet. Satellite images show a blur of light and no heat signature. Must be one of those ice comets."

Colonel Peterson seemed quite relieved, yet he had to find a way to save his dignity in the whole matter.

Col. Peterson: "Yeah. Yeah! That's it! Ice comet. Put that down in the logs. Everyone agree? Ice comet. Those pilots are all on report. This was no time to pull a practical joke. Santa Claus? Ha! Very funny. We'll see how hard they all laugh when they're busted and flying prop planes in South America."

Santa guided his sleigh to Israel. He had no idea how it worked, but thoughts were simply translated into the action of the sleigh. He thought about Beth in a hospital. He wondered if she was still alive and how to get her into the sleigh and back to the Boston Burn Center. It was in God's hands now. He left control of his life to Jesus years ago. Tonight would be no different, except every act was just more visible to the outside world.

As he passed over England, he slowed the sleigh. The shield created a supersonic boom behind its path as he crossed over France and headed towards Israel. NATO Command had been warned of the approaching ice comet. They followed its path and did not worry until all of a sudden the comet slowed down and changed direction, straight to Jerusalem. No comet or natural object could possibly do that. Immediately they launched intercept jets. In the surrounding countries, Saudi Arabia, Syria, Egypt, Iran, Iraq, everyone got nervous and launched their jet fighters to intercept. Each one thought it was a surprise attack by one of their foes. There had already been recent hostile fighting, but on Christmas Eve?

Santa willed the sleigh straight into Jerusalem. By the time he arrived and slowed down, the sky was swarming with high-speed jets, all armed and on edge each with their finger on the button waiting to see who would fire first. The Israeli jets headed straight for Santa. He was hidden by clouds and they couldn't see him, only his radar signature on their instruments.

Without warning their radar contact disappeared. Where was it? Santa was on the ground, well almost. His sleigh landed on the roof of the hospital. The sky above was a maze of jet trails getting too close together. Santa headed for the door that would lead him down the stairs into the hospital. The door was locked. He leaned all his weight into it and tried to knock it down but to no avail.

Santa knelt down on one knee and removed his cap. He prayed with both determination and love in his voice.

"Father, I have not come all this way to fail you. Give me strength Lord, give me strength. Guide me to her, Jesus. Show me the way. Amen."

He stood up, walked back to the door and pulled with all his might once again. This time the hinges gave way instantly and with a crack the metal door came loose and fell aside. Santa looked a bit stunned but smiled as he went down the stairs.

The hospital was busy but calm. Santa went to the elevator and took it to the ground floor. He walked up to the receptionist.

"Excuse me young lady. Could you tell me what floor the Burn Unit is on? I'm looking for a girl named Beth?"

The receptionist was chewing gum and listening to rock music bobbing her head to the beat. She did not even bother to look up to see who it was.

"Burn Unit - 3rd Floor. Take a right out of the elevator."

"Why thank you. Merry Christmas and Shalom."

He took the elevator and turned right to find Beth. He found room after room of families gathered together into small spaces and finally found a very small room at the end of the hall. He peered inside. Alone in the room was a child wrapped in bandages. It was hard to tell if it was a girl or boy. The child turned her head and stared at Santa, as he loomed, larger than life, in the doorway. He smiled.

"Are you Beth?"

The child nodded yes.

"Well then. I guess you know who I am. We can talk on the

way. I'm kind of in a hurry. Can we go now sweetheart?"

There was a faint whisper through the bandages.

"Yes Santa. Thank you for coming."

Santa gave her a big smile and then almost scolded her in a teasing way.

"No more talk about dying, by the way. I'm here to help you get better. Got that? Now, let's get you wrapped in a blanket and away we go!"

Santa had seen a wheelchair in the hallway. He went to get it and place it next to Beth's bed.

"I'm going to be as gentle as possible. I'll try not to put any pressure on your bandages. Ready?"

Beth nodded and reached her bandaged arms around Santa's neck. He carefully lifted her into the wheelchair and heard her wince in pain. He covered her with a blanket and went straight to the elevator. At the top floor he picked her up and carried her up the stairs. As he went through the doorway, he heard the sound of guns being raised and readied. When he opened the door going in, it had tripped a silent alarm for the Army to arrive.

They stood and stared at each other. From the other side of the roof, the reindeer trotted between Santa and the Army men with guns. They were stunned when they saw Santa's outfit and then the sleigh and reindeer. Cautiously, Santa approached the sleigh. The Army men pointed their guns at Santa. He paused for a moment and then laughed.

"It seems Jerusalem has changed a bit since the last time I lived here. We used to greet our guests with a little more kindness."

The leader of the Army men, a young Sergeant, didn't know what to do.

"Where are you taking her? Put her down and step back!"

"Her name is Beth. She sent me a letter. She has burns covering her body and she wants to die. I don't want her to die. I'm here to take her to the Shriner's Burn Center in Boston. They volunteered to help her. Neither of us can help her here, but they can. It seems your government doesn't want her to get help because Palestinian terrorists would be causing you embarrassment. How can a young helpless child embarrass you? If she must die, let it be fighting for her life, not from your political agenda. If she lives, let it be by God's hand. I absolve you of all your sins against her and will accept full responsibility. It is

Christmas Eve, a time to love one another and a time to give, not a time of war."

Santa slowly placed Beth in the back of the sleigh and covered her with blankets and mounted the sleigh and grabbed the reins. Santa turned his head towards the soldiers and pointed to the sky above, now swarming with jets.

"We could really use some help up there. How about an international escort? Israel was where I grew up. Israel was where Jesus was crucified. Israel has the blood of too many children on its hands already. The choice is yours. If any of you are fathers, don't you think it's about time you acted that way?"

There was a pause. The leader signaled the others and the guns were put away. Joshua, the Sergeant, pulled out a radio and spoke into it loudly.

"This is Sergeant Joshua. I'm on the roof of the hospital. I want you to listen and listen carefully. Link me to an open channel so that all the jets overhead can hear me. Got it?"

The voice at the other end sounded worried.

"Go ahead. You're now on the open channel. It's a bit critical up there."

Joshua covered his radio and turned to Santa.

"I was a father. A bomb in a shopping mall killed my children two years ago along with their mother. They were out buying me a birthday present. I know what it means to be a father. Now, what should I tell them? If I tell them who you are, they'll think I'm lying and before you know it, there will be World War III up there."

Santa just smiled. The reindeer started to stomp their feet and snorted, signaling Santa they were ready to go home.

"Do you believe in Jesus?"

"What do you mean? I'm a Jew in the Israeli Army. God has taken my family away from me. What does Jesus have to do with any of this?"

Santa chuckled politely.

"This is Christmas Eve. Tomorrow is my birthday too. I ask you to seek in your heart what to say and what to do. Ask yourself Joshua. Ask, What Would Jesus Do?"

Joshua thought for a moment. Then he took off his backpack and guns and handed his rifle to another soldier. Then he walked over to the sleigh. For a moment he touched the glittering surface to confirm it was real and then hopped into the back seat with Beth. He took a deep breath and spoke into the radio.

"This is Sergeant Joshua from the Israeli Army. I am in a special craft from America on a mercy medical mission for a young girl. It seems we are all responsible for hurting her. It is Christmas Eve. I think we all forgot what that really means. It's about time we stopped acting like spoiled children."

Joshua turned to Santa not knowing what to say next. Santa shrugged his shoulders and signaled him to keep talking. Finally Joshua spoke again.

"We are leaving Jerusalem and flying over the Mediterranean then over the Atlantic to Boston. I beg of you all, please give us clear air space. Anyone who shoots at us will have to answer to God, the President of The United States, the United Nations and to a helpless little girl who needs our help, and needs it now. For once, can we be messengers of peace on the eve of the birth of Jesus?"

There was silence at first. Then slowly the skies cleared.

"This is Major Mohammed from the Iranian Air Force. We do not shoot at innocent children. We have no quarrel tonight with anyone on a mission of mercy for any child. It's a beautiful night. Anyone want to join me or are you all cowards who have to shoot at women and children who can't fire back?"

"This is Major Bardeau from the French Air Force. We will escort you too."

"This is Colonel Hussein from the Egyptian Air Force. We'll take you to the open Atlantic then you're on your own. If anyone fires on you, I'll personally give them a Christmas present they won't forget. Praise Allah."

Santa lifted the reins. Joshua closed his eyes.

"Up and away my steeds! Back to the open ocean as fast as you can!"

In the night sky, Santa, a glowing sleigh and eight reindeer lifted into the darkness with Beth and Joshua in the back seat. Beth and Joshua held on to each other. It wasn't clear who was more frightened.

One by one all the jet fighters from different countries formed an armada. They surrounded the sleigh for miles. Only those closest to the sleigh could really see the object they were escorting. As the first jets saw what was really in the night sky, Joshua opened his eyes and held the radio close to his mouth. In a quiet voice on the open channel he spoke.

"Anybody going to report this or shall we all just do this quietly? I don't think any of us are going to risk our careers by saying anything. Do you?"

In the cockpits of the closest jets from Egypt, Iran, Saudi Arabia and Israel, all of the fighting men in unison shook their heads in silence.

Colonel Hussein finally spoke.

"Ah Joshua, could you ask your, well, your pilot, my daughter has always wanted to know something. How high can you fly?"

Joshua looked out of the sleigh to the city lights now more than two miles beneath them. Then quickly closed his eyes and slid low into his seat.

"Too high! Much too high!"

And throughout the air space could be heard the sounds of many a pilot laughing in unison, in different languages, yet tonight all the same.

The escorts peeled off one at a time, each one passing by to see for themselves. Each one gave a salute as they passed by Santa. When they returned home, a strange peace would grip the entire region. No one quite understood why.

It was almost 3 a.m. before Santa entered U.S. air space, on his approach to Boston. The U.S. had already scrambled several squadrons of fighters to intercept. This time, as far as they knew, it was some UFO or bogie headed directly to Boston and it had originated from the Middle East, clearly, a potential major threat.

Joshua listened in on his radio to the chatter of the pilots then finally he spoke.

"This is the UFO or bogie coming from Jerusalem. We are on a mercy mission. This is an emergency medical flight. We are headed to the Shriner's Burn Center in Boston. Can you give us clearance to land?"

This time they weren't as fortunate as when they were over Israel. The voice at the other end of the radio contact responded immediately.

"Negative. Negative. Identify yourself and change course

immediately. You are to land in Greenland. Do not go any further into American air space. We have targeted your vessel. We have missile lock. We have you scoped with a laser weapon. Turn immediately. Turn now or we'll shoot."

Santa overheard the radio talk and slowed the sleigh and dropped to the surface of the ocean, under the scope of the radar as the skis on the sleigh barely touched the tops of the waves. As far as radar was concerned they had disappeared. Satellite tracking lost them in the fog and clouds. Surface ships could see nothing on radar or sonar. The UFO or bogie had disappeared. The jets were ordered to do a systematic sweep of the area but found nothing. Santa skimmed into Boston Harbor by 4 a.m. east coast time. The sleigh headed for the Boston Burn Center and set down on the roof.

Joshua, glad to set his feet on firm ground, helped Santa to carry Beth into the hospital. They immediately went to the first floor to Admissions. It was Christmas morning. Joshua had used his satellite phone to call ahead to the hospital to prepare them to receive Beth as soon as they arrived.

Santa tapped on the bell at the counter. It gave a quiet ding. The nurse who came out to greet them was surprised by the odd sight. There was Santa Claus holding a child wrapped in bandages in a red blanket. Behind them was an Israeli soldier in uniform. She looked bewildered.

"May I help you?"

"Good morning. Sorry to come in so early. We contacted the hospital earlier. We've had a long journey. This is Beth. I believe your people in Admissions know about her."

The admissions nurse scurried to a back room and in moments two more nurses came in with a gurney to take Beth to the Emergency Treatment Room. Then the admissions nurse turned to Santa and Joshua.

"Did you park out front? You might want to move so you don't block the Emergency Entrance. This is going to take a few minutes to finish the admissions forms. Which one is the father?"

Santa put his white gloves on his belly and laughed and then put his arm around Joshua's shoulder.

"Well, Joshua, you wanted to come along for the ride. It can only be one thing. You lost your family so God is giving you another one. Beth is your daughter. Isn't that just perfect?"

"But Santa, I can't do that. I have no job here, no passport, no place to live, no …"

Santa interrupted by placing his hand over Joshua's mouth.

"God will provide everything, you'll see. Ask the hospital administrator. I'll bet he gives you a job right away and they have special housing for family or parents in need, while the children undergo surgery. Trust me, everything will be fine. Merry Christmas, Joshua. I have to get something from my, well from my car. I'll be right back."

Santa went to the roof and took the sacred small red sack from the sleigh hidden underneath the blankets. He knelt on his knees in the dark and prayed, asking Jesus to guide him to make sure the gifts of the cross were given to the right people.

Santa returned to the lower floor and found Beth and Joshua in the Emergency Room. Beth was being examined by the night nurse, who was changing her bandages. The nurse's name was Jeannie. She was a single mother with short brown hair. She had worked hard to survive over the past few years. Jeannie's daughter had pituitary cancer, a form of cancer that affects the brain. Her son had problems with drugs and found it difficult to hold down a job. She had come to Boston as a Critical Care Nurse and developed a specialty in working with burn patients such as Beth. She always wore colorful nurse's outfits, not the plain white uniforms, but blues and greens with pretty patterns which made her patients feel more at ease. She always had perfect, very decorative fingernails and wore little make-up since her face was naturally beautiful.

As Santa watched the scene of the three of them talking, he looked at the world with different eyes. Santa, after two thousand years of helping others, could see when people were in need. But more than that, he could also see when people were meant to be together. He was, after all, just a servant of God doing his special work on earth. He knew what must be done.

He walked into the white curtained area that separated them from the rest of the Emergency Room. Jeannie looked up and did not hesitate or skip a beat in her work.

"Hey look, Beth, Santa's here. And it looks like he's here for you. Isn't that amazing timing. I bet he's just delivered his presents to the children upstairs. Hi Santa!"

Santa smiled and tears welled up in his eyes. His work on earth would go on for just a little longer. It looked like this was a special night for him too. He became a re-energized Saint, in his love to help children in need all over the world. In a way, Jesus had given Santa a special gift tonight. Not the sleigh powered by forces no one on earth can fathom, but the gift of love. It is a gift that grows. The more you give the more you receive.

He pulled two small presents wrapped in colorful paper and string out of the sack. He handed Jeannie one of the presents and gave Joshua the other.

"Joshua, you hold this gift for Beth. When her hands are better she can keep it until she grows up and has children of her own. Jeannie, you accept this gift for yourself. You hold on to it and share it with Joshua. You will all be so blessed from this day forward. I can already see what your fate will be. How perfect. How wonderful! Thank you all for making my Christmas the best one ever. Well, it's my birthday too. I think I'll go home now. I don't really want to be flying in the daylight and its almost dawn."

He smiled at the three of them and then went over to Beth and whispered in her ear while Jeannie and Joshua opened their presents and looked at each other strangely.

"Beth, can you hear me?"

Beth nodded.

"I leave you in good hands. I think they make a nice couple don't you? I think they are going to fall in love, get married, and something very special will happen to you. You are going to have a lot of operations. They are going to be painful but you will get through them because Jesus loves you and so do I. Beth, Jeannie and Joshua are going to adopt you when they get married and love you as a very special gift. Is that all right with you?"

Beth's eyes lit up and she gave a great big smile. Then Santa put his finger over his mouth.

"Shhh. Don't tell. It will be our secret. Let them find out for themselves, but trust me, you'll see."

Santa stood up and gave Joshua and Jeannie each a great big hug and a kiss on both of their cheeks.

"Merry Christmas! Merry Christmas everyone! Ho, ho, ho!"

In the next instant Santa ran up the stairs and jumped into his sleigh. Dawn was approaching. Time to return to his workshop and get some sleep.

Within a year, Jeannie and Joshua got married and adopted Beth. Their wedding was an unusual blend of Jewish and Christian traditions. The guests never quite figured out why an old man in a Santa outfit was the best man at the wedding.

Beth would always have the scars from her burns on her body. When she had children of her own, they were beautiful inside and out and they loved Beth because she was so special and so loving. Nicholas would always have his scars on his hands and feet and the knowledge he had built the cross upon which Jesus gave His life for us all. But their scars were nothing to be ashamed of and nothing to hide. They would be concealed, but with pride. A pride that says loud and clear, I love you Jesus. I love you Lord. I am a child of God. Your will be done on earth as it is in heaven.

Santa's trip home from Boston on Christmas morning was uneventful. Colonel Peterson stayed up all night waiting for the ice comet to return. Sure enough right before dawn, the strange blip re-appeared on the screen. He had taken a special jet helicopter to the location where the radar blip first appeared on Christmas Eve. He waited in a field until the Command Center sent word the bogie was headed his way. He tracked it from his equipment in the helicopter and saw it land within two miles of where he was hiding in a field on the other side of the mountain. He put on his backpack and set off in the direction from which he saw the flash of orange sparkling light land in the forest. He was still angry about being embarrassed in front of his own men and was determined to get even and find out what was really going on here.

It took a few hours using his snowshoes but he finally located a group of houses and barns in the middle of nowhere. He watched through his high powered binoculars but could only see children playing outside, a few horses and smoke from the fireplaces heating the various structures on the property. He couldn't see any adults, weapons, vehicles or any danger. One of the children spotted him in the trees since his binoculars reflected the sun like two small mirrors. He realized he had been spotted, and decided to just walk in casually to see if he could find any subversive activity or signs of any secret

90

organizations.

Santa was asleep inside and his helpers were in their homes in the nearby town with their families on Christmas day. As he came close to the children, they did not run away as he expected. Instead they waved and welcomed him. As he approached the house they invited him in and offered him some hot chocolate and cookies and candy canes they had made for the holiday season.

One of the children was a young boy, about the same age as his son had been when he died. The young boy's name was James. He walked using two crutches and seemed very happy to have a stranger come to visit. After some snacks the children gathered around the kitchen table and started asking Colonel Peterson some innocent questions. They wanted to know if he was one of Santa's helpers or a mailman, or a merchant, or someone looking to adopt a child.

"Oh no, I'm not here for that. My son died a few years ago. I don't think I'll ever have a family again."

The children looked a little disappointed but mostly felt sad for him because they could sense he was hurting inside even if he couldn't see it himself. James thought it might be fun to have some contests outside to work up an appetite for dinner. Colonel Peterson could smell all sorts of things cooking in the ovens including breads, potatoes and pies. Although he was more interested in pumping them for more information he suddenly felt like a child again himself and went outside to play with the children.

He had a wonderful time. In fact he had never had so much fun. They made giant snowmen and dressed them in old clothes. They had contests to see who could hit the most tin cans lined up on top of the fence using snowballs. Although Colonel Peterson was a sharpshooter, he lost to a young girl who never missed. Then they decided to have foot races. They made up a winding route around the barns and workshops and then back to the main house, using red cloth strips tied to trees and posts to mark the way.

They decided to have two races. First all the girls, then all the boys. The girl's race was very close and the tallest girl won but not by very much. Then the boys lined up to race. Colonel Peterson was surprised to see James line up with everyone else. He shook his head side to side.

"Hey James, are you sure you're allowed to do this? Don't you think you might get hurt or something? How about if you be the judge at the finish line? I'll bet it will be a close race."

James looked at him rather strangely.

"I guess you don't live around here do you?" James said politely.

Colonel Peterson looked a little surprised.

"Why no, I don't actually. How did you know?"

James just smiled and invited him to join in.

"Why don't you join in the race? You're so tall it should be easy for you."

Colonel Peterson shook his head no.

"Aw, that wouldn't be fair. I'm much older and faster. How about if I just watch?"

James laughed and shrugged his shoulders.

"Okay, but you're missing out on all the fun if you don't try."

Colonel Peterson shrugged his shoulders imitating James.

"Well all right, here we go. Count me in."

The oldest girl started the race quickly.

"On your mark, get ready, get set, GO!"

Everyone shouted and screamed and jumped up and down. A few of the older boys were very fast and beat Colonel Peterson to the first flag and surprisingly James kept up with the front pack. They flew around the course and every now and then slipped a bit in the snow or on the ice. James used his crutches in the deeper snow almost like miniature pole vaults and could leap over logs and bumps. On a sharp bend around the barn fence, James took a spill and fell down hard. You could see he hurt his hands as he fell. But he got up quickly and ran and leaped on the crutches and caught up again. Everyone went wild watching from the finish line. On the final bend around a giant pine tree, James fell again and his crutches came out of his hands. You could see he had hurt his knees but he grasped the crutches from the deeper snow and stood up once again. By then the front-runners, led by Colonel Peterson, were almost at the finish line.

James rallied once more and everyone including the boys in the race started cheering him on. Instinctively, Colonel Peterson ran to the finish line, a ribbon strung between two posts and crossed it alone. He felt jubilant. He was smiling and feeling good about himself until he turned around. He saw all the other boys cheering James on. You could see his hands and one knee were bleeding a bit and he had a look of determination on his face. The other boys waited until he caught up and they all crossed the finish line together.

Colonel Peterson had a strange feeling. He learned an important lesson that day. Everyone carried James up in the air cheering and shouting, declaring him the big winner. Colonel Peterson watched as they all went inside to have some snacks and help James clean up before dinner. He stood alone. For the first time, in a very long time, he realized how alone.

All of a sudden all the emotions he had hidden from the death of his wife and son came flooding through his body. He was a combat veteran, the Commander of NORAD, but today, in a hidden valley surrounded by mountains where he had come to find evil or seek revenge, instead found himself sobbing on his knees, all alone. He started to feel all that pent up anger start to melt. He was angry with himself. He was angry with God. How could a good God let bad things happen?

As so many emotions and past events flew through his body and mind, he was startled to hear a deep quiet voice right behind him and then he felt a man's hand on his shoulder.

"So who wins the race? It is the fastest man? Perhaps in your world that may be so, but today, James won. Do you know why? Because he tried the hardest. He fell and got hurt but he got up and tried again. He never gave up. He fell again and got hurt but he still got up and continued. Not only did he continue, but he finished strong. That's what God wants us to do, finish strong. All of us have stumbled and fallen. All of us have made mistakes or taken twists and turns in our life that we shouldn't have or else fate interceded in ways we never planned for, like losing a wife and son tragically. Isn't it wonderful that a small group of abandoned children should understand all that when a man of such power and position cannot see it? Maybe there is a lot to learn from these children. Why don't you stay for dinner and then stay here overnight. I'm sure you won't be disappointed."

As Colonel Peterson turned around he stood face to face with Saint Nicholas. The sound of all the excitement had awakened him from his slumber.

"Tell me Colonel Peterson, are you here by accident?"

Colonel Peterson was stunned. His mouth dropped open.

"How could you possibly know my name? You almost sound

like you were expecting me. Do you have military communication decoders?"

Santa burst out laughing and covered his mouth.

"Oh, I'm sorry. I couldn't help it. That was just so funny, I thought at first you made a joke. I almost forgot. Oh, please forgive me. No, no. No fancy things here. I think you'll find that we're rather simple folk. Who needs all that cumbersome gear when you have guardian angels all around you?"

He pointed to Anna Marie hovering over his shoulder who had told him all about Colonel Peterson. He could see nothing but air. He thought the old man might be crazy or something. Nicholas understood.

"No. Not crazy. It's just that I see different things than you do. You only see the here and now of this realm. I see in both realms, the spiritual and the physical, and I see now and sometimes the future. It can get rather confusing and to some rather annoying. But let's not dwell on all that. Why don't you join us for Christmas dinner? It may be unlike any you have experienced before. Besides, do you have any better plans?"

Colonel Peterson smiled. A part of him was still a tiny bit skeptical but most of him started to believe. He pulled out is radio from inside his jacket.

"This is Peterson. I'll be back tomorrow morning. You copy, over?"

Radio Operator: "Roger that, Colonel Peterson. We'll wait for your command. Do you need any assistance? We have paratroopers armed and ready to drop into your zone on your command. Over."

Santa folded his arms on his chest and gave Colonel Peterson one of his famous looks. Colonel Peterson felt very small and embarrassed all of a sudden.

"That's a big negative. No need for that. Tell everyone to stand down and go home for Christmas."

Colonel Peterson paused for a minute. He realized that when he was in the kitchen there was little food around to feed so many children. The smells in the kitchen were all breads and desserts but no meats or vegetables. He wasn't sure what was really going on but he followed his long dormant instincts. He got back on the radio again.

"This is Peterson again. Do you have a lock on my present GPS coordinates?"

Radio Operator: "Affirmative. We have an exact location to within 15 feet."

Colonel Peterson paused for a moment and then nodded his head as if he had made some important decision in his own mind.

"All right, listen up. I want you to make a food drop tomorrow using this location but use a vector north, northwest at one mile from here. There's an open field for the drop zone."

Radio Operator: "Yes sir, but I thought you had supplies for yourself in the helicopter?"

Colonel Peterson started grinning.

"Don't ask any questions, just do it."

Radio Operator: "Yes sir. But how much should we drop?"

Colonel Peterson covered the radio and looked at Santa.

"How much do you need?"

Santa just smiled.

"You don't have to bring anything here. But if you must, just let your heart be your guide. We do not wish to be a burden on anyone."

Colonel Peterson looked over at the house. Inside he could hear the children singing French Christmas carols. He looked at the red cloth strips tied to the trees and the imprints in the snow where James had fallen and got up to run again. He looked at the buttons on Santa' coat and touched one of them out of curiosity. An odd sensation of warmth shot through his body.

"You know, I think we need to clear out all the food reserves in the bunker and get all new stuff in. I think it might have been contaminated or something. Drop it all here and truck in replacements tomorrow. Don't forget my hot chocolate and why don't you get in some eggnog for New Year's Eve? Got that?"

Radio Operator: "Yes sir. That will be about eighteen pallets."

Colonel Peterson nodded and chuckled.

"That's a great big Roger, over and out. Merry Christmas."

Radio Operator: "Merry Christmas to you too, sir!"

Santa scratched his head.

"I don't know these new terms you use. How big is eighteen pallets? Do you think that's enough for dinner for all the children?"

Colonel Peterson laughed.

"Now that's funny. Actually, that's enough for dinner for 100 for three years. It's all dehydrated and sealed. All you have to do is add water. Don't worry, it can last for many years. Hope you know someone who can use it around here. Boy, all this talk about food is making me hungry. Let's go eat."

Santa smiled.

"Well, that's very generous of you. Perhaps when you leave tomorrow, I can offer you something to return your kindness."

Colonel Peterson just shook his head. How could an old man and a bunch of abandoned children possibly offer him anything?

"Nah. No need for that. You don't owe me anything."

Christmas dinner with Santa was something to behold. The meal went on for hours, with singing, praying, talking and sharing stories. Each of the children told their stories about how they came to be there and what they wanted to be when they grew up. Santa watched Colonel Peterson intently as each child spoke. When James finally had a turn, Santa just smiled and nodded as he saw Colonel Peterson's reaction. James had lost his two parents in a car accident that left him crippled. There seemed to be a pre-planned symmetry to everything. Sometimes things work out for the best when at the time we just can't see it or understand.

After the children went to sleep, Colonel Peterson stayed up late talking to Santa. Santa explained to him who his early relatives were, Santa's two favorite children Rosie and Peter, and about the gifts of the cross. Finally Santa left Colonel Peterson alone in the kitchen. There was a wonderful peace and tranquility in the house. The only sound was the popping of the logs as they burned in the fireplace, glowing orange and sending heat throughout the house.

Colonel Peterson was still restless. He just had to know. He put on his coat and walked outside to the barn that had remained closed all day long. He pulled open the barn door and walked inside. A full moon reflected off the snow and lit the barn with a pale blue-white light. Inside, was the sleigh. He walked up to it and couldn't understand. It looked to him like an antique. There was no power source, no rockets, no communications equipment, just a wooden sleigh, carefully painted, beautifully maintained.

He heard some movement in the far end of the barn and saw the reflections of many eyes looking at him. At first it was almost a panic reaction, thinking he had stumbled into a pack of wolves. The glowing eyes surrounded him. Then one came forward slowly and he realized they were deer, reindeer. The largest of them sauntered up to him and nuzzled his belly by rubbing his nose against his jacket. Then all the other reindeer surrounded him and lay down on the hay and went back to sleep, assuring him everything was safe.

From what appeared to be a hole in the roof, a beam of white light bathed him. He looked at his hands and then lifted his hands into the light that seemed to beckon him and cleanse him. He lifted his eyes to the skies and finally got down on his knees. He clenched his hands into tight fists and brought them to his chest. He began to pray.

"Heavenly Father, I can't take the pain anymore. Make it go away. I miss my wife and son. I don't know why you took them from me. What did I ever do to deserve that? What did they ever do to deserve to die so young? Why them, Lord? Why not me? I don't understand. I have been so angry; it has consumed me like a burning fire. I need to give that to you tonight. Please Lord, make me a child again. Make me a child of God. Let me live my life in peace through you. Take control of my life. I bow down to you as my Lord and Savior. I can't do it myself anymore. I need you. I'm just so alone, so alone."

In the morning the children made breakfast and went into the barns and workshops to do their chores. They found Colonel Peterson fast asleep surrounded by the reindeer in the barn. He had his arm around the neck of one deer. As the children peered into the barn one deer began to lick his face. They all giggled as he finally awoke. He heard them laughing and when he realized why, he just stood up, brushed off the hay and had a big smile on his face. He looked up at the ceiling, expecting to see a big hole in the roof, but it was solid. He looked at his hands and finally understood that the light was from within.

Outside there was the drone of large cargo planes flying overhead. The children all ran outside to see the sky filled with parachutes and huge pallets of boxes. Colonel Peterson walked out into the snow and sunshine. He closed his eyes and leaned back his head. He felt new, alive, happy, and peaceful. He hadn't felt like that in years. The children ran out and got the horses and ropes and ran up to the field to bring back all that had landed. He continued walking and found Santa leaning against the barn with his arms folded across his chest. He spoke quietly.

"Ready to leave? I think you'll find everything you need in the helicopter waiting for you."

Colonel Peterson didn't understand but reached out his hand to wish Santa goodbye.

"Thank you for letting me stay overnight. Last night I went into the barn to see the sleigh. But it wasn't what I expected, just a bunch of tame deer, owned by a kind and gentle old man."

Santa smiled knowingly.

"It seems you didn't find what you were looking for but I think you found something else, something far more important."

Colonel Peterson looked up to the sky and closed his eyes and took in a deep breath.

"Yes. Yes, I did. It was long overdue."

Santa put both of his white-gloved hands on his shoulders.

"You're going to finish the race strong, young man. You fell down but you got up. That's all that matters. Go in peace. Go with God."

Colonel Peterson walked back to the helicopter. He noticed something rather odd. Along the same path he took originally, there were now tracks in the snow like skis with many pole marks. As he approached the helicopter he could see someone inside the co-pilot's seat. As he climbed on board and fastened his seatbelt he looked over at James who was smiling. No words really needed to be spoken.

Colonel Peterson flipped some switches to start the rotor and spoke loudly over the rising noise level.

"I'm in no rush. Want to take the scenic tour?"

James smiled.

"Sounds good to me. Can you teach me to fly?"

Colonel Peterson laughed.

"Oh, you just don't know how long I've waited for someone to ask me that. Yeah, I'll teach you to fly and lots of other things, too. I think you can also teach me a lot, James. I'm a bit rusty at all this, but I think we're going to be just fine."

They flew over Santa's house and saw a stream of tracks from the food drop leading back to the workshops with horses, reindeer and children forming lines in the snow.

Colonel Peterson adopted James on the following Easter. He

was just amazed at how all the paper work just sailed right through the courts with no resistance. He took James to the best military hospitals he could find. Less than a year later and after several operations and daily physical therapy, James was able to walk with just braces and without crutches. Every now and then he tries to walk without the braces. He falls down sometimes but he always gets up again.

Colonel Peterson and James became more than father and son. They became friends. Each brought out the best in the other. In our family, the family of God, that is what we must ask of each other.

Neither of them was ever lonely again. Even when they were by themselves, they could just pray any time to their heavenly best friend.

None of us are ever truly alone.

James 1:17
Every good and perfect gift is from above, coming down from the Father of the heavenly lights, who does not change like shifting shadows. He chose to give us birth through the word of truth, that we might be a kind of firstfruits of all he created. (NIV)

Chapter 13

Always Represent God

Nicholas loved northern Canada. Although it was a far cry from his native land near Jerusalem, he found the mountains a place of joy, peace and comfort. Away from modern cities and technological inventions, life was simpler and proceeded more at God's pace, not a hyped up world of electronics and videos. Nicholas would often take long trips carrying a big backpack filled with enough things to survive in the woods where he would find more than enough food. In the summer he ate berries and fruits. He was a good fisherman and would make fishing poles from pine branches, string and hooks he carried in his backpack. The natives in the area all knew who he was, for the legends of Santa's deeds of loving, caring and giving had spread far and wide even north of the Arctic Circle in the land of the northern lights. Sometimes Santa would stay overnight with various tribes of Eskimos and Native Americans. The young children would always stare at him at night when he removed his backpack wondering what goodies he might be hiding inside. He always left small gifts wherever he stayed overnight, in part to give thanks for the hospitality, and as a token of friendship. He learned many new crafts and in the process showed people a few tricks he had learned over the centuries.

In the spring after Santa's trip to Israel and the Boston Shiner's Burn Center, he decided to take one of his short journeys into the northern mountains that were still covered with snow. He arranged for some of his adult helpers to care for the children while he was gone. They had developed some rituals for these journeys. On the night before Santa left, he would gather all of the children and helpers and have an evening with a great feast and long prayers. Everyone loved those nights, though they would miss Santa for a few weeks, they looked forward to these celebrations. Nicholas always made sure each child had a special assignment before he left that he would write down as a reminder of what each of them was expected to accomplish in his absence. Sometimes it was learning something new in math or history, or memorizing bible verses. For the older children he would often assign projects like writing plays on a special bible story to let their imaginations and learning of the spirit come together in the wonderful creative energies of youth.

Tyler grew up in a small town in Texas. He was loved by his parents and grew as a Christian from the time he was born. He was not as strong as the other boys in his class but he was very handsome. He was not the smartest in regular schoolwork but in bible studies he soared. His grandmother, who cared for him as a baby, read the bible to him every week and sang gospel songs that made him smile. While other boys played basketball, football and competed in wrestling, Tyler found the only sport he really liked was archery. To get athletic scholarships, all of his friends stuck to baseball, football and basketball. The other boys worked out on weights as their parents tried to prepare them to compete and get some national recognition. Tyler read books and went to bible study camps.

After the world learned of Santa's feat in going to Israel, many young adults became confused about whether or not to believe in Santa Claus. Some adults even struggled with the clear evidence from radar to visual sightings by pilots from all over the world. Some from the Middle East and Asia, who did not accept the fact that Jesus Christ is the Son of God and died on the cross for our sins, were particularly challenged to accept even the concept of a St. Nicholas, as a spirit who taught that it is a wonderful blessing to give to others.

Tyler was struggling with being teased endlessly at school about his love for archery. He wanted to get away from his small town for the summer instead of going to camp or working at the local store and cleaning at night to start saving money for college. His father worked hard and many late hours to provide for his family and save for his education. Like most parents, it was a difficult, endless and frustrating task. At first his father wanted Tyler to try football or basketball to earn a scholarship but accepted the fact that Tyler was built for a different destiny.

During his prayers, Tyler repeatedly got a message in the form of a vision. He dreamed about this message all day and every night. He knew God had set out before him a task that seemed impossible. He did not know how he could ever accomplish it but he had faith. In desperation Tyler wrote to Santa in the spring. He never expected an answer. He didn't even know how to address the letter. He went to the post office on his bike and when no one else could hear he went up to the clerk on duty and sheepishly asked could he please send a letter to Santa and how should he address the envelope. The man behind the counter did not flinch or hesitate.

"No problem. Just put a first-class stamp on it and address it to St. Nicholas and I'll make sure it gets there. Kind of old to be writing to Santa, aren't you?"

Tyler didn't care what anyone thought. He just put on a stamp and wrote the name as instructed and handed over the envelope. He watched as his letter was postmarked and then saw the clerk put it into a mail bag, not the dirty white canvas bags like the others, but a clean red sack hanging all by itself in the corner. Satisfied he had done what he could, he rode his bike home and waited each day for the mail to arrive.

Santa returned from his journey to visit his northern friends in the forests and mountains to find a small stack of mail waiting for him. Most of Santa's letters were handled by his many helpers, but those that presented unique challenges were given to Santa to read personally. He went through the stack slowly, treasuring some thank you letters from parents and children alike, especially those who had lost hope until they received a special bible from Santa with a personal message. At the bottom of the stack was the letter from Tyler. Santa went outside to watch the sun set over the mountains and read the letter as he sat in his rocking chair, glancing up to catch the special moment when the golden rays of the sun skimmed over the mountain peaks to create a scene so gorgeous, if it were a painting you wouldn't believe it was real.

"Dear Santa,

My name is Tyler. I live in a small town in Texas. I have wonderful parents and all that I need to do, I do well in my life. I go to bible studies and I know how to pray. I am very good at it and often lead my Sunday school class at church. I am much better in church than I am in our public school here. They don't let me pray there you know, but I can talk to God silently when I want to and they can't stop me.

102

I know you may think I'm crazy but when I prayed for God to tell me what to do for my future, and I asked how I could serve Him, He told me to write to you. I am not a child asking for toys or gifts. I am just wondering if you can help to lead me to a destiny to serve God. I think that's why He told me to write to you. I get average grades in school. I am not very good at sports, except for archery. I know the tryouts for the Olympics are coming soon and, well, I don't know how to put this Santa, but I believe that God wants me to go to the Olympics and represent Him, not my country, but Him. I know all of this sounds crazy and probably this letter will never find its way to you, but I just had to try. You must be very special in God's heart if He wanted me to write to you for such an impossible task. Although you may never be able to help me, I will pray for you from here, that you may continue to bring joy and hope to children all over the world.

God bless you Santa.

In Christ,

Tyler

The phone rang at Tyler's house. Tyler's father, Richard, answered and then listened intently to someone at the other end of the line.

"Yes, Tyler is my son, but there must be some mistake."

"Colonel Peterson, I'm sure my son didn't apply to any program in Canada for this summer and even if he did, we couldn't afford anything like you're describing."

"That's very generous of you but the airline tickets alone would be very expensive and ..."

"Could I have your number and we'll call you back? It sounds wonderful but I'm sure you understand we need to look into this carefully."

"Alright Colonel. I've got it. Thank you very much. We'll call you back. Again, thank you."

Richard hung up the phone slowly and shook his head in disbelief.

"Tyler, that was a Colonel Peterson from NATO Command Center, stationed in Canada. He said you were chosen to go to a special camp to get training in archery so you could compete in international competition and they would take care of your airfare and all expenses if you wanted to go. Do you know anything about this?"

Tyler's mind raced. Could it be? No way! Must be some amazing coincidence.

"I didn't apply to any camps but I did write for help on archery training, and this sounds great. Can I go Dad?"

Richard looked puzzled.

"I'll make some calls and see if all this is safe and proper. I've got friends down at the police station who can check to see if all this is legit, then we'll talk some more."

Late that night, Tyler heard Richard and his mother Sandy arguing and strained his ears to listen.

"We can't send him to Canada before school ends."

"They said they provide schooling in addition to the athletic training. It sounds like a once in a lifetime opportunity. I love him too and wouldn't think of leaving him somewhere unless it's absolutely safe. The guys at the police station said this Colonel Peterson is one of the top officers in NATO with an impeccable reputation. His own son went to this place. They've contacted the Royal Canadian Mounties who verified that everything is fine. It's a chance he may never get again. Let's make the decision his. This is no easy program and it's a long way from home. Come on, Sandy. You know this would be every boy's dream to go there."

"I don't want him getting his hopes up and then going up against men who are so much better than him, that when he comes home he'll feel like a fool for going and end up mad at us for letting him go. He's still my baby and always will be."

"Sandy, let's face it. We can't afford to send him to college without some kind of scholarship or miracle. Maybe this can get him a scholarship and even if it doesn't, he deserves the chance. Otherwise he'll always wonder, and could be angry with us for holding him back on his one big chance."

"I just don't want him hurt. He's a very sensitive boy."

"I agree Sandy. But no matter how close you hold him, one day that boy will be a man and leave our home to go out on his own. It's our job to prepare him for that time. Funny, I guess when you think about it, we love him so much we want him to be strong enough to get out on his own, yet we want him here."

All loving parents go through this struggle. You don't know the pain of those decisions until you have to make them yourselves.

At breakfast the next morning, Tyler's eyes followed every move his parents made. He had learned that sometimes to get what you want from your parents, you have to give them time to realize that you're growing up.

As Sandy made omelets, she casually asked Tyler a question, although she already knew the answer.

"Tyler, are you sure you really want to go away to this camp? It means leaving school now and finishing this term in Canada. You won't have that summer job to earn money for college and you won't know anyone there like you do here. And if you get homesick, we can't just pick you up like an overnight at a friend's house in town."

Tyler looked to his father for approval. His father nodded yes. Tyler shouted for joy, jumped up and ran to his room and started packing. Sandy cried. She said it was nothing, just a little burn from the stove while making breakfast, but Tyler knew much more than his parents thought. Most parents don't realize how amazingly perceptive their children are. They want or expect them not to know, but they do.

The day of departure Tyler watched the school bus stop and pick up his friends as he waited for his father to take him to the airport. He wouldn't see his family for months and for a moment he felt sad and a little afraid of the journey he was about to embark upon, but he knew if it was because of his letter to Santa, it just had to be good. He also knew the schoolwork and training combined would be difficult but he had already resolved, no matter how tough it was he wouldn't give up.

The drive to the airport was a bit hurried. Richard had to get to work and taking Tyler would make him very late but it was worth the effort. When they arrived at the airport it was jammed with traffic. The instructions they received by letter said Colonel Peterson would meet Tyler in front of the entrance to the long term parking area. As they got closer Tyler could see a military jeep and some men in uniform in front of the gate to the parking lot.

When they pulled up Tyler jumped out and grabbed his bags and his bow and arrows. Colonel Peterson took Richard aside and talked for a few minutes. Tyler couldn't hear them but saw them both smile and shake hands. Richard walked over to Tyler.

"Well son, this is where I say goodbye. You are in good hands. They'll take you from here."

There was that awkward moment. All young men have it with their mothers and fathers. You want to hug goodbye but not in front of other people, especially a military officer. Tyler didn't want to look like a wimp so he simply shook his father's hand. Richard was startled but smiled, then he took a step back and saluted his son. Tyler grinned and saluted back. Then his father couldn't help it, he gave his son a big hug and kiss on the cheek and whispered into his ear.

"Whatever you do son, I want you to know that we're proud of you and have been since the moment you were born. Promise you'll write each week or your mother and I won't sleep. Safe journey."

As Richard drove off, Tyler turned around to see the men in uniform scanning his luggage and then opening everything up to check it carefully. They gave Colonel Peterson the thumbs up and put the luggage into the jeep. Colonel Peterson looked at Tyler and smiled.

"You ever flown before?"

Tyler wanted to impress the Colonel and act very casual at the same time.

"Oh sure. I flew to Disney World with my parents. It was fun. Flying is no problem for me. It's like being in a bus."

The uniformed men turned to Colonel Peterson and laughed. Tyler didn't understand why until they entered the military hangar.

"Then you should have no trouble with our flight today. The person you wrote to said I should take good care of you so I thought I'd get you there quickly so you can start your training. Hop in."

They drove through a maze of gates, check points and finally into a military hangar. Inside was a sleek black jet unlike any Tyler had ever seen before. Silently the men in uniform placed his luggage in the belly of the small jet. Then they brought a special flight suit for Tyler and fitted him carefully. It was one of those new fluid pressurized suits he had read about. They helped strap him into the seat behind the pilot.

His heart was racing. It was hard to believe all this was happening. Colonel Peterson climbed in and the cockpit canopy closed tightly around them. Colonel Peterson started talking to the tower and Tyler could hear everything on his own headset. The engine fired up. Tyler could sense the raw power of the thrusters even through his seat and the suit. The jet started to move forward. When he glanced outside he saw his bow and arrows on the hangar floor.

"Colonel Peterson, stop! My bow and arrows. They forgot to load them. Please, I need them. That's the whole purpose of this trip."

Colonel Peterson chuckled and tried to calm Tyler down.

"The one who sent me gave me specific instructions to do that. Don't worry, if it's really your path, you'll make another bow when you get there."

Tyler was still a little concerned.

"Make one? You don't understand. That's a really expensive bow and the arrows have colored rings to register to shoot in competition and the arrows are aluminum. I can't make those. The bow has a special computer designed damper on it for vibration..."

Colonel Peterson interrupted.

"Tyler you're just going to have to trust me on this. Forget the bow and concentrate, when we get to cruising altitude do you want to take the stick?"

Tyler was a blend of excited and confused, but he knew what to do. As the jet pulled out of the hangar, he took a deep breath and prayed, asking God to protect him and Colonel Peterson on their journey. As he opened his eyes while his head was still bowed down he noticed an emergency sign with the inscription – "Pull To Eject".

"Hey, Colonel Peterson. What's this red handle on the floor for?"

"I wouldn't recommend that you pull that. It will eject you from the jet. Hopefully you won't need that today."

The take-off was awesome. Tyler's body felt like it weighed a ton as his whole body got pushed back into the seat. The climb was very steep, nothing like the commercial flight he took to Disney World. In minutes he was high above the clouds going north. The Colonel rolled the jet over a few times and then flew upside down for a while. Tyler wished he hadn't eaten breakfast.

"You all right back there Tyler?"

"Sure. What a take off! Are we going as fast as a commercial jet now?"

Colonel Peterson laughed.

"Very funny. In a minute you'll feel the jet shake a bit. It does that as we pass from sub-sonic to super-sonic speeds. It's classified how fast we can really go but let's just say that if you were on a Concorde trying to catch up, you'd be lost in the vapor trail."

The flight was fast and beautiful. They landed on a military base and transferred to a jet helicopter. This leg of the flight was noisy and seemed so slow compared to the scram jet, but at low altitudes they could see mountains, lakes, rivers and trees just beginning to bud. Quickly the forest below turned to mostly pines and the mountain peaks still had snow.

They landed in a large field early in the afternoon. Colonel Peterson helped Tyler unload his bags and gave him a backpack frame to strap the luggage onto his back to carry.

"You see that smoke over that hill? That's where you're going. I've got to get this copter back to the base. You'll be fine. Just keep your eyes on the smoke trail and you won't get lost."

Tyler got that nervous feeling again.

"I thought you were coming with me?"

"You're a man now. I thought that's what you wanted. You'll be fine. I'll see you when you're ready for the next step in your journey."

Tyler didn't understand.

"Thank you very much for the ride. Is the smoke coming from the campsite? I thought you would be bringing a lot of other students. Am I the first one this season or am I late?"

"For anyone who wants to serve God, it's never too late. If you keep focused on why you really came here, you'll be fine. Don't let the attention or focus remain on you. It's Him."

Somehow it all made sense to Tyler and suddenly he felt at ease, almost like when you spot your home after returning from a long trip, that same comfort and warmth flooded his spirit.

As Tyler set off for the origin of the smoke trail, Colonel Peterson took off and quickly disappeared. It was suddenly very quiet, very peaceful. Tyler's mind now focused on the reasons for his journey. Was he really going to meet Santa Claus? Was he real? Why else would he have been brought here except for his letter? Why did they leave his bow and arrows back at the airport in the hangar? Was he really going to a summer camp with lots of other young athletes to be trained to be good enough to be selected for the Olympic tryouts? If he got that far, how could he represent God? Wouldn't they force him to be on the U.S. Team?

As Tyler continued his walk towards the smoke trail he thought about whether he would ever be good enough for international competition. He had only won local high school tournaments and competed with varsity teams from Texas and Oklahoma. What about men in college and older men who were bigger and stronger? The other teams would have access to all sorts of high tech equipment to design and manufacture the bows and arrows. How could he make his own bow? Maybe Colonel Peterson was mistaken and Santa had arranged for a brand new bow, one of gleaming metal all polished to a beautiful mirror finish.

His luggage started feeling very heavy by the time he spotted the house in the forest surrounded by gardens and open fields of long green grass. When he finally arrived at the house the sun was almost setting. The cool mountain breezes felt refreshing. As he approached the house he saw several children sitting on the porch reading. He wondered where all the hordes of other people might be and where the target range was and how odd that there were no paved roads to be seen anywhere, only dirt trails. He put down his luggage on the porch of the house.

"Hi there. You must be Tyler."

He turned around to see a tall young woman about his age, standing behind him. She had perspiration on her forehead and was dressed like a runner only she had no running shoes on, just a pair of moccasins worn down from many miles of use. She had beautiful long black hair, braided on both sides, and cheeks that were red and skin that was a deep golden, not from exposure to the sun but her natural color. Tyler was a bit smitten by her natural beauty and spoke softly.

"How did you know my name?"

"We've been expecting you. We have the same teacher."

Tyler didn't quite understand. Maybe she meant they had the same coach. Odd to have the same coach for a woman runner and a man in archery but everything about this day was far from normal.

"My name is Blue Wings, but my friends here just call me Blue."

"Are you an Indian?" Tyler asked in an innocent voice.

Blue Wings spoke in a polite but almost correcting tone of voice.

"There are no Indians here. My forefathers have been in these mountains for many centuries, long before the British, French and Vikings crossed the great oceans."

Tyler smiled, understood and tactfully changed the subject.

"Do you know who I am supposed to see here and where I stay?"

Blue Wings wiped the perspiration from her forehead.

"Forgive me. You must be tired from your long journey. You can stay in the main house tonight and tomorrow I will take you to your teacher. Some of Santa's helpers inside can answer your questions. We have a big family meal together about 6 o'clock every night. Everyone here cooks, cleans and does their own laundry. Maybe you can show us Texas-style cooking and tomorrow I'll show you all the food we can gather from the forest. I'll take you to your teacher in the mountains after breakfast."

Tyler was confused about all this. He had expected an archery coach. Maybe that's what a teacher meant in the local language. He had expected a camp filled with athletes in training. Instead he found orphaned children, who were being cared for by Santa's helpers. Would he see Santa? He wondered if Santa's sleigh was in the big barn. Where were all the reindeer? Where was the machine shop he would need to build his own precision bow? He had so many questions it just made him tired, thinking about it all.

He slept peacefully in the clean cool mountain air. He had dreams about what God really wanted him to do. Why would God direct a young man to represent Him in the Olympics? Maybe it was just a fanciful dream or wishful thinking. How could he know for certain? Maybe God had not really spoken to him as he thought, but what purpose would it serve otherwise? Was he just dreaming about fame and not what God wanted him to do to bring more people to Christ or was this a test of his faith? Though Tyler was not the strongest, nor the brightest student, above all others for his age in school, his faith, his prayers and his spiritual gifts were strong. He understood the armor of God and he wore it well.

In the early dawn he looked out of his window to see reindeer eating grass in the meadows surrounding the barn. High up in the sky he could see eagles flying. In the early morning quiet, he could hear the faint sounds of an owl in the distant trees and a distant howl, perhaps a dog or even a wolf. He suddenly realized he wasn't in a small town in Texas but the wilds of northern Canada. Maybe there were bears and wolves running about. He thought making a bow seemed like a good idea today, just in case nature got too close.

Tyler helped make breakfast, cooking pancakes using a blend of flour, milk, eggs and a little onion. Everyone loved them and wanted more. They had homemade jams that tasted great with the hot pancakes. He helped clean up after breakfast, patiently waiting for his archery instructor to come get him for his first lesson. Tyler would learn many lessons this day, none of which seemed to involve archery.

Blue Wings found Tyler after the breakfast cleanup.

"Come on. Time to meet your teacher. He's not too far away. I'll show you the way. Watch closely so you can find him by yourself. I'm training to run the marathon. You mind if we run there today? Don't worry, I won't go too fast."

Tyler shrugged. He really had no choice in the matter.

"Sure. No problem. How far are we going? Down one of those dirt paths to a nearby archery range?"

Blue Wings was already jogging outside.

"No, we're going up the mountains. It's about an hour or two depending on how many times I have to stop for you."

Tyler's mouth dropped in disbelief, and he muttered to himself.

"Oh great. You had to write to Santa, huh? Hope this teacher has a jeep to drive me back in. Sure hope he knows how to teach archery."

He struggled to keep up with Blue Wings and at the same time tried to memorize the path if you could call it that. It was more like a maze through trees, around giant boulders, across meadows, crossing streams and up and around the mountain far away and out of sight from Santa's workshop, if indeed it was Santa's place. After all, so far there were no signs of Santa anywhere.

About two hours later after many stops so Tyler could catch his breath, they reached the peak of the mountain. Blue Wings was barely breathing harder than normal and looked like she had jogged down the driveway to pick up mail whereas Tyler was drenched in perspiration and his legs and feet were sore. He thought he was in good shape but he quickly learned that most of his notions about fitness and training had no relevance in this raw wilderness.

"You did fine for a first day out Tyler. Think you can find your way back? Your teacher is waiting for you. I'll see you at dinner. I have to start my training now. This was just a warm up for me. Are you going to be alright?"

Tyler looked a little sheepish and realized he was totally lost.

"I'll be okay. I think I can find my way back. I'll keep looking for the chimney smoke in case I get lost."

With no further words Blue Wings disappeared in an instant, running faster and faster, smiling at the beautiful day and all the great bounties in nature. She would eat berries and fish during the day that she caught using spears she made from dead branches. She cooked the fish near the ponds and lakes ever careful not to attract bears or wolves from the scent of the cooking.

Tyler walked to the very top of the mountain peak that still had some snow. The view was spectacular. He could see for many miles in the clear northern air. The smell of pine filled each breath. He sat on a flat rock and rested, enjoying the view.

A quiet, gentle voice broke the silence.

"This is the land of my Father. The forest remains almost the same here except for a few men who have cleared land for homes and taken away the trees planted centuries ago."

Tyler turned around to see an old man sitting next to a bear as they both gazed out looking at the far horizon. Tyler kept looking at the man, then the bear and wondered if the bear could climb trees.

The old man sat quietly patting the head of the bear that had a wonderful coat with a golden blonde color from his huge black nose to his short tail. The bear got up on all fours and slowly sauntered over to Tyler who was frozen in his tracks, debating whether to run, jump to the tree tops below or pick up a stone to defend himself. It was the largest bear he had ever seen. Before he had time to choose, the bear nuzzled his nose into Tyler's belly and moved his giant head side to side almost tickling Tyler. It was one of those magical moments boys have in their lives, one he would always remember. Suddenly, he wasn't afraid. He patted the bear's head and scratched underneath his huge jaw. The bear opened his mouth revealing gigantic teeth, then sat down and closed his eyes, enjoying the attention. In the coming months, the three of them would become best of friends. Tyler would name his giant friend Golden Bear. Together, they would form a most

112

unusual bond, the type that only an animal and a boy can truly understand.

Tyler stared at the old man who sat quietly on top of the rock at the peak of the mountain.

"Are you my archery instructor? Blue Wings said I would find you here, except she called you a teacher. I assumed that meant for archery."

The old man just stared out to the surrounding mountains.

"I know something about archery. If you want to learn, I will pass on to you some of the knowledge I have about many things."

Tyler was baffled and confused. Why did he come all this way? Was there some misunderstanding or mix-up? Did his letter get mixed up with someone else's? Colonel Peterson clearly came to Dallas to bring him here, but why? Maybe this was a test of his patience. Was Blue Wings just teasing him and left him alone in the forest with an old man and a bear to see if he would get frightened and run back to the shelter of Santa's home?

Tyler had learned years ago from his grandmother that it is at moments like these that we all need to go to the Father and ask for guidance and patience and let Him show us the way.

So on top of a strange mountain with Golden Bear at his side Tyler got on his knees and prayed out loud.

"Heavenly Father, I thank you for this wonderful day and bringing me to this strange and beautiful place. High on this mountain I feel closer to you. Here, there is a calm and peace. I am not sure what you want me to do, Father. I want to praise you and glorify your name. You told me to represent you. I thought it was through archery. It is the only thing I'm good at, you know, but if I am to serve you in another way please show me. I do not know why you have brought me to the mountain today with this old man and Golden Bear, but please bless them and protect them on their journey Lord. I know we must be close to you and listen hard. Guide me now Father. I am yours always. You lead and I will follow. Amen."

When Tyler opened his eyes, he saw the old man and the bear both kneeling in silence. He never saw a bear on his knees while bowing his head before. The old man spoke quietly in a soothing, deep, almost melodic voice.

"Show me your hands."

Tyler held out his arms and showed the old man his hands.

"These are the hands of a boy. When you are ready, look at your hands again. On that day, you will be a man. You pray to the Father with a pure heart and show yourself to be a man in the spirit. No one comes to the Father except through me. Your gifts are strong. If you wish to serve, you must become stronger and wiser far beyond your tender years. If you are truly chosen, then you will know it in your heart. You will never give up even when all seems lost you will continue to serve the Lord. You are about to embark upon a difficult journey. Are you truly ready, young Tyler? You will face many trials and dangers. The Evil One will seek you out when He realizes you are a threat to His dominion of evil. You cannot escape it, not even here. Do you truly want to serve? If you have doubts, now would be the time to leave."

Tyler smiled.

"I am not sure I understand everything you are saying. I am not afraid to serve. I have given control of my life to Jesus Christ. He is my Lord and Savior. I do not fear the Evil One for I am already saved. I already have the victory. I just don't know what God wants me to do now. I pray all the time so I can listen and praise His holy name. In school it is hard for me to be myself. The other kids tease me. I am an outcast in my own town except with my friends in church. I am not the strongest or tallest or faster but for some reason God has led me to believe I can serve Him by becoming good at archery and representing Him in the Olympics. Maybe all this sounds crazy to you or maybe you're the only one who it won't sound crazy to, I don't know."

The old man laughed and patted Tyler on the head.

"Yes, you are crazy, crazy in love with the Spirit. The vast unspoiled beauty of this land is a testimony to His greatness. I understand and see more than you may think, young Tyler. I am a tough teacher. My yoke is heavy but my burden is light. I will ask the impossible of you, physically, spiritually and mentally, but your journey begs for the impossible. I see now why the giver of the gifts asked me to train you in our ways. Your letter touched his heart because you did not ask for something for yourself but how you could serve your God. The Father is the potter and He has placed you as clay into my hands. Perhaps you can be shaped, we shall see."

Tyler looked a bit confused but felt warm and happy inside. As

114

odd as it seemed, this must be the path God wanted him to take. The old man looked serious and again looked into Tyler's eyes.

"You can call me Chief Daniel. If you are willing I shall show you how to become whatever it is you want to achieve. Each day you will meet me here. Each day you will have training but nothing like you have ever known before. You must trust me that no matter what you think or how strange the tasks, you will do it. Each day we will talk. Ask questions. Never hold back what is in your heart. To love the Lord you must develop body, mind and spirit. You are much stronger than you think, young Tyler."

Golden Bear stood up and started walking down from the peak of the mountain. He found a patch of snow and rolled in it. It was a wondrous sight to see such a huge animal being so playful.

Chief Daniel stood up and looked into the surrounding forest.

"Things are not always as they seem Tyler. That is your first lesson today. When you learn what that means you will have gone from boy to man. For today though, time to begin your training. You will spend much time in the forest. There is beauty, wisdom and danger around each bend in your path. You must learn to see, hear and feel far beyond yourself. You will no doubt be challenged while you are here. If ever you are in danger, do not be afraid or too proud to shout for help. Call your friend and he will protect you."

Chief Daniel pointed to Golden Bear rolling on his back in the snow.

"But he is just a bear. How can he hear me from far away and why would he come to me?"

Chief Daniel folded his arms.

"You are not listening. What was your first lesson?"

"Things are not always as they seem."

"Very good, very good."

It took Tyler a while to adjust to Chief Daniel's unique way of teaching. Nothing was ever direct like in school. He rarely answered questions as expected. Rather, Chief Daniel would ask Tyler other questions urging him to grow and stretch the limits of his imagination and earthly knowledge. Much of what Tyler learned was in the realm of the spirit. There are no books written to answer the questions he sought. It seemed on many days Chief Daniel went to elaborate yet simple measures to help Tyler grow.

In the weeks that followed the first meeting, Tyler began an extensive round of physical training. Every day he ran up and down mountains. Chief Daniel taught him how to fish and find food in the forest. Then he showed Tyler how to make an axe and how to make a shelter from branches, grasses and mud. Tyler learned how to chop down a tree to use the logs to make strong shelters for protection from a winter snowstorm, rain or hail.

Each day Chief Daniel gave Tyler lessons in philosophy and life and read from the bible. Strangely, Chief Daniel never had to look at the verses. He just opened the bible and handed it to Tyler. It was as if he had written the verses himself. They had long talks about worldwide differences in religion. Tyler talked about his love for Christ and how he understood the trinity, Father, Son and Holy Spirit. Soon, Tyler began to expand his horizons and his eyes opened to a new world all around him. He slowly felt connected to all living things and saw part of their purpose in God's greater plan on earth. His sense of sight, hearing and smell leapt to new heights. He could find berries in the forest by listening to the song of pine sparrows as they spoke to each other. He learned to fish by finding deep pockets in the streams by watching how the surface of the water changed the size and shape of the ripples and swirls on top of the water.

After a month of training, Chief Daniel surprised Tyler one day. "Today you shall begin to make your bows and tomorrow you will begin to gather what you need to make your arrows. What must you do first?"

"Chief Daniel, I thought you didn't know too much about archery. How are you going to help me build a bow and make arrows?"

"I have never shot an arrow or made a bow before. What does that matter? I'll ask the questions. All you have to do is seek the answers. What could be easier than that?"

Tyler was trying hard to have faith in Chief Daniel. The physical training was indeed going very well and his other training on spiritual matters was also doing remarkably well, so why shouldn't he trust him on the next step in the journey?

"Did you ever wonder why people around here call me Chief Daniel?"

"I assumed you are a Chief in your local tribe and that Daniel is a common name used here just like it is in my home town."

"No. You are still not seeing with open eyes. You have come far but there is a long way to go. The journey never ends. I am the journey."

Tyler felt like he had disappointed his new friend. Golden Bear who was sitting listening to them talk, lay down on the ground and covered his eyes with his paws.

"I was taught in the bible about a Daniel who had absolute faith in God. He was put into a den of lions and survived overnight until the King released him at dawn. His faith kept him safe all night. Chief could mean one of greatness or maybe a man of great faith in the face of all danger."

Golden Bear sat up quickly and nodded his head. Tyler thought more.

"The first day when Blue Wings told me to climb to the peak of the mountain to find my teacher, I just assumed it was you Chief Daniel."

Chief Daniel broke out in a broad grin, showing his perfect white teeth, glistening in the sunlight.

"And now, what do you think?"

"Now I see each man chooses his own path in life. If I keep praying and focusing on God, if I walk on the narrow path, then I am letting the spirit guide me. So in a way, each of us who seeks God is our own teacher."

"Very good. From now on, do not assume or presume. Seek to feel in your heart and soul what is right. Always ask yourself, what would Jesus do, in all situations you face in life. Then, you will always be on the right path. It doesn't mean you will be free of problems or dangers, rather that you shall go forward with integrity, honesty and living in the light."

Tyler started to see more clearly now. Chief Daniel looked at Golden Bear and then spoke directly to the bear.

"Old friend, you are to be the guardian for your new friend. Until he leaves, you shall be together to protect him from the coming evil."

Golden Bear nodded and rolled on his back, exposing his enormous belly and held still. Chief Daniel looked at Tyler in expectation but this time Tyler understood without words. Golden Bear, as a sign of faith, trust and friendship, exposed his vulnerable belly. Tyler leaned over and rubbed the bear's thick fur and patted him and then gave Golden Bear a gentle hug around his neck.

As Tyler stepped back, Golden Bear rolled back up and sat in front of Tyler. He roared and then opened his powerful jaws, with teeth that could crush bones or bite through a skull in a fight. His large black nose was shining and saliva dripped from the soft flesh of his gaping mouth.

Tyler's eyes opened wide. He looked at Chief Daniel to confirm what he thought he must do. Chief Daniel nodded. In an act of faith, Tyler placed his hand inside the open jaws of the giant bear. He looked into Golden Bear's eyes. He realized they were not the jet black eyes he had assumed they were. Instead, staring back at him were two pale yellow eyes with black centers, unflinching, unmoving. Tyler felt his hot breath. The surface of the tongue was rough but underneath was soft. It was a bit gooey and uncomfortable and his hand and shirt got soaking wet but when Tyler finally removed his hand and arm, there was a feeling of jubilation. Tyler would later realize that this moment of faith and bonding would save his life and that of Blue Wings.

Chief Daniel began walking. Tyler and Golden Bear, now side by side, walked behind. Tyler wondered if he was just an old gentle bear or was there more to what was happening than he could see. Chief Daniel took them to a new spot deep in the forest in a small valley next to a small fast moving stream. He showed Tyler all the different kinds of trees and how each one served a different purpose.

"I have never made a bow, Tyler, but many of the greatest warriors in centuries past have used this tree."

He pointed to a small tree growing amongst the rocks in very little soil.

"As you see, the seeds landed in a place with little earth, yet this tree grows straight and strong. It is difficult to cut down, harder still to fashion into a bow, and nearly impossible to make arrows with because the wood is like iron. When you are finished, I will show you how to seal the wood and change it into a tool of neither wood nor metal but something unique, almost spiritual in its very nature."

Tyler spent a long time picking just the right tree for the bows and ended up using the small straight tree Chief Daniel had shown him. It had branches that naturally curved in the shape he had seen designed by the manufacturers of bows. Chief Daniel drew in the soft mud near the stream, the size and shape of the bows the ancient warriors used to hunt deer, buffalo, wolves and bears.

Tyler spent the rest of the day cutting the trees and branches using an axe he had made from a sharpened stone. He fashioned two bows of slightly different shapes and sizes. The longer bow was for greater distances and the shorter bow was for under 50 yards. On the first day, for the arrow shafts he simply cut and split the wood into long square pieces. He would later carve and sand them into smooth circular shafts. By the end of the day, Tyler was exhausted. He could not run home as usual, carrying his newly cut pieces for the bows and arrows. He crossed paths with Blue Wings late in the afternoon. She helped him carry the newly cut wood back to the house. After a big dinner, Tyler fell asleep very early.

The next day he ran swiftly to the mountain peak, eager to gather more materials for his bows and arrows. Chief Daniel was waiting for him with Golden Bear at the peak.

"Your arrows will need wings to fly to the target. What would be the best thing you could use?"

Tyler thought carefully.

"Most people now use plastic formed into imitation feathers. They put them on very straight using epoxy. In the forest I think we could use the feathers of a bird but I am not sure of which bird and whether to take the feathers from the wings or the tail. What do you think, Chief Daniel?"

"The arrow is but a straight shaft. To make it fly to do your bidding and God's will, the great warriors of the past knew they must do two things. One is to use only the feathers of the eagle. Second, was never to align the feathers straight along the shaft but rather to cause a gentle spiral as the arrow flew to its target."

Tyler smiled and put his hands on his hips.

"Hey. You told me you never made a bow. How come you're an expert all of a sudden?"

"I am an old man with many children and grandchildren. I was here before the world was created. Your task is not to make the greatest bows but to represent God as He told you to do. So your task is to figure out the best way to do that. I cannot guarantee success, young disciple, only that we shall try our best to give you every skill you need from our combined wisdom. In the end, it is up to you. You have already put your future in the hands of God. I know what He has planned for you. No matter how you do, I will never be disappointed, because I see and we both know we have all done our best. So, are you ready to climb today?"

"Climb? Where am I going?"

"Ah, Tyler, sometimes you are just so funny. You must climb to get the feathers you need. When you see the eagles, just ask him for the feathers so you will receive them as gifts."

"Ask him? I don't think I'm ever going to understand you, Chief Daniel."

Tyler spent the next few days climbing several mountains and going close to the nests of several eagles. On each trip he brought with him some freshly caught fish. He held the fish high above his head so the eagle could see and then tossed it on a nearby rock. When the eagle swooped in to see if it was safe, Tyler held up a single feather Chief Daniel had given him. Tyler twirled the feather and asked would the eagle please give him some feathers to use for his arrows, and that no harm would ever come to the eagle or any other animals from the feathers he would place on his arrows.

Each time the eagle took the fish and flew away. Tyler waited patiently at the same place and sure enough a few hours later each eagle would return with long feathers in their beaks and leave them on the rock where they had gotten their fish.

Each night he worked on carving the bows and arrows. He fell asleep sometimes at the workbench, not to awaken until the kitchen was filled with the sounds and smells of breakfast. In the coming weeks under Chief Daniel's guidance he finished the bows and arrows. He glued the feathers to the shafts using a blend of white latex excreted from some wild weeds, mixed with pinesap. It formed a waterproof glue that was very strong. They blended a wax to seal the wood made from bees wax, the boiled juices of some roots and then blended it with the powdered black ashes from burning the wood carvings and scraps from the original trees Tyler cut down. When they were completed, the bows and arrows were deep black and glistened in the late spring sun.

One day when Tyler woke up early, he saw an old man with long white hair and a beard sitting in a chair in his room. He was wearing black boots and had rosy cheeks.

"Are you Santa?"

Tyler couldn't believe his eyes. He had almost forgotten about the letter that had brought him here in the first place.

"Nice to see you Tyler. I hear from Chief Daniel that you need some help to finish your bows and arrows. I will work with you today to complete them in a way suited to your task. Let's have some breakfast and then go out to the workshop."

Tyler was in awe of Santa. No one would believe his story now. Between Golden Bear, the eagles and Santa, how would he ever be able to tell his parents of his experience without sounding like his imagination had run wild?

Santa smiled at Tyler as his violet eyes glistened.

"So, tell me young man. Why did you write that letter?"

Tyler looked a bit confused and humble at the same time.

"I don't know why God asked me to write to you other than to ask for your help to make a dream come true. The dream He put into my heart was to go to the Olympics and to represent Him. I am good in archery and good in prayer. That is my spiritual gift. However, I don't know how I can represent God, since I am an American and to be honest Santa, I am sure there are men all over the world who are better at archery than I am right now. Many have wealthy sponsors with all kinds of money and high tech equipment. I am but one boy from Texas with a dream God whispered to me. All I know is, I can't give up. No matter what it takes, I am going to try my best. I don't understand the training Chief Daniel is giving me, but I do know it is giving me strength, making me happy inside and it is reaffirming to know that anyone who wants to sacrifice in order to serve God in some way grows even if they don't win with ribbons and medals."

Santa stroked his beard and nodded and stared into Tyler's eyes. He remembered centuries ago when he was young and full of unswerving faith, strong in prayer and had to learn of giving gifts.

"The others may have all the high tech equipment but they don't have God and they don't have me! Don't worry. No contest. Let's go get a good breakfast so we can keep working all day. Have you ever forged metals before and created molds to use to cast?"

Tyler shook his head no.

"Good. Today is your day to learn then."

After breakfast they went out into the barn. It was dark inside. Santa walked over to the sleigh and signaled Tyler to join him. He knelt down and prayed for a long time silently and then out loud. As Santa spoke Tyler could feel a wind inside the closed barn. It was like a gentle whirlwind circling them next to the sleigh. His body tingled all over and he got goose bumps and Santa spoke louder and louder.

"Lord guide me now, your old humble servant. Show me how to help this young man be a representative of Christ to billions of people throughout the surface of this planet. My time here on earth is almost over Father. I know you will call me home soon. Your gifts of the cross are so few now. I must be certain you want me to use them for this purpose. Give me a sign Lord. Let us know this is your will and then your will be done."

Then silence. The wind stopped. Tyler almost held his breath. He could sense a wonderful moment in his life was in the process of revealing itself. He strained his ears. He had learned to hear the rustle of leaves in distant trees, the cry and song of a bird miles away and the grunts of Golden Bear from far away. He tilted his head, trying his best to pick up a faint sound. It grew louder each moment.

All of a sudden there was scratching on the roof of the barn. What could it be? Santa and Tyler walked outside the barn and looked on the peak of the roof. There were the eagles that had given Tyler their feathers. As they looked up at all the eagles perched on the roof, a white dove flew into Tyler's hands. He carefully cupped both hands around the dove then gently stroked his head. Two of the eagles suddenly flew from the roof and perched themselves on Tyler's shoulders. They flapped their wings and made threatening screeching sounds and looked like they were going to pounce on the dove. Tyler slowly placed the dove inside of his jacket to protect it. The eagles flew all around Tyler's head and body looking for the dove. Tyler remained rock steady. He wouldn't run. He would not be threatened. He protected the dove as his own.

In a minute, as quickly as it all started, it ended peacefully. The eagles flew away. Tyler slowly reached into his jacket to let the dove fly free. He couldn't find it. He started to panic. He quickly took off his jacket then his shirt thinking the dove was hiding or worse, it may have gotten smothered. He looked at Santa in quiet desperation for an explanation. Santa just grinned.

"Do you remember when Christ was baptized by John the Baptist, a white dove appeared in the sky? That dove is now inside of you. Call it purity of spirit, call it ultimate faith or by any other name, it is now a part of you. When your service to God, this task He asked of you, is almost over, the dove shall fly out of you and bring you the peace and the knowledge that God is inside of you always."

They went back inside the barn and closed the door. Santa walked over to the back seat of the sleigh. There, hidden underneath was a red sack that glowed in the darkened room. Santa reached inside and removed a small tubular object wrapped in colored paper and tied with colorful string. He handed it to Tyler. As soon as he held is in his hand it was almost like getting burned.

"Ow! Santa, it feels hot. What is it?"

"This is the last of the nails used to place Christ on the cross."

Tyler looked horrified.

"Oh my God. I shouldn't have this. Should I even touch it? Is He going to be mad at me now?"

"No, my child. He understands. Now you try to understand. He wants you to take that nail and forge it into a gift for all of mankind. We are going to use it to make a part of your bows, the part that each arrow rests upon before you release it to fly to its target. Then the tip of each arrow must be coated with a very thin layer. You must make that mold to cast the metal. You will understand it's meaning if you go the distance Tyler."

"Go the distance? You mean if I do what God wants me to do?"

"Something like that Tyler. Something like that."

They spent all day forging the one large nail into the arrow rests for each bow and then the delicate thin tips for each arrow. Tyler was not comfortable touching the nail or the metal parts that came from it. Each time he touched them he prayed in a loud whisper.

"Please forgive me Father. Please forgive us all."

After the sunset, Santa and Tyler emerged from the barn. The late spring air was cool and moist. Santa hugged Tyler tight.

"God bless you Tyler. I envy you on your journey. Perhaps it would be too much excitement for an old man like me. You may not see me again for a while but I shall see you. When you have your first son, think kindly of me. Some day, the son becomes the father. Always keep your faith. Finish the race strong. Never let the Evil One scare you away. The victory is already yours. No matter what happens after today, remember that son."

Tyler watched Santa walk into the house. He would not see him again for several years. Many times though, he felt his presence. Years later he would journey back to Santa's house for a wedding.

In the weeks that followed, Tyler and Chief Daniel and Golden Bear spent hours each day perfecting Tyler's aim, technique, strength and endurance. Tyler started to grow a scanty moustache, as he became more of a man than a boy.

Chief Daniel was an odd selection for any coach. Each day began on the mountaintop with prayers and talks about life and the purpose each of us must strive to find. He showed Tyler how to use the wind as a friend when shooting from great distances by watching the flicker of leaves in distant trees signaling the approach of a puff of wind. He taught him to stand firm with his legs and feet secure to insure his aim was steady. He showed him the ways of the ancient men of faith who blessed the bow before they used it and blessed each arrow before it flew in the air. He made the bows, arrows, winds and earth all blend into one spirit, one energy, that Tyler must command to secure an eminent place in the Olympic events to come.

Each day he ran with Blue Wings. She ran like the wind itself. All seemed hopeful and beautiful. It was almost like living in a dream. That is, until that day in the forest Tyler would never forget.

It was a day like all others. There was only a week left before Tyler and Blue Wings would leave to compete in the Olympic tryouts. Tyler had just finished his early morning session with Chief Daniel when he heard the first scream. He stopped in his tracks and didn't breathe, straining to hear the direction of the scream. He recognized Blue Wings' voice even though she was clearly panicked and in trouble. The second time he heard her voice, he determined the direction. He quickly threw down his bows and arrows and tore off his jacket as he began to run as never before. He quickly reached Blue Wings at the edge of a field. She was standing next to a pine tree with low branches. She was surrounded by wolves. Tyler froze in his tracks for a moment, and then shouted.

"Blue Wings what should I do? Can you make it up the tree?"

"If I move they'll attack and tear my flesh before I can grab the first branch. Did you bring your bow and arrows?"

Tyler felt like a fool.

"No. I just ran here to find you as fast as could."

The wolves circled closer to Blue Wings.

"Tyler run away quickly or they'll kill us both. Run now, Tyler."

Tyler didn't move. He would not abandon his friend. He would never abandon his faith. He prayed out loud in a fast voice.

"Oh Father, tell me what to do. Please Lord, don't let her die like this. Take me instead Jesus, please just take me.

Tyler closed his eyes for a moment and suddenly knew what to do. He took in a deep breath and yelled again and again at the top of his lungs.

"Golden Bear! Golden Bear! Come quickly. We need you."

"Golden Bear! Where are you? Please come now!"

As he finished screaming, some of the wolves left the circle around Blue Wings and formed a circle around Tyler. They snarled and bared their fangs. Slowly the circles of predators got tighter around them both.

Tyler was not sure at first. He thought he heard a strange sound in the forest. Whatever it was, it was headed his way at incredible speed. Slowly the sound built to a crashing and rumbling sound combined. In the forest he could see some movement in the tips of the smaller trees. Then like a team of horses thundering around a racetrack came the sound and sight of Golden Bear making a straight line to Tyler and Blue Wings and the wolves, now in a frenzy.

For a moment the wolves ceased their howling and jittery frenzy, then they all bolted together to meet Golden Bear in the middle of the field, intercepting him before he could reach Blue Wings. Tyler quickly yelled to Blue Wings.

"Quick, climb! Climb as fast as you can."

At the same time he picked up a big dead branch, wielded it like a club and ran towards Golden Bear and the wolves. In moments, the battle began. The wolves tried to bite Golden Bear on his hind legs to cripple him. Quickly though, Golden Bear would swerve around and use his huge paws to swipe at them. When he connected for the first time, Tyler froze for a moment. There was a sound of cracking bones as the ribs of the first wolf were crushed like small brittle sticks. There was a quick loud yelp and then you could see blood flying as the swipe tore open the side of the wolf. The smell of blood drove both Golden Bear and the wolves into a torrent of fierce fighting.

As Tyler joined the fight, he realized his gentle friend had incredible raw power. He had to protect Golden Bear from behind so the bear could use his powerful front legs and jaws to fight. Tyler swung with all his might striking some of the wolves in the head. They yelped and backed off, but only for a moment, then surged back in. The fight lasted a long time. The wolves would simply not stop attacking. More than a dozen lay on the ground dead or dying. Tyler and Golden Bear were covered with blood and both were exhausted.

Towards the end, Tyler had his back leaning against Golden Bear. One of the wolves finally succeeded in gashing into Golden Bear's side. The bear howled in pain with a sound so loud it echoed in the distant mountains. It was a deep and serious wound.

Tyler doesn't remember to this day what happened next. He remembers kneeling in prayer and asking Jesus to give him strength to defeat his enemies. Blue Wings could no longer stay up in the tree while her friends were in danger and climbed down to join the fight. All she told Tyler later was that she saw him jump up and start yelling something about having the faith of Daniel. He yelled this over and over again. At the same time he was swinging wildly with his club until he used it to ram down into the throat of one of the wolves. Then with his weapon stuck in the throat of the enemy, he used his arms to pick up the wolves and dash them down hard onto a rock in the field. The last of the wolves fled, seriously wounded, into the forest. When calm was restored, Blue Wings and Tyler hugged Golden Bear who was laying on the ground bleeding badly, his golden fur stained with deep red blood.

Wolves, dead and dying lay strewn on the ground in a circle all around them. Tyler was covered with blood and perspiration. He was crying and praying at the same time.

"Please Father, don't let him die. Heal him Lord. He is more than a bear, he is my friend, he saved me so that your will could be done. Don't let it end like this, I beg of you."

Blue Wings looked carefully at Tyler.

"Oh no, Tyler your arm. You are bleeding too."

"I know. It doesn't matter. We have to save him."

They heard some noise behind them and spun around fearing it was the wolves returning. Instead, it was Chief Daniel. He carried Tyler's bows and arrows.

"Please help me Chief Daniel. What can we do?"

Chief Daniel examined Golden Bear and then Tyler's arm.

"Today you learned the true meaning of love. Love is not what you think, children. Love, true love, contains a strong element of sacrifice. Each of you has shown the other what love is today."

Looking down at Golden Bear who was panting in pain, Chief Daniel spoke gently and assured his friend.

"Don't worry old friend. Today is not your day to die."

They worked together and built a shelter over Golden Bear. He was too huge to move anywhere. Chief Daniel made a blend of herbs and roots he gathered in the forest and boiled them in a small pot he found. Around nightfall it was time to close the wounds. Chief Daniel gave the needle and thread to Tyler. He knew what he had to do.

"Sorry my friend. This is going to hurt but we have to close up your wounds or they'll get infected."

Golden Bear lifted his head and looked at Tyler and moaned. Tyler had never sewn an animal wound like this before. The hide was thick. Blood was everywhere. It took a long time but he finally sealed each gash as best he could. Then he washed the stitches and wounds with the blend Chief Daniel had made. It stopped the bleeding. Golden Bear fell asleep for the night. Then it was Tyler's turn. Chief Daniel handed the needle and thread to Blue Wings. Tyler looked into her eyes.

"Don't worry. I know it's going to hurt but it has to be done."

Tyler pulled up his shirt and stuffed part of it into his mouth so he would not make any loud sounds. Blue Wings was crying by the time she finished.

"It hurts me too, Tyler."

She spoke softly through her tears.

Chief Daniel then washed Tyler's wounds.

"Don't worry. They are only skin tears. It did not damage any muscle. In a week you'll be fine. You will now have to train harder than ever this last week, to build muscles and strength to compensate for your losses today. But tomorrow, only rest."

Years hence, Tyler would bear on his arm tiny dots around two scars, one long, one short, that formed the cross on his biceps. Each time he saw it, he was reminded of faith, love and sacrifice. More than that, he would think of his friends, Santa, Chief Daniel, Blue Wings and Golden Bear. What man on earth could ask for better friends?

Daniel 6:16-23

So the king gave the order, and they brought Daniel and threw him into the lions' den. The king said to Daniel, "May your God, whom you serve continually, rescue you!" A stone was brought and placed over the mouth of the den, and the king sealed it with his own signet ring and with the rings of his nobles, so that Daniel's situation might not be changed. Then the king returned to his palace and spent the night without eating and without any entertainment being brought to him. And he could not sleep. At the first light of dawn, the king got up and hurried to the lions' den. When he came near the den, he called to Daniel in an anguished voice, "Daniel, servant of the living God, has your God, whom you serve continually, been able to rescue you from the lions?" Daniel answered, "O king, live forever! My God sent his angel, and he shut the mouths of the lions. They have not hurt me, because I was found innocent in his sight. Nor have I ever done wrong before you, O king." The king was overjoyed and gave orders to lift Daniel out of the den. And when Daniel was lifted from the den, no wound was found on him, because he had trusted in his God. (NIV)

Chapter 14

The Olympic Vision

In Los Angeles, at the same time Tyler was healing, one of his major competitors in the Olympics, John Bradley, was finishing his preparations for the Olympic tryouts. One of his commercial sponsors had been in touch with the American coach to make sure John would make the team in return for a big donation to the Colorado Springs training center.

John drove his Lincoln Town car to the local country club where the golf course had set up a special practice range for him. At noon, he dined with fine china and crystal goblets under an umbrella on the terrace of the fancy members-only restaurant. He met with his sponsors routinely to discuss promotional ideas. They instructed him on how and where to affix their company logos for maximum exposure. He paid for nothing and was guaranteed several million dollars in endorsements if he won a gold medal. His manager had lined up a number of major companies to reap the benefits of his victory, everything from breakfast cereals to sneakers to automobiles. No one in the U.S. could beat him, or so he thought. His major competitor was Hans Goldschmidt from Germany.

Hans was 24 years old, in the peak of his health and at the top of his field. He had competed in archery since he was eight years old. He was a six time national champion. His body was picture perfect like on a cover of a men's muscle magazine. His enormous build was the result of years of private training and coaching in his own gym. He took many supplements over the years to pump himself up. He had blonde hair, deep blue eyes and had accumulated wealth through merchandising and endorsements. He dated a long series of famous women, mostly international models with stunning bodies and beautiful faces.

Backing Hans was a host of high technology companies and some universities doing research on every way possible to improve the man and his machine. His unique bows were intricately designed by supercomputers, with a series of special counter-weights, balances, dampeners and high precision sights. His arrows were made of a new foamed metal alloy that made them ultra light yet strong for the long distances that would decide the Olympic event. They designed special electro-optical glasses for him that adjusted the lens for different lighting conditions to optimize his resolution and contrast of the targets and bow sights. He was solely concerned with his public image, money and the accumulation of material objects. He scoffed at anyone who went to church. Hans did not know the spirit. His numerous trainers included psychologists who imprinted in his mind daily the will to win, and repeated constantly the image of him accepting the Olympic Gold medal. Each day beautiful women in bathing suits gave him muscle massages after he used the tanning lights to maintain his bronze tan.

Tyler had no manager, no psychologists, no fancy cars, no commercial sponsors, and no high tech university computer geniuses to design his equipment, no personal gym and no prior experience in competition other than his small high school in Texas. How could such a boy ever hope to compete with the likes of a John Bradley or Hans Goldschmidt? Moreover, though Tyler had trained hard, it was only in some remote mountains with a bear, an old man and a young woman runner, not giant stadiums filled with spectators and television cameras. Tyler did have one advantage the others did not possess. He had faith, not in wealth, power or high technology, but faith that God wanted him to represent the Lord in the Olympics for reasons Tyler did not yet fully understand.

The time for the U.S. Olympic tryouts had come. Colonel Peterson and Richard had arranged for Tyler's transportation to Colorado Springs and for Tyler to stay on a nearby Air Force base since he could not afford to stay at a hotel for the tryout week.

The day of his departure was hard on everyone. Blue Wings and Tyler exchanged gifts they had made for each other. She would compete in the Canadian trials for the marathon. If all went well and they both qualified they would see each other again. Otherwise, this may be their last moment together. They walked together with Golden Bear, who was healing quickly, to the field where the jet helicopter would pick up Tyler. Chief Daniel had said his goodbyes the day before. Just as Tyler saw him departing, an odd thing happened. As

Chief Daniel started walking down the mountain for a moment Tyler thought he saw something different, something like a man in a long white robe and not the old Native American wearing only a simple cloth around his waist.

Tyler and Blue Wings hugged each other tightly as the helicopter landed. Blue Wings had tears flowing down her cheeks. She turned to walk away. Tyler kept watching until she disappeared into the forest.

Colonel Peterson and Tyler were both quiet during the trip to the NATO Air Base and then the longer flight to Colorado Springs. After they landed, Colonel Peterson drove Tyler to his host family for the Olympic tryouts. Tyler walked Colonel Peterson back to his jeep. The two looked at each other and stared for a moment.

"Colonel Peterson, no one is going to believe me. What do I say? What should I tell my parents and grandparents?"

"More than anyone Tyler, I learned my lesson on things such as these. To your parents and grandparents, speak the truth, no matter what, no matter how wild, always speak the truth. As for the outside world, speak by your actions not your words. Let your deeds show who you are. Just keep praying for guidance and you will be fine. Remember all the gifts from Santa came from Christ. I do not know what happened in those mountains or what gift you received, all I can offer as advice is to use your gifts wisely. God bless you, Tyler. We'll be watching and rooting for you."

The week of the Olympic tryouts went quickly. Tyler spent most of the time waiting. He went last each day since he was young, unknown and without a coach or manager. The first few days were the short distances. Tyler used his short bow. At first everyone laughed at the weird looking wooden bow. All the others had fancy sights and metal dampeners and made Tyler's bow look like a joke in comparison to theirs. Yet each day Tyler tied with the best score and that was always John Bradley.

The last few days were the long distances. This would weed out the competition. Tyler used his long bow which was as tall as he was and very heavy. His arm hurt where the wolves had torn his skin but he persisted diligently, never speaking, just concentrating on his shooting.

When the tryouts were done, the highest score of the trials and the highest score ever for the pre-Olympic competition was achieved by a young man from Texas. The following day before boarding the flight home, Tyler went to the Olympic office to pick up his package of instructions and schedules for the summer Olympics. He waited in line with many others. When it was his turn they handed him his big envelope.

"Ah yes, Tyler, that's in archery isn't it? Yep, here's your package. You're down as an alternate. You'll only go if one of the other men gets sick or injured or can't make it. Congratulations."

Tyler was stunned.

"Just sign here that you accept your selection as alternate and that you'll follow all the rules and regulations of the U.S. Team."

They handed Tyler a pen but he stood with his arms crossed.

"There must be some mistake. I had the highest score. I won the trials. The scores were posted yesterday."

There were many athletes in line behind him and the U.S. Officials handing out the packages had no time to argue or debate.

"Look kid, the scores don't matter. Each coach picks his own team based on who he thinks will best represent the U.S. Team in the Olympics. You're young, unknown, no coach, no manager, and no sponsor. Consider it an honor to be chosen as an alternate. Just sign and wait to be called in case someone gets sick.

Tyler stood firm. He handed back the package and the pen. He did not sign.

"I love my country. One day I hope to serve my country in any way I can. This is wrong and simply not fair. Can I please speak to the archery coach about this?"

"Look, either sign or leave. No one talks to the coaches after the final selection list is posted. Those are the rules."

Tyler knew about faith and love. He knew this was not the way of the spirit so he quietly turned around and walked away. The official yelled at him as he was leaving.

If you leave now, without signing, they'll assign someone else the position of alternate and they'll never let you try out again."

Tyler kept walking.

The flight home was lonely for Tyler. He just stared out the window. When he arrived at the airport gate, his grandparents greeted him to drive him home. They could see his sorrow and confusion in his eyes and body language as he walked into the gate area.

Tyler told them what happened on the ride home. He didn't want to face his parents. He thought they would be angry and disappointed with him. When he pulled into his driveway, the outside of the house was decorated with the U.S. and Olympic flags. His parents had made him a huge cake with Olympic rings on it. The local newspapers were there to take his picture. Tyler got out of the car and faced the surge of people rushing to congratulate him. He raised his arms signaling for everyone to stop.

"Before any of you go any further, there is something I have to tell you all."

He turned to his parents.

"Sorry, mom. Sorry, dad. It's just something I have to do. I'm not sure I understand myself. Please just help me through this, okay?"

His parents held hands and nodded. They were always proud of him.

"I want to thank everyone for your enthusiasm and for planning a welcome home party but there is nothing to celebrate. I won the tryouts in archery. I scored the highest ever in the pre-Olympic season, but I was not chosen for the team. They put me down as an alternate. I refused to sign because I knew it was wrong to deny me just because I am young, or unknown or have no coaches or sponsors. I love my country. I always will. What I wanted from the beginning was to represent God. I thought to do that I had to get on the U.S. Team. I was wrong. I'm sorry I got you all excited only to be disappointed. I am not giving up. Somehow I would still like to go to the Olympics. If I can't wear the stars and stripes, maybe I can still find a way to represent God. He has no flag, no country, but it's all I want to do."

The crowd remained silent. A few walked away and went to their cars. Slowly, the crowd dispersed. A few photographers took Tyler's picture as he stood with his head bowed in front of his house. They would be printed in the local papers. Tyler's family went inside and shared a meal and a big welcome home cake. They were still very proud of him, in fact, far more proud of Tyler than they ever were before. His grandparents left the house early, but before they left they spoke to him privately in his room.

"We're both very proud of you. You stood up for what you believed in. But much more than that, you spoke up for the Lord, for everyone to hear. There is probably no other young man in the world who ever won Olympic trials and said they want to go to represent

God. That, in and of itself is a remarkable achievement."

"Please don't give up. You didn't come all this way to be stopped now. We're going to go home and make some calls. One way or another, you're going to the Olympics. We want you to practice and train now harder than ever, every day, without fail. Believe in your heart you will succeed and pray like you have never prayed before. God will do the rest. If you're meant to go, you will."

Tyler went to bed early. He was exhausted from the trials, from the trip and he still felt a sense of disappointment, yet at the same time he still thought something wonderful was about to happen.

His grandparents spent most of the night and the next day making calls all over the country. They were determined to see Tyler's dream and God's calling for him, come true. They contacted the leaders at Promise Keepers, Women of Faith, the Soul Winning Workshop, churches of every denomiation and other groups of spiritual men and women. They networked with politicians and religious leaders alike. Finally, at dinner, Tyler received a call.

"Hello, is this Tyler?"

"Yes. Who's this?"

"My name is Reverend Greene. I understand you want to represent God at the Olympics. Before I help you on this, can you please tell me what led you to say this?"

Tyler was a bit concerned about this call. He remembered what Colonel Peterson had said about telling the full truth only to his family for fear others would not understand. He carefully explained that God had given him a personal message to represent him in the Olympics. He didn't know how but he thought the only way was to make it onto the U.S. team. He left out the part about St. Nicholas, Chief Daniel and Golden Bear. After talking for a long time by phone about the bible and Tyler's personal beliefs they said a few prayers together.

"Tyler, I believe you have a gift to share with us all. I'll call you back later. I need to make a few calls to some folks overseas. I have an idea about how we can do this. If I can get you there, you realize the whole world is going to be watching you. Everything you say, everything you do, will be scrutinized in minute detail. Think you can handle that?"

"Yes sir, but I have to tell you I don't have any money to fly overseas and stay at hotels and stuff. I got this far on charity from other Christian men and women. My dad has a good job but not enough to pay for everything I would need for something this grand."

"Tyler, if you believe God has called you, all you have to do is pray for His help. Whatever you need, He will provide if He truly wants you to fulfill this task He has set before you. You do your part and He'll do his. Trust me on this. God bless you Tyler."

"Thank you for believing in me Reverend Greene."

"I'll call you back or else have someone else give you a call later. Well, maybe much later given the time zone difference. Goodnight."

The phone rang at three o'clock in the morning. Tyler knew it was for him.

"Hello. Is this Tyler?"

The voice at the other end sounded distant. The man spoke with an Italian accent.

"Yes. Who are you?"

"My name is Archbishop Berti. I'm calling from the Vatican in Italy. I hope I didn't call too early. This is the only time I could reach you today, so I thought to try to catch you in now."

"That's alright. I understand."

"An old friend called me to tell me of your desire to come to the Olympics. I trust him completely so I must trust that your desire is pure and sincere. What you are asking is very serious. We must all be certain this is done properly. This has never been done before you know."

Tyler was a bit confused.

"The Pope has arranged with the Olympic Committee for you to represent the Vatican. It is recognized officially as a country but no one has ever used that to go to the Olympics. I know your desire is to represent God. This is a way to beat the system and do God's will. You do not have to wear our flag, nor wear a cross, nor march in opening ceremonies with a sign saying you represent the Vatican. We do not expect you to say you are Catholic but that you are a Christian. The Vatican will pay for all your expenses and you will travel under the protection of the Pope. We will provide a bodyguard. Make no mistake about this Tyler. Many people will want to stop you now or see you fail. This is a lot for a boy your age. You will have to act like Christ, put up with a lot of nosy aggressive people from the media and after all this, I sure hope you do well in the competition. No one here expects you to win. We do expect you to act with kindness, grace and humility. I know this is all coming fast but my time today is limited. What do you say? Ready to take a trip to Rome?"

Tyler wasn't sure how to answer.

"I have to get permission from my parents but I'm sure they'll say yes, Archbishop Berti."

"Wonderful! Then it is already done. My friends from the Catholic Church in Dallas will contact you later and arrange your flight. I may not see you but I will continue to watch over you like a mother and her newborn baby. You are in my prayers now and every day. In the name of the Father, the Son and the Holy Spirit, bless you."

The next day was fast and wild. Tyler spent part of the day packing. They rushed to Dallas to get a passport and picked up the airline tickets from the church. The Archbishop, as promised, sent a bodyguard to accompany Tyler until his safe return home. His name was Bubba. He was not as big or as strong as Golden Bear, but about as close to it as possible for a human.

Before it could all sink in, Tyler was in Vatican City. He met up with Archbishop Berti at his room in the Vatican complex. It was all a blur. At the end of the meeting, everyone seemed satisfied Tyler was indeed the one to be the first ever to represent God at the Olympics. As they got up to adjourn the meeting, the Archbishop spoke in a kind voice.

"No matter what happens during the Olympics, I want you to know that hundreds of millions of Christians from all denominations will be praying for you. Many people, not just other athletes, will look upon you with jealousy and maybe anger. You must show them what it means to be humble and gracious."

Tyler nodded in agreement and then the Archbishop continued.

"Whenever you feel yourself yielding or compromising, remember the full armor of God. Every time you step into the public eye from now on, until the Olympics are over, there will be someone taking your picture and pushing a microphone in your face. Any wrong move, any improper gesture, will be recorded and spread instantly worldwide, anything to discredit you."

"I understand. Thank you for giving me the chance. I will do my best. To tell you the truth I'm a little scared about all this!"

"Ah. That's good to know. That's healthy and normal. You

know, even now, when I get up to say Mass in front of a lot of foreigners instead of my usual parish, even I get a little nervous. Each time I get up in front of a filled stadium, I get that queasy feeling in my stomach. Then, I think about Jesus sitting in the back row. He's listening to me, but more importantly I know He's smiling at me, encouraging me, and helping me go on just by feeling His warmth and presence. If you want, you can tell everyone they can contact me for information for now to relieve you of the burden of speaking in public so you can concentrate on your archery. At one point though, if this is truly your calling and your tasks given to you by God, then you should say something, perhaps to encourage other Christians your age to be as courageous and as open in loving God and His Word as you are now."

They all nodded and the meeting ended with all of them holding hands and praying together. The Archbishop spoke in English, Latin and Italian.

The next week went quickly. The Archbishop had Tyler taken to a monastery in a remote part of Italy where he practiced and trained hard every day. He ran up and down the slopes of the grape vineyards and did hundreds of push-ups and pull-ups to keep building his strength where the wolves had damaged his arm. At night, he scrubbed floors on his knees and cleaned dishes in the kitchen. Everyone treated him like just another monk except for his free time during the day to train.

All too soon the day came to go to the Olympics and to his place in the Olympic Village. He flew on a regular commercial jet. His room at the village was small and close enough to walk to the archery stadium and dining hall. Everywhere, he went, Bubba was his shadow. The Archbishop was right about one thing. Someone was constantly trying to interview him and take his picture. He politely spoke to them and told each one the same thing.

"Would you please allow me to concentrate on the competition before I speak. I would be honored to interview with your station once the competition is underway."

The first week of competition was mostly at the short distances for eliminations. Each team got their turn and slowly the field was narrowed to twenty competitors for the qualifying round. Now each shot would count and the pace slowed down and tensions skyrocketed. Every time the competition began, swarms of interviewers went to cover Hans Goldschmidt and John Bradley who were favored to win and for a while the oddity of a young boy from the U.S. representing God and the Vatican wore off.

The semifinal rounds cut the field to ten men. Tyler barely made the final cut. The next day would be the finals in the woman's marathon early in the morning and Tyler went to the stadium for the finish. He had seen Blue Wings several times at the Olympic village and they ate together when they could.

Blue Wings and Tyler were both a bit lonely and felt out of place with all the press and major international competitors. The favorites to win the women's marathon were runners from Japan and Spain. They were interviewed every day and wore high tech running suits. Blue Wings wore a short red skirt Santa had made her from the ancient scarlet cloth he used to carry the gifts of the cross. It was plain in the world of fashion but very special to Blue Wings. She had come in second at the Olympic trials in Canada and her faster teammate was not even favored to be in the top ten.

The crowd in the stadium watched on a giant screen to see the race from far away. Blue Wings was back in the pack of runners with several women hundreds of yards in the lead. Blue Wings was a very strong sprinter for the finish so she was not yet concerned. Suddenly a photographer moved out into the running lanes to take a quick picture. The runners jumped out of the way and in the rapid movement Blue Wings got stepped on from behind and fell on the pavement. Tyler put his hands over his eyes. He just couldn't look.

Blue Wings got up and for a moment just calmly brushed herself off. She was now several hundred yards behind the main pack but she started running again, at first limping, then running at a fast pace to try to catch up. On the giant screen Tyler could see her knee was red and scraped rather badly. The crowd started cheering as the leaders entered the stadium tunnel. When they first emerged, Blue Wings was nowhere in sight. The runners would have to go around the track twice to the finish line. The leaders were half way around the track when Blue Wings finally entered the stadium. The crowd cheered her wildly. As she passed by, Tyler screamed at the top of his lungs.

"Do it for Golden Bear. He saved your life. Show him you are worth it! Run, Blue Wings, run!"

Blue Wings could hear Tyler's voice above the crowd. She did not turn her head but focused hard on the track and the runners ahead of her. She dreamed she was running down the mountain and the wolves were chasing her. Suddenly, she put on a huge burst of speed. Her stride stretched out, her arms pumped and she breathed fast and deep.

By the time the other runners began their last lap, Blue Wings was only about fifty yards behind. With each stride she was getting closer but she was close to exhaustion. They made the last turn. There was only the straight part of the track left to go. Once again Blue Wings could hear a voice. This time it was not Tyler but Chief Daniel.

"Go the distance. Finish strong. Fly like the eagle. You can do it, my child."

She was confused. Chief Daniel was thousands of miles away or so she thought. Yet his voice was crisp, clear, as if he was running beside her. She made one last burst for the finish line and flew into the air at the last second to try to reach the ribbon first. It was a photo finish. The crowd got very quiet as they waited for the committee to examine the videotapes carefully and to determine if there were any fouls in the running. They finally posted the times on the giant board. By one-hundredth of a second, Blue Wings won. The crowd cheered. Blue Wings fell exhausted and in pain and immediately doctors tended to her wounded knee. Bubba tapped Tyler on the shoulder. It was time to go.

The archery stadium slowly filled as the competition began. Today, all the shooting would be from the long distances. The networks from all over the world interviewed the top men and each showed all of their high tech equipment. They went into elaborate details on how the bows were computer designed with new metal alloys and precision machining. They interviewed Tyler briefly, and asked him about his strange long black bow.

"Oh, I carved it from a tree with my friend. It was the first bow I ever made. I made the arrows from a small straight tree, using feathers from some eagles and glue I made from weeds and herbs."

The interviewers just smirked and chuckled. They quickly let their audience know their opinions.

"Well, no real competition here. It's just a young boy with a brave heart. In fact, it's amazing he got this far. Must have been with a lot of luck. Definitely no match for the likes of John Bradley and Hans Goldschmidt."

Tyler just smiled politely. Bubba stepped in front of the cameras signaling the interviews were over.

For the first time ever, at the end of the day, there was a three-way tie. The Olympic Committee met that evening and ruled they would allow a special shoot out the next morning, just fifteen arrows each, all from 100 meters, more than the length of a football field.

Tyler had dinner with Blue Wings and then went to the medals ceremonies for the woman's marathon. It was a heart-warming ceremony, with Blue Wings bandaged up limping to the center podium. When they put the gold medal around her neck, she bowed politely and then blew Tyler a big kiss. Bubba folded his arms and gave Tyler a stern look but to no avail. He was jumping up and down clapping and shouting for joy.

They walked Blue Wings back to the Olympic Village. A number of press people stopped her along the way for video interviews. Bubba and Tyler quietly stepped aside so Blue Wings could be the center of attention. Finally, one of the interviewers turned the camera to Tyler.

"We understand you told the U.S. Committee you wanted to represent God. Wasn't that just a cover up because they picked you as an alternate and not a member of the team? God has nothing to do with this, does He? You just wanted some attention and if you lose tomorrow you're not going to get it. Well, I see our time is up for now."

They ended the interview not allowing Tyler to respond. Tyler stood silently at first, staring at the interviewers and the TV cameramen. He spoke kindly but firmly. Quickly they turned the cameras back on.

"Are you so afraid of the truth that you must hide it by doing things like that. Isn't it bad enough for students like myself that they have banned prayer in school? I know it must be comforting for you to insult and try to disgrace a young man on international television and make him look self-centered when you know in your hearts that is the farthest thing from the truth. Yes, you are right. I may not win tomorrow. The other men are older, stronger, more experienced and have the backing of millions of dollars of high technology and commercial sponsors. I did not ever intend to come here for selfish reasons. It is not winning a medal that is important. It is showing the world how important it is to pray, to love God and to represent His way of love and peace in a world in turmoil."

Tyler paused for a moment and smiled at Blue Wings.

"You may use laws to ban school prayer and promote atheism as the new world religion, you may slander and defame young men and women who want to try to be like Christ, but you cannot stop me and millions of God's children from loving Him, from serving Him in ways that please Him. If all of this brings just one more soul to salvation, to accept Christ as their Lord and Savior, and know in their hearts that He loves us all, then this trip was worth it. I may leave with nothing but I shall pray tonight that for all of you out there, that I can be an instrument to let Him touch your heart, so that tomorrow you will leave with everything, everything you will need for the rest of your life. May God bless you and keep you safe and loved in His arms. I serve an awesome God. Tomorrow, arrows may fly to their target but that is not what God wants you to see. I don't know what will happen tomorrow, only that God has performed many miracles already to bring me this far. God has a miracle waiting for each of you, if you only repent and give your life, all your worries to Him. Let Him be the one true God you have been searching for all of your life. God is not dead. He is here with me and with you right now. Do not focus your eyes on me or worldly things. Rather, seek the fruit of the spirit. All of you are God's children. Isn't it about time you started acting that way?"

By the time Tyler had finished speaking dozens of camera crews from around the world were focused on him. Dozens of microphones were thrust towards him trying to catch every word. When he stopped talking, Blue Wings took off her gold medal and put it around his neck and gave him a kiss on the cheek. They held hands and then got on their knees and began to pray. They each took turns, praising God and thanking Him for everything, but most of all for being the center of their lives. When they both said together "Amen", there was not a dry eye in the crowd.

Tyler stood up but Blue Wings was having trouble. Her knee was in great pain. It would take months for it to fully heal. Bubba saw her problem and bent down and picked her up and carried her back to the athletes' dorms. Tyler held her hand the whole time while cameras followed them and the world began to see just how wonderful faith in God could be.

The morning of the final tiebreaker was cool and overcast. Tyler's grandparents had sent him some tee shirts to wear under his shooting jacket with messages sewn in large red letters, to encourage him. Secretly, the church had taken up a collection and paid for them to go to the Olympics with Tyler's parents. They sat quietly in the stadium not wanting to divert any attention to themselves and trying to let Tyler focus on his archery without being concerned that his parents and grandparents were in the audience.

John Bradley went first. Once he stepped up to the shooting line and shot his first arrows, a fifteen-minute clock started, visible for all to see, giving all of them a strict time limit to shoot all their arrows. He took his time. Millions of dollars of endorsements were riding on this moment for him. He did well, but a few arrows struck the red and blue circles around the yellow bull's-eye, giving an opening, an opportunity, for Hans to do better.

Hans stepped up to the line. Many in the crowd began to cheer as he raised his hands and waved, and then signaled the crowd to cheer louder for him. Tyler couldn't look. In fact he sat on the warm-up bench with his head bowed, quietly praying the whole time.

As the fifteen-minute clock ticked on, it was clear Hans was shooting a near perfect round. In the distance, the clouds got darker and thunder could be heard. When Hans was through, the Olympic referees checked the target carefully. He had thirteen arrows in the yellow center and only two in the red. He had beaten John Bradley and made it almost impossible for Tyler. It would be an Olympic and World record and a miracle to beat Hans. The thunder grew louder. Many in the crowd had umbrellas, and kept looking up to the sky.

The announcer called Tyler's name. When he stood up, the crowd got strangely silent. Tyler took his huge bow in both hands and raised it to the sky, then got down on one knee and bowed his head. The match of high tech versus God had gotten the attention of the media. After Tyler's speech the night before was broadcast all over the globe, hundreds of millions of people tuned in to the final match. By the time he stood up from his prayers more than one billion people worldwide were transfixed to their television sets. On the street, people gathered in front of stores with TV sets covering the scene. People in offices stopped working. Farmers in their fields came in to watch with their families. Politicians stopped their debates and hurried to their chambers to watch the final event. Everyone in Texas was watching, in stores, offices, bars, restaurants and those in cars were listening on the radio. Since the first man landed on the moon, there were never so many people watching and listening to a single event, watching a young boy who only wanted to represent God.

By the time Tyler approached the shooting line, the thunder was getting quite loud. Bubba rushed up to the referees and judges and asked for a ruling on what would happen if it started raining. Would they let the rain stop and hold the fifteen-minute clock out of fairness to Tyler? The committee met quickly. The coaches from Germany and the U.S. ran over and protested the delay and said they would sue and hold back their country's Olympic contributions if they didn't force Tyler to shoot immediately and that there was no way they should stop the shot clock, those were the rules. Political might, financial and commercial pressure once again over-ruled the righteous thing to do. The committee ruled he had to start right away and must continue even if it started raining. Every archer there knew if it started raining it would be impossible to hit the target accurately from that distance. The raindrops would alter the path of the arrows, making them heavy and the unpredictable winds would make each shot difficult at best.

The President of the Olympics got on the loudspeaker system and announced their decision that Tyler must shoot now and they would not stop the shot clock in case of rain. Many in the crowd booed at the unfairness while others, who despised all this attention on Tyler and God, started clapping.

Tyler stepped to the line. He kept his jacket on at first, and pulled his first arrow from his scarlet quiver. He drew back and fired quickly. The first shot hit dead center. The crowd suddenly became hushed. All was quiet. The thunder rolled louder and closer. In rapid succession, Tyler drew his mighty long black bow and in five minutes had released ten arrows. All of them struck the yellow. As he pulled back on his eleventh arrow, it began to rain. He had trained in the mountains and even in light rain. He knew how to compensate for the raindrops.

Tyler watched carefully for any movement of the wind by looking at the flags on top of the stadium. He carefully gauged wind speed and direction and compensated his aim, then released. Once again, yellow. The crowd started to murmur. The commercial sponsors for John Bradley and Hans Goldschmidt began to pace back and forth and spoke out loud and were caught on camera talking, even scolding, them.

"You better pray for heavy rain or you're washed up. If that kid beats you, no way are you getting any endorsements."

Lightening flashed. The thunder pealed. It started raining harder. Tyler took aim again for his twelfth arrow. He released. A sudden gust of wind and rain swept over the field and pushed the arrow just enough to strike the red circle. Now, to win Tyler would have to hit dead center for his last three shots. The light rain turned into a steady downpour. Umbrellas popped open, raincoats were put on, some put newspapers over their heads, but no one left the stadium.

Hans started clapping and celebrating. Nothing could beat him now. His coaches were slapping him on the back congratulating him. The shot clock ticked away. Tyler did not flinch. His steady gaze and determination captured the hearts of millions. He held the bow in one hand and removed his jacket halfway and then switched arms and let his jacket fall to the ground. There, for all the world to see was his simple tee shirt. No commercial sponsor, no flags, just a simple saying stitched in cloth. On the back of his tee shirt, getting soaked in the rain, in scarlet letters it said: "Open the floodgates of heaven."

The crowd stood up in silence. There were only five minutes left on the shot clock. As raindrops soaked his shirt and hair, as his face got drenched with raindrops, Tyler felt a familiar presence. He turned to his right over to where Bubba stood. There, next to him, stood Chief Daniel.

"Bubba look. It's Chief Daniel! How did you get here?"

Bubba looked straight ahead and pointed to his watch. He could not see Chief Daniel. Tyler looked up on the giant stadium screen. He could see himself and Bubba but not Chief Daniel. From somewhere in the stadium Tyler heard another familiar voice. It was his grandmother. He looked up and saw his parents and grandparents. Tyler quickly signaled by hand and mouth.

"Don't you see Him?"

As he spoke, he pointed to his eyes for the word "see" and then to Chief Daniel for "Him". Then he put two fingers behind the top of his head to indicate the feathers in Chief Daniel's hair. His grandmother shook her head no. Instead she put her hands over her heads and made a circle with her fingers. No, not a circle Tyler thought, a halo.

Tyler turned again to Chief Daniel. He saw Him for the first time clearly. He wasn't an old Native American warrior with braided hair and feathers. It was Jesus, standing in a white flowing robe.

"You have done well, Tyler. Time is running out now. You must act quickly. Do you remember the dove and the barn when you were with St. Nicholas?"

"Yes, but how did you know? No one else was there?"

"I am everywhere my child. It is time to release the dove."

Tyler remembered that moment with Santa when the white dove had disappeared under his shirt. Then he remembered the paintings he saw in Sunday school at church of when John the Baptist baptized Christ and a white dove flew into the heavens above them.

"Know that I am with you always."

In a flash, the image of Jesus disappeared from Tyler's vision. He knelt down and prayed. Precious seconds were ticking away on the shot clock. As he prayed he felt something tickling his belly. At first he squirmed then laughed and stood up and lifted up his tee shirt. A white dove flew high above his head. The crowd in unison let out a loud sound of awe.

No one knows for sure how it happened. The non-believers claimed it was the lightening and static electricity. The people of faith say it was a miracle. For whatever the reasons, something very odd happened at that moment.

At the start of the Olympic games, thousands of doves had been released to symbolize peace. They had all flown away. Yet, at that very moment they all returned. Instantly they formed an inverted "V" between Tyler and the target. The highest birds wings deflected the raindrops to the birds below and slowly it made a momentary dry path to the target. The only sound that could be heard was the whirling of wings, rain drops striking feathers and the clap of thunder.

Tyler quickly jumped up. Only fifty seconds left on the shot clock for three arrows. He drew his mighty bow, raised his elbow, steadied his feet, watched the flow of wind and held his breath. Just a little rain was coming through the torrent of doves above. He released. Right on target, right into the yellow. He drew again. The wind was swirling and it took a while to aim and compensate for the force of the air but he finally released. Again, the arrow struck home. Twenty seconds left.

Tyler's hands were sore. He stopped a moment to look at them. He remembered what Chief Daniel had said. These were no longer the hands of a boy but the hands of a man doing God's work.

He drew for the last time. At that very moment people from the crowd began to cry out. They all started pointing towards the target. From where the arrows had entered the paper and hay target, the tips of the arrows made from one of the nails that held Jesus to the cross centuries ago, began to ooze a streak of red. The target was bleeding. Tyler saw what was happening. At the same time at the corner of his eye he saw the shot clock tick down to nine seconds.

Tyler drew and held his breath. His arms began to quiver from the strain of pulling his giant bow. The wounds from the wolves felt hot on his arms. He glanced over to where Jesus had stood before. He could not see Him but he knew for the rest of his life, Jesus would always be there. That thought made him smile. For a fraction of a second his arms stopped quivering and in that moment he released.

You could see the arrow speeding on its way. The eagle feathers slowly spun the arrow onto a steady path. The doves above fluttered the raindrops away from the path of the arrow. In the next moment you could hear the loud smack as the arrow tip tore through the yellow of the target, dead center. Fifteen holes continued to bleed. The world seemed to stop. Everyone was shocked at all the events. The target bled, the rain continued. Then, a bolt of lightening jumped from the clouds and struck the target. The arrows all fell to the ground and the paper and hay started to burn. In the same instant the doves scattered and the rain once again fell on Tyler and the target and extinguished the flames and all traces of the blood that had oozed from the arrow tips.

The crowd did not know what to do at first. Tyler's grandparents started to clap. Two loud claps and stomped their feet twice.

"Ty -- ler," stomp, stomp.

"Ty -- ler," stomp, stomp.

The crowd caught on quickly. All over the world, people stopped whatever they were doing and clapped, shouted and stomped. The stadium shook from the vibration of thousands of people stomping in unison. Soon the sound was deafening.

Tyler just bowed his head and prayed to thank God. He never raised his hands, never took any of the praise or glory. That was all left for his God.

Immediately, the Germans and the U.S. coaches and sponsors filed protests. They wanted Tyler disqualified. One said using the doves to protect the target was illegal. The other said since the arrows fell to the ground all the shots should not count. Quickly, it became an international controversy.

Every station in the world played and replayed the sequence. Everyone had their own opinion and analysis. People studied the rules. Petitions flooded the Olympic Committee, judges and referees. They finally announced that the awards ceremony would be the following morning, pending a decision by the judges.

Tyler came to represent God. He did the best he could. It seemed there were forces of evil trying to stop him everywhere he turned. He finally understood that the wolves were sent to stop him. Friendship, love and sacrifice had saved him. The rain was sent to ruin his chances at showing God's grace and to force him to leave in disgrace and controversy. Instead, the dove of peace and baptism saved him along with his unyielding faith in God. Finally, the lightening struck all he had accomplished in one last desperate attempt to break up the upwelling of love and joy that began to spread all over the planet. Indeed, Tyler had no idea of the cascading effects of these events.

That night, the President of the United States called a press conference. It was unlike any other in history. The White House Press room was packed. Cameras from all over the world jammed into the space filled with anticipation. Security was extra tight. Tensions were high. The Press Secretary entered the room and all was hushed.

"Ladies and gentlemen, the President of The United States has called this special news conference to address all the good people of America and the world. In an unprecedented manner, the President has requested this conference be aired worldwide, on every station. This conference will be recorded in its entirety and rebroadcast, copied and flown to other nations and leaders in every country. Given this unusual circumstance, we are asking for your cooperation to listen quietly until he is finished. Then we will attempt to have an orderly question and answer period. For this, please raise your hands and wait to be called. Anyone just standing up and calling out to be recognized will not be permitted to return to any future press conference. Does everyone understand the ground rules tonight?"

Silence swept the room.

"Good. Before the President enters, the Supreme Court justices have been summoned here along with the Attorney General, the Solicitor General and the President of the U.S. Olympic Training Center in Colorado Springs."

Silently the justices and others entered the room. Murmurs filled the air. Speculation ran wild.

"Ladies and gentlemen, honorable members of the Supreme Court, members of the press, I give you the President of the United States."

The President entered the room looking very somber, wearing a black suit. You could tell by his face, he had gotten little sleep and perhaps he had been crying, as his eyes were moist and red. His pants showed a little carpet lint over his knees indicating he had just been on his knees, perhaps in prayer. He spoke calmly, but determined, slowly increasing in volume as his speech continued.

"My fellow Americans, to all good people of all nations, to men, women and children of all faiths, all denominations, I bid you welcome and thank you most sincerely for taking the time to join me tonight on this historic occasion. For those watching this from a recording, the time of this conference is 9 p.m., July 20th. A day I hope we will always remember."

He looked at his typewritten speech and slowly scanned the faces of the audience. They did not come for a canned political speech. They were longing for a leadership no president had given them for a very long time. He looked over to his wife and children standing off to the side and smiled. Carefully, he lifted the papers of the prepared speech and tore them in half, then in half again. Nobody moved. You could hear the faint click of cameras taking pictures of this unfolding scene.

"I had a speech prepared. Looking at your faces and my family, I think it's about time a President spoke from his heart, a heart touched by God to do the right thing."

He paused and took a sip of water, smiled and gave the speech of his life. He thought he was throwing his political career out the window. Little did he know it would catapult him into another term with the greatest margin of victory in American history, taking all Electoral votes and the vast majority of the popular votes. At this moment, he could not see the future though, only what he knew God wanted him to do.

"A month ago, a young boy from Texas, my home state, entered the Olympic trials in Colorado Springs. No one had ever heard of him before except in his small hometown. He went up against the best American archers, who were backed by universities, sponsors and a host of commercial interests. He won. Then we cheated him. All he wanted to do was represent God. He thought he could do that by representing the United States. After all, were we not founded as one nation under God? Tyler was given a chance to sign as an Alternate. Rather than admit defeat and resign to an Olympic Committee fraught with outside influence, he refused to sign. He did the right thing."

The President took a deep breath and gathered confidence.

"Through a remarkable network of loving, caring, spiritual people, a way was found to fulfill his dream of going to the Olympics for God. Vatican City, in a true stand for righteousness, took the historic step of allowing him to compete under the flag of the Pope, not representing the Catholic Church or the Vatican, but acting as a humble servant of God. For this courageous act alone, we must all be eternally grateful to His Eminence The Pope and the Cardinals, Archbishops and others who made this all happen so quickly."

He looked with disdain at the Olympic Committee members.

"I vow to the American people and every young athlete listening to me tonight or at any future time, this will never happen again. I have tonight instituted a Congressional Ethic Committee to oversee our Olympic stewardship. Their job is simple. First, keep it fair and keep it open to all people, of all ages, of all races, creeds and physical descriptions."

The room burst into applause.

"Second, commercial sponsors and business promoters of any kind will no longer be allowed any contact with our Olympic athletes during competition. Third, the United States will no longer sponsor, promote, send or permit any professional athlete from entering Olympic competition. The Olympics began as a wonderful international spirit of competition and cooperation and has turned into an ugly quest for the most medals. Well, dear friends, tonight all that ends. I return the Olympics back to you, all the people, as an event filled with amateur athletes who express the ideals of freedom, spirit, friendship and who will give a warm welcome to all members of the

Olympics from all nations. From now on, a Dream Team will take on a new meaning. It will not be the cream of the crop of the best overpaid professional athletes in any sport, but rather a team who dreams of showing the world the best elements of the human spirit, compassion and international friendship."

The packed room instantly jumped to its feet and burst into applause, giving the President a long, standing ovation. The President signaled them to be seated.

"That was the easy part."

He smiled and looked long and hard at the Supreme Court justices. Who knows? After his speech he may face them again due to impeachment. He was going to cross the sacred line tonight, big time.

"Now for the hard part. I address you all on the issue of prayer, government and God. Tyler wanted to represent God. I don't know about you but I think he did a remarkable job, one that makes us all very proud. When Tyler returns to school this fall, I want him and all American children to enter a new place, under new government, under new rule. I want Tyler to go to a school that does not outlaw school prayer. I want all American children in public schools to have that option, that time, that opportunity to pray to the Lord, if that is what they choose to do. When any public school has a football game or any sporting event, I want them to make it not only legal and proper to pray, but encourage all of them and all of you to do so as well. As far as our halls of justice, Congress and the White House, I urge you all to consider, please America, bring God back. I can, as your President, no longer allow our heavenly Father to be evicted from our schools, our courts and our governments. As a country we made a horrible mistake. We allowed the Supreme Court of the land to render a series of judgments and rulings that have undercut the moral fabric of this nation. I have summoned this court to be here tonight for all the world to see."

He pointed to each justice one at a time.

"I beg each of you to consider that your actions are responsible for destroying American values, Godly values, and diminishing us all in the eyes of God. Let every American see you and know who you are so they can all pray that you will have a change of heart and set the record straight and once again make us in act, in deed, in law, one nation, under God, with liberty and justice for all."

150

All across the country, men, women and children of all faiths began to absorb the enormity of the moment. Tears flowed. Shouts of joy filled houses coast to coast. Finally, a President who is bold, who loves the Lord and is not afraid to stand up and be counted as a man of God, a man of integrity.

"Ladies and gentlemen. Would you please stand and bow your heads? I want to warn you now, at every press conference I have, I will begin and end in prayer. Every time I give a State of the Union address, I will, I repeat, I will begin and end in prayer. You may sanction me, sue me, oust me, impeach me, do as you will, but from now on, move over Attorney General, move over Supreme Court justices, I will pray because that is what the leader of the free world and the greatest nation on earth is supposed to do. Now will any who wish to do so, please join me in closing this session with the Lord's Prayer."

He began slowly.

"Our Father." Few spoke up with him.

He started again in a louder voice.

"Our Father." He stopped, as more were willing to join him.

No one knows how or why. Few will forget what happened next. The President's family joined him on the podium, all held hands and bowed their heads. In restaurants, shops, stores and places all around the world, people stopped whatever they were doing and knelt or bowed their heads. For the third time, the President began to pray, as all the members of the Supreme Court stood in unison and joined in the Lord's Prayer. No one knows for sure, but estimates are over one billion people recited the Lord's Prayer in unison. Santa and all his children stood in joy, weeping that one of Santa's special gifts had yielded such an astounding accomplishment. When the prayer was done, everyone remained standing.

"To begin this new era of cherishing God in our lives, I want to ask everyone in the world to join me in a candlelight vigil. Let every church open their doors. Let there be prayer and song and rejoicing all over the world in every temple, church, mosque, shrine and meetinghouse. We may call Him by different names, but there is one true God, and we all ask Him tonight to forgive us from straying from Him for so long. And to young Tyler, wherever you are, it doesn't matter what any Olympic judge or committee says now. You wanted to represent God. You did. In my book, in the eyes of the world, you have given us all a great gift and for that, thank you and God bless you."

Dawn came to a new day and a new era all over the world. In Tibet, the monks chanted all night. In China, the Buddhist shrines overflowed. In Israel, every Temple was filled. In America, church bells rang all night long. The world celebrated a return long overdue.

Tyler packed up his bags. He met Blue Wings for breakfast and then Bubba loaded their van to get ready for the trip to the airport. First, they would walk to the stadium for the medals ceremony. Tyler was prepared to be disqualified and no matter what was decided, he would act graciously and politely and then quietly return home. He had not seen the President's speech. He was sleeping, exhausted from all the excitement.

Bubba kept Tyler in the security tunnel until the announcement was made for the archery finalists to come to the podium. All three men were called. Tyler was a bit surprised. Bubba and Blue Wings escorted him to the podium stage and then stepped aside.

The President of the International Olympic Committee, an older silver haired Russian woman, stood in front of the microphone. She had seen her churches closed by Communists and had suffered for years in grave danger, holding secret religious services at her home. For her, this was a private moment of triumph. Her short speech was translated into English, Italian, Spanish and Chinese.

"The Olympic Committee has received hundreds of petitions on the subject of the archery competition. We must base our rulings on the rules and regulations established and written by each sporting event. After great deliberation and soul searching we have made the following decision." Tyler took a deep breath and reminded himself no matter what, to act like the man God wanted him to be.

"First, there were formal protests by the American and German coaches calling for the representative from the Vatican to be disqualified on the basis he used doves to interfere with the event. This is truly a unique event in Olympic history. In the rules and regulations no one may interfere with the sports equipment or competitor. We extend this word "one" to include any animal and even a mechanical device. However, the doves did not make the bow, the doves did not pull the bowstring or aim the arrows and the doves did not otherwise engage with the competitor. In fact, it is we, the Olympic Committee, who brought the doves to the stadium in the first place at the opening ceremonies. True, they somehow deflected the rain but we can only interpret their presence as a distraction to the competitor that he may or may not have brought upon himself. And against this there is no rule, no regulation and therefore, no violation. Thus, the committee discharges these first protests as invalid."

Tyler gulped sensing what was coming next.

"As for the matter of the lightening bolt and the arrows falling from the target, once again we must turn to the rules and regulations. The competition was video taped by many people. Analysis of those videotapes shows that all but one arrow struck the center and one arrow struck the red. The only question is the last arrow. The rules require the arrows must remain in the target long enough for the judges to determine its position. We therefore rule on the basis of the video evidence that the arrow did strike the center. We take the bolt of lightening as an act of nature or forces unknown, it was not the responsibility nor under the control of the competitor."

There was a long pause and then the big screen scoreboard lit up.

"Finally, it is the unanimous ruling of the archery judges and the entire Olympic Committee that the American and German competitors and coaches did both unfairly, improperly and illegally involve themselves in these protests. Their sponsors tried to influence our officials into disqualifying the competitor from the Vatican and their coaches threatened to boycott future Olympics unless we ruled in their favor. Neither this nor any future Olympic Committee nor judges will tolerate this kind of unsportsman-like conduct. Thus, we have ruled, all sponsors and their agents may have no direct contact with any Olympic officials until the games are over, and any violation will disqualify the competitor. We have therefore disqualified both John Bradley and Hans Goldschmidt. However, since they made it to the three-way tie round, we shall award them both medals of Honorable Mention."

The big score board immediately posted their names and next to them, Honorable Mention. The two men shook their heads in disbelief and went to the podium and were handed their medals then stood next to the podium flanked by security guards. Tyler was left standing alone in front of the podium. Everyone could see the officials scurrying back and forth and whispering. Finally, the Russian official came up to Tyler and whispered something in his ear. He whispered back. Tyler signaled for Blue Wings to come over to where he was standing.

All of them huddled and whispered and finally nodded their heads in agreement. The official once again stood in front of the microphone.

At that moment, hundreds of millions of people were glued to their TV sets. The suspense was agonizing. People driving their cars pulled over to the side of the road waiting for the results. All of Texas held their breath. In Tyler's hometown no one moved. All business stopped. A hush fell over the world.

It seems they had a technical problem. Normally at the awards ceremonies they play the national anthem of the country taking the gold medal. What do you do when a country wins who has no national anthem? Blue Wings went to the microphone with the Olympic Official. The Official stood quietly until the crowd, in total silence, stood up in anticipation of the announcement.

"This year in the men's archery competition, due to the fact that two of the three finalists were disqualified and with the highest score ever achieved by an international competitor, and with the greatest of grace and sportsmanship ever witnessed in our lifetime, the winner of the bronze, the silver and the gold medals, goes to…"

She couldn't finish the sentence. The crowd was already going wild. All over the world people were shouting and dancing for joy. Church bells rang, cars and trucks beeped their horns, and people hugged and threw hats into the air.

In the mountains far away, St Nicholas was in his workshop, when two of the children came running in to tell him the news. He just smiled calmly and patted the children on the head.

"I know my children, I know."

"But Poppa Nicholas, how can you know? They just announced it on TV."

Santa went back to his work and spoke in a gentle voice.

"Because I have the faith that can move mountains and some day, you will too."

On a nearby mountaintop, Golden Bear let out a roar so loud all the birds and animals in the area stopped in their tracks. He knew too.

As Tyler took to the podium, everyone in the stadium started to say his name by clapping and stomping. But Tyler's grandparents had a better idea. Slowly, a new wave started, until everyone had joined in.

Clapping twice, then stomping their feet.

"JE - SUS." stomp, stomp.

"JE - SUS." stomp, stomp.

The stadium shook. The earth shook. The stadium filled with doves appearing out of nowhere and swooped and circled Tyler then flew to the top by the thousands.

Blue Wings took the microphone. Since there was no national anthem music to play, they decided she would sing. The crowd slowly quieted down from the wild celebration. Three medals were placed around Tyler's neck and Blue Wings began to sing. Her voice was soft and sweet. She began to cry. Tears filled her eyes. She could not see the crowd any more but could feel their presence. She started to sing but three times had to start again, overcome by emotion and tears. Finally, on the third time, everyone in the stadium sang with her. So did the whole world. The song, the feelings, made the world whole, made the world one. When you accept the living presence of one true God, the words don't matter anymore. It is a language we all understand. The world, in unison, sang Amazing Grace.

Tyler never raised his arms to be recognized for his achievement. After the medals went around his neck, he knelt on his knees and prayed. He just wanted to thank God for this opportunity to represent Him. He prayed he had done what God had asked and for guidance on his future.

After the song was over, Tyler stood and walked off the podium and immediately went over to Hans and John. He took off the bronze medal and placed it around John's neck. He took of the silver medal and placed it around the neck of Hans. The crowd murmured for a moment and then finally clapped in approval. They all shook hands and then Tyler, Blue Wings and Bubba walked to their van and went to the airport.

Tyler would have returned home to celebrations that would have rivaled the greatest in history. However, he told reporters and his parents he did not want parades or parties. Rather, he simply asked everyone instead to celebrate by going to church to praise God. So much wisdom for a young man. The churches on the following Sunday were overflowing.

When Tyler returned home he asked his grandfather and father to join him in the garage. They had a workbench set up there. He told them about how he made the arrows and how the tips were made from a nail that put Jesus on the cross and how Santa helped him to mold them and put them on the arrows.

His grandfather smiled and put his arm around Tyler's shoulders. "I think you know what we have to do. We'll help you."

The three of them nodded and spent hours slowly removing all the tips from the arrows and the bow arrow rests and placed them in a red cloth and sewed it shut. They mailed it to Colonel Peterson along with a brief note.

> *"Would you please return these to their rightful owner? Thank you for all your help. God bless you.*
> *Love, Tyler."*

When Santa received them, he carefully re-melted them and forged them back into the shape of the original nail. He wrapped it in paper and string and put it back into the bag of the gifts of the cross.

That weekend, Tyler and his father and grandfather went camping, to have some quiet time together. They talked all night about what would be the right thing to do now. What would God really want Tyler to do? No doubt the high school coaches assumed Tyler would win every competition and put their town on the map. No doubt the Main Street merchants assumed Tyler's reputation would boost business and they could merchandise tee shirts, memorabilia, videos and sports equipment.

The three men of God held hands, prayed and sang songs late into the night. They all knew what must be done. In the early morning light, Tyler quietly placed his bows and arrows into the fire. They burned slowly but with great brightness. Tyler spent the next school year at a religious retreat where he took his studies seriously for the first time in his life. This would keep him out of the public eye and put the focus back on God. He finished high school back in his hometown. All the girls in his class chased after him, but he was not interested. After he finished college he got married to the woman God had put in his life. It was a simple ceremony. Santa performed the service with a local minister. When Nicholas read from the bible, the New Testament words came alive, as if he was there when the words were written and

156

saw everything happen. Perhaps he did.

The wedding reception was at Santa's house. Everyone played with the children. As a result of that day, a few of the children were adopted and ultimately flew to new homes in Texas.

The wedding pictures taken by the family were most remarkable. One of their favorites was Santa scolding Golden Bear for licking the frosting off the top of the wedding cake. The one picture they treasured the most was when Tyler and Blue Wings kissed when Santa pronounced them husband and wife. In the final developed photograph was an image of Chief Daniel smiling looking down on the newlyweds.

Before Tyler and Blue Wings left for their honeymoon, Santa took them into the barn with the sleigh. He pulled out one of the last gifts of the cross from his glowing scarlet sack hidden in the back seat of the sleigh. He handed a small wooden box to Blue Wings.

"One day soon, you will have a son and daughter. When they are ready, give them this. You will know when. Just listen to your hearts."

Santa's eyes filled with tears. The drops fell on the small wooden box. Blue Wings took the gift and gently placed it in her cloth pocketbook.

"Tyler and I have already decided our first born son will be named Nicholas and our first daughter will be named Danielle."

Santa smiled and took out a handkerchief to wipe his eyes. He did not know if he would still be around to see the birth of the children of this new age of prayer and open love of God, that swept the world in the wake of the summer Olympic events. He did know that wherever he was, he would always be with Jesus.

After all, he was Christ's Santa, a man who in all his time on earth put the needs of others first.

Luke 9:46-48

An argument started among the disciples as to which one of them would be the greatest. Jesus, knowing their thoughts, took a little child and had him stand beside him. Then he said to them, "Whoever welcomes this little child in my name welcomes me; and whoever welcomes me welcomes the one who sent me. For he who is the least among you all – he is the greatest." (NIV)

Chapter 15

The Last Journey

By the time Blue Wings and Tyler got married at Santa's workshop, the red sack containing the gifts of the cross was almost empty. After centuries, the wood and nails had all found their way into the lives of many families who passed it on to the next generation.

Santa had provided homes for thousands of children over the centuries. As time passed, more and more international organizations sprang up to provide shelter, clothes and food for needy children. Shelters also grew in number to provide for the homeless and for battered women needing a safe place to stay with their children. His good works, ideas and deeds over the centuries had yielded wonderful fruits.

Special hospitals for children had been built in countries all over the world, especially in America and Europe. More and more people worldwide donated their time, money, talents and energies to these hospitals to continue to expand the number of people treated each year, especially those with no funds of their own.

Although grateful for all he had accomplished, Santa began to feel lonely. He wanted to join God in heaven. He had lived or out-lived many generations, seeing children, grandchildren and thousands more spring forth from his love and efforts. He missed his wife. He saw the bag of the gifts of the cross dwindle to just one left. As he prayed each day, he sensed that both he and God knew his time to be called home was soon to come.

After much prayer and many meetings with Santa's enormous network of helpers, he decided to close down the orphanage in northern Canada. He found good homes for the last of his children and from then on, other agencies would take over to handle the on-going number of children in need of loving, caring families. His reindeer remained close to his house and still took shelter in the barn on cold winter days, where Santa left fresh hay and water to drink.

Golden Bear and Santa often took walks and fished together.

They formed a unique and lasting friendship. Each night when Santa was home he would go out to the barn and open the red sack and ponder the last gift of the cross. The sack barely glowed in the dark now but he always felt warm in its presence. The sleigh was getting rusty and needed some repairs and fresh paint. Santa missed sitting in his rocking chair at sunset to watch the children play. He missed going out into the forest to pick a Christmas tree and decorating it to the delight of many boys and girls. He missed singing gospel songs with children on Sunday and hiding Easter eggs.

The huge network of Santa's helpers took care of answering his letters now. He still wrote to many of his children but they had grown up, had children of their own and eventually died leaving him even lonelier.

As Christmas approached, he felt the urge to travel once more. This Christmas he would give the last gift of the cross. He spent time fixing up the sleigh. In fact, he made it more beautiful than it ever had been from the time of his first historic flight.

After the sleigh was beautifully restored, Santa loaded it full of huge sacks of all sorts of hand-made gifts. He overfed the reindeer to make sure they all had thick coats and enough fat to withstand one more great journey, the last journey.

He invited all his friends from the northern tribes and asked them to take anything they might need for their families from his house and workshops. He gave them blankets, linens, children's clothing, beds, workshop tools, furniture and other things he no longer needed. They were all grateful yet at the same time sad, sensing the reason could only mean that he would soon be leaving them. Together, they made several festivals as each tribe came to visit. They left him food and unique gifts he could leave for other children on Christmas Eve.

He contacted his friends at NATO Command Center for the last time to let them know not to be concerned with an unknown radar contact on Christmas Eve. He told them this time he would leave very early in the afternoon and would travel a northern route over the pole. He was going to fly directly to his homeland in Jerusalem. The military network of believers quietly made sure no one would mistake him for a hostile target this time and even offered Santa an escort, but he refused knowing he would be too fast for them, and that he needed to make this last journey alone.

On the morning of his last Christmas Eve on earth, Santa quietly prayed in the house for a few hours. He called some of his favorite animals to the house including Golden Bear and gave them food and said goodbyes. They seemed in some strange way to understand. Though animals may not have been given an eternal soul like God gave to Adam and Eve, and all their descendants, animals do have feelings. Is it not ironic that of all God's creatures, it is the dog that loves unconditionally, placed on earth to be man's best and most loyal friend?

Santa hitched up the sleigh at noon and fed the reindeer one last time. He filled to overflowing the bright new sleigh and left open the doors to the barn so animals could find shelter. Santa's helpers would return to his house in years to come along with many of his children and find it in perfect condition. Each visitor would stay there for a week or so to recapture wonderful memories and re-acquaint themselves with the beauty of nature and then return to their new homes. Before they left they would clean, or re-paint, do repairs, fix-up, wash, re-plant and do many tasks to leave the house and workshops in better condition then when they arrived. Over the years, his house became almost a shrine, a holy place to remember what it means to be blessed enough to give, give of yourself, to give to others and in return receive blessings beyond earthly measure, all within the spiritual realm.

St. Nicholas led his faithful team of reindeer out of the barn. You could sense the excitement and anxiety in man and reindeer alike. The reindeer pawed the ground and snorted and shook their heads to let off waves of sounds of jingle bells that echoed in the pine trees. A slow gentle snow fell leaving a beautiful cover of white over the land as far as the eye could see. Santa knelt down and the reindeer watched and listened. Puffs of white mist came from each hot breath through shiny black noses.

"Oh my dear heavenly Father, I think we both know, this is my last journey. I do not know what you would have me do tonight but as I have done for centuries you lead and I will follow. You are the Grand Master of the Universe, you are the creator and giver of all things. I love you Lord. I always have. I always will. I am returning to where it all began. I seek your holy presence tonight Father. I shall travel to where the cross first took you from us on earth, the cross I made, and the nails I forged. Forgive me, Lord. Tonight, the last of those gifts of the cross I shall give to one you shall choose. Guide me that I may do

160

your will. Help me see your vision of who should receive the last gift. My body, my heart is now over two thousand years old. The body may be old but I remain on fire for you Father. I have never been lukewarm. I cannot be. You have blessed me above all men beyond measure. I have started through you, thousands of orphanages, hospitals, homeless centers and so many good things to help others. It is so wonderful, so blessed to give. How great thou art to give me the opportunity to do so much during my time on earth. Guide me tonight. Let tonight be my final destiny, then take me home, bring me to you forever, so that I may dwell with the souls of so many of my children already called home to you. Make the sleigh swift and bold tonight Father. It is truly a miracle how you transform simple wood and metal things into gifts that go on giving forever. Save a place for me dear wife. For tonight I sense I shall finally join you in heaven."

Santa stood up, took a deep breath, slowly scanned his familiar mountains and home for the last time, and then climbed into the sleigh. Though the sleigh was overloaded with gifts, Santa could sense its huge power. Today it seemed filled with greater energy than ever before. The metal tracks of the newly refurbished sleigh caused sparks to fly into the air and on the ground left a trail of fire and smoke in the snow before it lifted off the ground, racing at speeds greater than ever before. He flew over the North Pole and directly into the air space above Europe.

He stopped first in Italy and landed at the Vatican. He grabbed one of his sacks and walked into one of the churches there giving a service with children acting out a little play about Mary, Joseph and Jesus. The people in the church were stunned as Santa walked in and went right down the center aisle. Archbishop Berti was giving a special service to the poor and homeless. He looked up and smiled. St. Nicholas smiled back. Santa just lay the sack of gifts at the base of the baptistry in the front of the church. The children looked at Santa in awe. They had seen many of Santa's helpers but they knew, they could sense, this was the real Santa.

With a quiet dignity, Santa knelt down on one knee, said a short prayer, winked at the Archbishop, and then walked out of the church. The children all ran outside to see Santa mount the sleigh and right before their very eyes, the sleigh sparkled and glowed as an aura of light surrounded it and then lifted into the sky at incredible speed.

They waved goodbye and thank you and said "Merry Christmas" then ran inside where Archbishop Berti handed out all the gifts, some made from the tribes of northern Canada, some hand-made by Santa himself. They were all loved and appreciated. It made them extra special to know that Santa Claus himself had delivered them to their church for the Archbishop to distribute. The parents were especially grateful for without those gifts, they had nothing to offer their children this year but the hope of a better year to come.

Nicholas directed the sleigh to Israel to where he had lived as a young man and the place where Jesus died on the cross. Tonight His birth and life and rebirth would come full circle for Santa Claus. As Santa dropped down over the night sky in Jerusalem, he felt for the first time, truly out of place and out of time with the rest of the world. Hidden in the pristine mountains of northern Canada, life was simple. The place he lived as a young man was now totally foreign. There were cars, buses, trains, planes, lights, buildings, towers, satellite dishes, barbed-wire fences, all things polluting the once natural beauty of a great city. He could see areas that had been bombed or destroyed, checkering the landscape like a war zone. He felt the pangs of loss and anguish, fear and longing in all the people. An old man in a sleigh with reindeer, bundled up for winter snow and stormy breezes was indeed out of sync with this strange new world.

Santa saw a procession of children walking down a street carrying candles and a cross. He directed the sleigh to land on a small side street near the religious gathering. He carried the remaining sacks of gifts and went to the corner, standing amongst a crowd of people watching the procession. They were singing beautiful Christmas songs, carols, religious songs in English and other languages. As the children passed by, Santa started handing out the gifts. Tears came to his eyes. He knew it was the last time he would enjoy giving the small joys of hand-made toys.

The procession led to a lovely church that was filled with children and parents enjoying a special Christmas service. Santa emptied his sacks. There was but one gift left to give, hiding under the back seat of the sleigh.

As he handed out the sacks of toys, a young girl looked up to Santa and smiled. She didn't know for certain who he was, only that he was a kindly old man giving joy to young children. He had nothing more to give so she reached out her hand and held Santa's hand tightly as she tugged him so he would join her in church. He was hesitant at first, but her smile was too overwhelming. Hand in hand they walked to church together.

Often in our lives we see things happen and assume that it was just an amazing coincidence. Perhaps, but more often than not God has a plan of action in our lives that is difficult to see and understand. Some argue that all is a plan. Others argue that man exercises free will and the results are from our choices, not God's plan. Who can say for certain?

After Hans Goldschmidt did not succeed at getting his Gold Medal at the Olympics, his life changed dramatically. The commercial sponsorship dried up, the glamorous models no longer flirted for his attentions. He no longer posed for pictures and ads. He dropped out of the mainstream he had thrived in for many years. Often at night he would stare at the Silver Medal Tyler had handed to him that he mounted in his glass trophy case. He would take it out and touch it and think about those days over and over again. He became sad and lonely. His friends slowly drifted away. He realized they were not attracted to him nor really even liked him as a man but rather they were attracted to the glitz, glamour and flash that surrounded him. Slowly, God started touching his heart. Santa had quietly sent bibles with a personal message written inside to both John Bradley and to Hans. Both were experiencing the same kinds of changes in their lives.

John and Hans both needed to discover the roots of their slow transformations. Both realized it had to do with God, the Bible and Jesus. They had spent their lives scoffing at Christians and anyone who went to church. They worshipped money, not God. Both decided this Christmas to come to Israel for a personal pilgrimage.

Hans and John visited the place where Jesus was buried in the tomb and rose again. They went to the place where Christ was born. There was an emptiness, yet a yearning in their hearts, a desire of men seeking greater joys and purpose in their lives.

As Hans and John struggled to find meaning in their lives, they happened upon the Christmas procession and whether by plan or coincidence, John, Hans and Santa all ended up in the same church that evening. The singing was sweet, innocent, gentle and soothing to the spirit. Listening to the music, watching the children sing, and after their long separate journeys of faith, all three men knelt to pray. John prayed for God to show him the way to a future that had hope, one where he wouldn't feel sad and lonely anymore. Hans prayed for God to take control of his life. All these years he had tried to do it all and he had only succeeded in deluding himself and ruining his life. Santa prayed for something no one else on earth could offer. For the first time in his ancient life, he asked Jesus to please make him a mortal man again. He no longer wished to be immortal but to come home and be in heaven to rest and rejoice forever.

Each man in their own way would have their prayers answered on that Christmas Eve. God answers our prayers in His time, not ours, and sometimes we get what we need, not what we want, for that is the nature of God's way.

As the Christmas celebration service was ending, most of the children gathered at the front of the church. They had finished singing and each had walked around the church to show off the little costumes that they had designed and sewn themselves. Up above them, leaning against the wall, was a giant wooden cross, a reminder of how God sent His only Son to earth to save us all and give us eternal life through the sacrifice of Christ on the cross.

The church was old but well maintained. It was built in a time of relative peace and calm. The designers of the building never envisioned a time when there would be war in the holy places. They placed the cross carefully but assuming there would never be a need to secure it from the blows of bombs and weapons. It just leaned high up against the wall, with a small wooden block to keep it from sliding and falling down.

With no warning, there was a faint sound of a boom and then a flash of light followed by the sound of shattering glass. In the next instant, part of the wall fell to the floor. A shell had struck the church. A few of the parents in the front pews were badly hurt from falling glass and pieces of the wall. One of the children let out a cry and pointed to the top of the wall. The giant cross was leaning over and about to fall. In the next moments of panic several men rushed to the front of the church and pushed the children back and covered them with their bodies to shield them from the cross as it plunged to the floor of the church.

The cross struck hard. One of the men was badly injured. His name was Joseph. He was in the front pew and had jumped up to protect his young daughter who had escorted Santa into the church. Her name was Christina. Her mother had died a few years ago from a random act of violence. To Joseph, Christina was his world. He would do anything to protect her. After his wife died, he vowed to show Christina the kind of love God wanted all of us to share with each other. Now Joseph lay on the ground unconscious with his kidney crushed by the falling cross.

John, Hans and Santa strained to lift the giant cross off of the chest of Joseph. It was heavy, too heavy for any one of them to lift on their own, but in unison they were able to move it safely off of Joseph. There was crying and weeping in the church and yet at the same time an odd quiet, as if the earth stood still in time. At the instant all three men touched the cross they each felt a wave, a pulse, go through them. It was a blend of an electric shock and warmth, almost like a burning sensation. It traveled from their hands deep into their bodies and soul, giving them mild pain, goose bumps and a flash of internal heat all at the same time. None of them realized it then, but it was at that very moment that God answered each of their prayers in a way only a loving God could possibly achieve.

In just a few minutes the sound of sirens could be heard as police and ambulances rushed to the scene. John, Hans and Santa went around the church offering comfort and first aid as best they could. Christina sat down next to Joseph and started to cry.

"Please, please don't leave me. Please somebody help me."

She sobbed uncontrollably. Joseph could barely move and slowly drifted off into unconsciousness. John went over and held on to Christina, trying to calm her and assure her that everyone would be all right. For John, this moment became a new starting point in his life. For so many years, he had been a self-centered man. He had wealth and fame and instead of using it to help others, he only thought about himself. His journey, his pilgrimage to find the place of birth of Jesus, to find God in his life, had succeeded. From that moment on, he learned how to grow and care far beyond himself and about giving the ultimate gift of life.

Santa watched Hans go around the church. He could tell with a glance that Hans himself was struggling to find meaning and purpose in his life. He carefully observed how Hans truly cared for all of the children in the church and wanted each of them to find comfort and not to be afraid anymore. Nicholas noticed that Hans had a large frame and a very strong body as well as a newly found gift of love to give to others, to give of himself openly and freely. It struck him at that moment what God must have had in mind all along. He took Hans aside and put both his hands on the top of the large shoulders of Hans. He looked long and deep into his eyes and saw inside a soul struggling to grow, desperately seeking God and needing a new purpose in his life.

"Hans, I can see in your eyes a need to do something here. Would you like to help, not just tonight but every day of your life in ways you could never have imagined possible? Would you like to spend many years being a man of God and a man who shares his love with children and their parents all around the world? Can you accept that your being here at this moment is no coincidence and that you are destined for a higher purpose in life?"

Hans looked at Santa as if he were a little crazy, yet at the same time had this strange sense that he understood. Santa took him by the arm and led him out of the church and down the side street where the sleigh and reindeer were anxiously waiting. Hans looked at the sleigh, then at Santa, then at the reindeer, then back at Nicholas.

"You're kidding right? There is no Santa Claus. That is only a myth, a legend, a children's story. No one could live on and on like that. And even if they could, how could an old painted piece of wood with a bunch of reindeer fly. That's impossible. Isn't it?"

Santa laughed so hard it brought tears to his eyes.

The reindeer seemed to understand what Hans was saying and pawed the ground and snorted, anxious to get him up into the sky and show him a few tricks of their own. After tonight, Hans would never doubt again and would never say anything negative about the sleigh and Santa's reindeer.

Santa reached in underneath the back seat of the sleigh and removed the last gift of the cross. He could see how everything fit together now in perfect harmony. He unwrapped the last gift box made from the wood of the cross. It contained the last nail from the cross, the one he has re-forged to help Tyler in his quest to represent God in the Olympics. He handed them with great care and dignity to Hans, and then cupped his hands over the gifts and over the kind hands of Hans and knelt down and began to pray.

"Heavenly Father, how great thou art. I see your master plan now, for me and for this man struggling to find you in his heart and soul. My Lord, I now come before you as a Saint, an immortal man for the very last time. Father, please accept these gifts of the cross that you gave to all of mankind and bring to Hans, give to him immortality and your special love, your power to do good all over the world. Let his heart fill with the love of children and the desire to see them find good parents, good homes, food, clothing and shelter that they may learn to know you and love you as I do. Fill him with the power and authority over your sleigh which can transport the body from one place to another at great speed that your will could be done on earth. Give him the courage of a thousand men and the heart of a man of God. Let him be from this day forward, a Promise Keeper, a man of integrity, a man who seeks you every day, your wisdom, your power, your glory, and through this young man Father, let great works of charity be done throughout the world. Take all of my wisdom, my immortality and let it be in him from this day forward to carry on your good works. We ask this in your Son's precious, precious name, Amen."

Hans could feel the electricity begin to build in his body the whole time St. Nicholas was in prayer. By the time the prayer was finished his whole body was a giant swarm of electricity and energy. Quickly his body began to glow in a spectrum of colors. First, tiny blue dots and sparks flew from his skin and exposed hands and face. Soon that turned to oranges and reds and purples until there was a huge glow and aura surrounding him. The reindeer looked up to him in awe and slowly backed up for a moment almost afraid of the sheer power they could sense emanating from this new creature of God.

All around the side street the wind began to increase in a steady pace until it was the roar of the ocean in a tempest or an approaching tornado. Pieces of paper flew high into the air and the windows in nearby houses and stores shook and rattled. Bolts of lightening flew from heaven down to the street all around them and thunder clapped in endless peals at a deafening level. Hans could barely stand. He felt his body collapsing and found himself on his knees weeping for joy at the wonder of it all. Santa never let go of his hands and the gifts of the cross until the wind had subsided and the thunder and lightening ended in a sudden calm.

They both stood up and looked at each other and smiled. Santa was now just Nicholas, a kindly old man who had served God for two thousand years. Hans had become immortal though he had yet to do the deeds of a man chosen by God. That would come in the centuries ahead. Hans looked at Nicholas not knowing what to say.

"But where do I go? What do I do now? I am not worthy of such an honor. Surely there must be some mistake, surely God should have chosen another. All my life I have been a selfish man. I know nothing of giving, though I would so much like to learn. I could never be St. Nicholas. The reindeer will not listen to me. I don't know how to fly or make gifts. There must be a mistake."

Nicholas just chuckled.

"No. My God, your God, the only one true God, does not make mistakes, people do. He has chosen well. Yes, I see it now. There could be no more perfect choice than you, dear Hans. He has given you all the power you need. All you need to do is believe in Him and believe you can do His will if you try hard enough. Just open your heart and it shall be filled as never before. You will be amazed at how wonderful you will feel. It will take time to learn to guide the sleigh but it is rather simple really. Just think of where you want to go. If it is God's will, He will take you there. The reindeer must be cared for like your own children. Treat them well, especially on Christmas Eve. Soon you will have so many children you will be overwhelmed at the joy they will bring to you. I envy you in your new journey. You asked for a purpose in life. You wanted meaning in your life. Well, now you have it. Good luck Hans. And God's speed."

Nicholas walked down the street and turned to go back to the church. He had unfinished business there. Hans stood and stared at the sleigh. Slowly he went all around it and touched it, then patted each of the reindeer. As he circled the sleigh, the enormity of the event finally overcame him with joy and excitement all combined. He got down on his knees and began to pray. He thanked God for giving him a new chance in life to find happiness. He asked for guidance. He asked God to take control of his life and promised to do his best in whatever tasks were set before him.

Hans gathered strength and felt a wonderful sense of joy in his heart, one that he had never before imagined existed. He mounted the sleigh and grabbed the reins then sat down in the sleigh, ready for the ride of his life. He thought about where to go. He remembered from his childhood, a special place his family had in the Black Forest. The property connected to the large protected forest. There would be no people to see or discover the sleigh or reindeer. He could build cabins or houses for workshops and places for children to stay until they found homes. From there he could build a new network of Santa's helpers and begin a new era of giving. He closed his eyes and placed a vision of the forest location in his mind. Instantly the sleigh lurched forward, the metal glides sparked on the pavement and then the sleigh quickly lifted up into the night sky over Jerusalem. It gathered speed each second as Hans was thrown back hard in the front seat. In the new era, the sleigh would travel at speeds so fast it was difficult for those on the ground to see anything other than a blur of light in the sky like a meteor or comet. The reindeer remembered what Hans had said in the side street and decided to have a little fun of their own. Several miles above the ground traveling at over two thousand miles an hour, the reindeer arched their backs and kicked up, making the sleigh do a giant loop in the sky, which for a moment, put Hans upside down. He would be careful in the future to treat the reindeer with the greatest of respect.

Nicholas re-entered the church. There were many people helping the wounded, and it looked like everyone was going to be all right, everyone that is, except Joseph. He saw John and Christina holding on to each other as the medical team attended to Joseph. He could hear them saying that it looked like Joseph's kidney was crushed and that the bruises already visible were a sign of internal bleeding. It was very serious. It was not clear if he would make it through the night.

As Nicholas stood over them, he was touched at how John cared so deeply for Christina and Joseph, two people whom he did not know before this fateful night. John took something out of his wallet and handed it to the emergency medical team. It was an international organ donor card.

"Please, show this to the hospital and call ahead. See if my blood and tissue type matches his. I will donate my kidney if he needs one."

Nicholas had heard about the organization from some of Santa's helpers. He knew it was a large and growing network of people throughout the world who wanted to give the ultimate gift of life. The card allowed hospitals to take certain organs from their bodies in case they died in an accident or in a hospital. It required fast action on the part of the hospital to harvest the organs, so the cards allowed for this rapid action. As a result, all over the world thousands of organs each year were donated to people in desperate need of kidneys, lungs, hearts, and many other vital organs. For those who were kind enough to donate their organs, God took these good and loving souls into heaven with a special joy in His heart. If that our bodies could serve the needs of others by giving life and hope where there was none before, then it was an additional blessing beyond being taken into heaven with Jesus.

The medical team radioed back to the hospital. They checked Joseph's records and then the data from John's donor card. In minutes they called back to tell them they were not a match. Christina began to cry, fearing the worst, that now her father would also be taken away from her and she would be left alone.

Nicholas stepped forward, with his hat humbly in his hand and spoke quietly to the medical staff, all the while keeping an eye on Christina and Joseph's rapidly failing body.

"Excuse me. Would you please take Joseph to the hospital right away? I will ride with him in the ambulance. When you check, you will verify that my blood and tissue type match his perfectly. I will gladly give of my body to save this man to make sure Christina will wake up tomorrow morning and still have a father who will care for her, along with her new found friend John. I think John has found a new calling in life now. He will want to spread the news of how to give the gift of life to others all around the world in a way that only a true Santa's Helper could do with God's blessing."

The medical team did not hesitate or ask questions. God touched their hearts and in a flash, without question, they accepted the fact of the tissue type match. Later at the hospital, the blood and tissue were confirmed to be a perfect match. When the doctors operated they could not understand how the kidney of such an old man was in such perfect condition. In fact all of his organs were in perfect condition as if he were a teenager living in perfect health. There were murmurs in the operating room and conjecture about who was this man dressed in a red suit and black boots, but no one knew for sure. He had signed the operating waiver to give permission for the operation, simply, Nicholas of Antioch. John knew in his heart who he was, and vowed that night to take it upon himself as his new life's journey to spread the word far

170

and wide about how to provide a gift of life to another person even if your body, your shell, should die suddenly without warning, that others may live and find joy in their families, with the family of God.

There was a loud crash in the Black Forest that Christmas Eve. Apparently Hans needed some practice on landings. The reindeer turned their heads at the rookie driver. Next time Hans would remember that after he placed a vision of where to go in his head he needed to put a vision of how to do a safe landing, otherwise the sleigh had a mind of its own and would land anywhere in that area, trees or no trees. The sleigh needed a little repair after that night but that was the least of Hans' thoughts and worries. He jumped out of the sleigh and immediately got down on his knees and prayed, thanking God for a second chance, thanking Jesus for giving him the power and authority to bring joy to children all over the world. We all have that power and authority, although each of us chooses a different path, a different way of doing God's will.

The next day, John sat with Christina in the hospital lobby and played under the Christmas tree that was full of pretty lights and ornaments. John bought her some things from the hospital store. It wasn't much but it was not the amount of money spent but the thought that counted most. He spent some time speaking to the hospital administrators in the coming days about their organ donor programs and how they might be able to form a stronger international union with donors in all countries. Ironically, this would lead to a great expansion of organ donor cards all over the world and ultimately to many unique situations. In the near future, Jewish and Palestinian families would sit together in the hospital waiting rooms as men and women of different faiths donated their organs to save others. Over time, it moved the hearts of many people as they saw more clearly that we all share one planet, one earth and that though there are differences in how we dress and act, our bodies given to us by God are all the same inside. Slowly but surely, many good bonds were formed with men and women and children of all faiths as they united to give the gift of life to others. It began as a simple gesture on a Christmas Eve in Jerusalem and ultimately became a tidal wave of love that covered the globe.

Nicholas of Antioch recovered quickly from his surgery. In fact the hospital was totally baffled that his body healed almost overnight and he was walking about wishing people Merry Christmas the next morning. Joseph also recovered quickly and, in fact, a few weeks later he felt better than he had in many years. After all, he had within his body part of a man who was once a Saint, a man chosen by God to forge the nails and the cross upon which Jesus Christ gave his life to forgive the sins of man before the eyes of God.

Hans and John would end up meeting many times in the future, having a little reunion of their own. They talked about that day in the Olympics when God revealed himself so openly to the world. They talked about that night in the church in Jerusalem and how a personal pilgrimage had ended up leading each of them in different directions yet to the same goal of giving love to people, particularly children, all over the world. Together, they planned new ways to expand the organ donor programs to as many countries as possible. John helped bring Hans new ideas about toys for children. In a marvelous plan of God, it would come to pass that two women, twins, about their ages, came to a hospital drive to help sign up more people for organ donor programs. They met with John and Hans and God touched all of their hearts and before long there was a double wedding. In this way, John and Hans would remain friends for many years and together do God's work on earth with great energy and enthusiasm.

After his remarkable recovery from the surgery, Nicholas found his way to the Black Forest. God guided him to the right place. He spent the remainder of his years showing Hans how to make marvelous toys and gifts for children. He often went with Hans to gatherings at hospitals and at orphanages. He still loved to see the faces of the children when they received an unexpected gift.

When God was ready, he did something rather unusual, for a most unusual man. Nicholas of Antioch never died, at least in the way you and I know of such things. Rather, like a rare few in the bible, one day, God just reached down and picked up Nicholas in His gentle hand and brought him straight to heaven. There he found a giant celebration as he was reunited with his wife and thousands of his children who had grown up under his care, along with thousands and thousands of people who had been touched by the gifts of the cross that he had given over the centuries which were passed on to the next and each succeeding generation. Church bells on earth rang that day. Tyler, Archbishop Berti, Blue Wings and many others eventually would join Nicholas in heaven and together they would rejoice in God's heavenly light for eternity.

As for Hans, some children say they have seen him late on Christmas Eve, placing gifts in their stockings or leaving presents under the tree. Some in Europe called him Father Christmas. But the name Hans liked best was the name that gave him joy in simple ways. He loved it when his children simply called him Poppa Nicholas or simply father. He had but one Holy Father, the one who gave him an immortal soul. Over the centuries he would learn some of the same pains and sorrows and joys that the original St. Nicholas had learned. It was hard seeing his wife and children grow old and go to heaven, leaving him behind on earth. He went on, knowing he served a great purpose. He served the will of God. He spent the next two thousand years giving all his time and energies to the gifts of the cross, not those of wood and metal but those of love and kindness, peace and righteousness, and the gift of prayer. And when he finally grew tired, he would pass on the sleigh and immortality to yet another chosen by God.

So we return to the beginning. Each of us must answer in our own way whether Santa Claus is a man, a spirit or something just so wonderful it cannot be described in simple words.

Each of us has the power and authority to do wonderful things in our own lives. We can find our own spiritual gift and share it with others. We can each be kind and loving people. We can each provide the gift of life to others when our shell remains behind and our soul reaches up to God in heaven. Perhaps that is one way each of us can be Christ's Santa, the person God wants us to be. Each of us has a spiritual gift. Part of our journey in life is to discover that gift and then offer it to others.

God bless you all, and to all, a Merry Christmas.

1 Corinthians 12:4-6
There are different kinds of spiritual gifts, but the same spirit. There are different kinds of service, but the same Lord. There are different kinds of working, but the same God works all of them in all men. (NIV)

Epilogue

The Gift Of Life

What is the gift of life? Who can give it? Why doesn't everyone partake in this blessing?

The gift of life is when someone volunteers to donate an organ to another human being. It is an amazing gift to give to another and one that takes thought, heart, spirit and a commitment to the larger family of people on earth.

Anyone can ultimately give this gift by signing an organ donor card. There are instructions on how to do so on the following pages. Once you have filled it out, carry it with you always. There are no limits to age or gender. If your heart is big enough to make this gift possible then you have taken a giant step to becoming one of Santa's helpers, giving like he did of himself. If you are young, it will require parental permission. However, it is the young in age and the young at heart who must carry this adventure to everyone around them. It is you who must take the lead and you alone can make this happen. It is truly a unique gift to put on your Christmas list at any time of the year.

Why doesn't everyone partake of this blessing? This is difficult to answer. Most people just don't have the chance or the time or the means to sign a donor card. So you must provide that time, that chance to others. There are plenty of ways you can do that as an individual, or as a school, or as an organization, big or small.

All those who take the time to sign up to give the gift of life have made an important decision in their lives. It is in one way simple and in others more complex. All of those who enjoy this blessing are saying that they believe their soul will reside in heaven and that the body is not a part of their spiritual self. It does not matter of what religious faith you are, for all embrace the truth of recognizing, like Santa does, that there is a God in heaven and the spirit inside is separate from the body. Different religions and churches may use different names and have different forms of worship, but the gift of life transcends all of those differences and unites us as one people on this planet when it comes to giving this treasure.

What can just one person do? Each of us can make a huge difference in someone's life through this unique gift. Sadly, each year, more than 6,000 Americans die while waiting for organ transplants. Many are children. Worldwide it is many times this number. The waiting list for organs is now about 83,000 people in America and worldwide over ten times that. It is estimated that 60 percent of those on the waiting list will die waiting while millions of viable organs are not donated nor volunteered by people while they are still healthy. The waiting list grows by about 12% a year in the United States and more in other countries.

It is numbers like these that have attracted Santa and his helpers across the globe to focus their attention, and yours, on creating a new wave of organ donations through registration of people of all ages. It would appear that the adult world with all its political issues has been unable to solve this problem. So it is now left to the children of our country and the world to organize and show their parents and other adults how to do things in a way that would make Santa smile.

Each of you reading this book can do something. Each of you can volunteer to donate organs after your body has given up your spirit or soul. Each of you can help organize at a local school or college to get students and other people within your town to sign up. It doesn't take money and you don't have to go anywhere to do it. It only takes love and respect for life. The kind of love that Tyler had. The kind of faith that Santa has and wants each of us to enjoy.

For those achieving a certain level of registration, certificates will be awarded along with documentation that you can use to help build your own future or just so that you will feel great about yourself and your friends for working together on this vital gift of life program.

This is something you can bring to your local organizations in your city or town. It is perfect for so many kinds of activities, such as Boy Scouts, Girl Scouts, National Honor Society, Rotary, Masons, churches, businesses, sports teams, and just so many other organizations where people gather to enjoy the company of others or to learn.

How can you organize more people to sign up? It is really very easy. You can copy the Organ Donor Cards in this book and keep a list of all of those you sign up. They fill out a card and keep it and you simply have them sign your master list with their name and address. We have a wonderful program for all who get others to sign up to be a future donor. You will be awarded certificates based on the number of people you sign up. All of this does not cost any money, just your time and effort to make it a success.

Certificate Program

For all those who get people to sign up as organ donors, upon receipt of your list, we will send you a certificate as follows:

Bronze Certificate: For achievement in getting 5-50 people to sign up.

Silver Certificate: For achievement in getting 51-100 people to sign up.

Gold Certificate: For achievement in getting 101-200 people to sign up.

Platinum Certificate: For a miraculous achievement of > 200 sign ups.

Instructions
For Organ Donor Card

Here is an organ donor card that you can use for yourself and you can copy for others. People signing up need to fill out the information requested on each line of the card. This includes the name, address and phone number of the future donor. Then is the name of their next of kin such as a mother, father, brother or sister along with their phone number.

It is important that they sign and date the card and check off whether to donate all of their organs or just specific ones. Finally, there is a space for people to witness the signature if they are under the age of 18. In that case a parent or legal guardian must sign and date the card indicating their approval.

That's it!

We really would like to find out about everyone who signs up for this program, so please make a copy of your organ donor list after it is filled out and mail it to the publisher at:

Christ's Santa
Life's Journey Of Hope Publications
P.O. Box 1277
Groton, MA 01450

--(Cut)
ORGAN & TISSUE DONOR CARD

Print Name: _____
Address: _____
_____
Phone: _____

This is a legal document under the Uniform Anatomical Gift Act.

--(Fold)
I hereby make this anatomical gift, if medically acceptable, to take effect upon my death.
My wishes are indicated on the reverse side.
Emergency contact phone numbers.

Next of kin: _____

Relationship: _____

Phone: _____
--(Fold)
I hereby wish to donate:

☐ Any needed organs or tissues
☐ Only the following organs/tissues _____

_____

Donor Signature	Date Of Birth
City & State	Date Signed

--(Fold)

Witness (1)	Date Signed
Address:	

Witness (2)	Date Signed
Address:	

If under 18 witness must be parent/legal guardian.
--(Cut)

179

--(Cut)
ORGAN & TISSUE DONOR CARD

Print Name: _____
Address: _____
_____
Phone: _____

This is a legal document under the Uniform
Anatomical Gift Act.
--(Fold)
I hereby make this anatomical gift, if medically
acceptable, to take effect upon my death.
My wishes are indicated on the reverse side.
Emergency contact phone numbers.

Next of kin: _____

Relationship: _____

Phone: _____
--(Fold)
I hereby wish to donate:

☐ Any needed organs or tissues
☐ Only the following organs/tissues _____

_____

_____ _____
Donor Signature   Date Of Birth

_____ _____
City & State   Date Signed
--(Fold)

_____ _____
Witness (1)   Date Signed
Address: _____
_____

_____ _____
Witness (2)   Date Signed
Address: _____
_____

If under 18 witness must be parent/legal guardian.
--(Cut)

--(Cut)
ORGAN & TISSUE DONOR CARD

Print Name: _____
Address: _____
_____
Phone: _____

This is a legal document under the Uniform
Anatomical Gift Act.
--(Fold)
I hereby make this anatomical gift, if medically
acceptable, to take effect upon my death.
My wishes are indicated on the reverse side.
Emergency contact phone numbers.

Next of kin: _____

Relationship: _____

Phone: _____
--(Fold)
I hereby wish to donate:

☐ Any needed organs or tissues
☐ Only the following organs/tissues _____

_____

_____ _____
Donor Signature   Date Of Birth

_____ _____
City & State   Date Signed
--(Fold)

_____ _____
Witness (1)   Date Signed
Address: _____
_____

_____ _____
Witness (2)   Date Signed
Address: _____
_____

If under 18 witness must be parent/legal guardian.
--(Cut)